BLACK SOULS

SABINA GABRIELLI CARRARA

THE GREEN BAT

CONTENTS

ISBN-13: 978- 1-9162660-2-5

To my mother, the strongest woman I know and yet the most compassionate.

PROLOGUE

Poor girl, I had never seen someone in such a state of shock before.

Not that I can blame her: the sight of me with my face smashed lying in a puddle of blood must have been atrocious, and it will probably haunt her for the rest of her life unless she finds an excellent and skilled psychiatrist.

I had been that lucky in the past. Sending me away to doctor Strein's clinic was probably the only good thing my sister ever did for me. It took years, but I eventually got back on my feet, and I felt good like I had never before.

I have always been different from Mara. I was not born with her strength. Mother knew it, and she protected me for as long as she could, but then she had to go, and I was on my own. Everybody used to say I was the spitting image of mother. The problem was, not only were we similar in our features; we shared the same pain. A pain of the mind that made us different from everybody else.

Father never wanted me around: to him, I was nothing but a constant reminder of the weakness and the darkness that had infected the family. I didn't know any different; that was all I knew. All I had always been, but Dr Strein cured me, and I discovered the world could be a bright place. A place filled with happiness except my sister took it away from me, again, for her convenience. It's so ironic that in the end it will be her to die with the blackest soul. Unfortunately, a miserable consolation because I will never know the meaning of love. I will never hug my daughter again, and I will never seek my revenge.

When they zip up the body bag, I will go back to be that ghost I've been all these past years.

Mara's evil seed had spread and rotted the ones around her.

1

PONTE ALTO - ITALY

Mara had just changed into her nightdress. She was planning an early dinner, maybe in front of the TV as she liked to do every once in a while. She had cursed her late husband, Renzo, quite often because of his habit of eating his meals in front of the TV while watching the soccer games. Now, she had discovered the pleasure of a good meal and a good TV show at the same time. If only he could see her!

Summer had fully arrived and the evenings were bright, making it even more unnatural for her to change for the night that early. It had been a long day and she was exhausted.

Mara had retired the previous year and officially passed the control of the family business, The Kopfler Grand Hotel, to her daughter Giulia. In reality, she had kept a considerable share of the company always intending to stay in the loop of the business. For that reason, she had wanted one of her men to manage the hotel, Roberto Assi. He was her eyes and ears. That day she had spent most of the afternoon with him discussing the expansion plan Giulia wished to set in place. Mara actively opposed the project. One reason above all was the contractor Giulia had chosen: Carlo Rampelli. Rampelli was a local businessman who had made his fortune in mysterious ways. Unfortunately, he was Giulia's boyfriend as well. Mara disapproved of his professional reputation, as well as of his private life. Carlo had a clandestine affair with Giulia for years before recently leaving his wife: whether for love or merely replacing one golden goose with another. This last was the theory Mara Kopfler believed.

The Kopfler Grand Hotel was one of the oldest in the entire region. Mara's grandfather built it overlooking the lake on one side and the town centre on the other. Over the years it became one of Ponte Alto's most prestigious and luxurious resorts. Its impressive architecture and its strategic setting made it the symbol of who held power in the community.

Mara had just put away the dirty dishes when she heard the front gate bell ringing. It was Giulia.

What was she doing here? She was not expecting her.

"Mum? Where are you?"

Before Mara could answer Giulia was in the sitting room.

"Why are you already in your nightgown? Are you sick?"

The thought that her daughter could be concerned for her pleased Mara, but not for long.

"I stopped by this morning, and Edda told me you went to the hotel. Not to meet me, obviously!" Giulia added to answer her mother's surprised expression.

Mara was tired, and the last thing she wanted to do was arguing with her daughter.

"Yes, I just briefly stopped by to see Roberto and ask how Sandra is doing. And besides that, I don't think I have to justify my movements to you."

Giulia knew how much her mother admired Roberto's wife. She liked Sandra herself and never understood how she could stay married to a slimy person like him. When Sandra fell sick with cancer, everybody who knew her was extremely sad.

"Oh, OK," Giulia replied, bringing her tone to a more

cordial level, "I just stopped by because I need your signature on some papers for the bank. Here, mum, I have a pen," She then scattered a few documents onto the coffee table, hoping her mother would sign without too many questions.

Giulia was the CEO, but anything out of the ordinary required her mother's signature. Something not easy to obtain if Mara didn't believe it was in the best interest of the business.

Giulia and Carlo had carefully planned the extension of the hotel. It was indeed a hazard, but still, Giulia strongly believed in the project. She was sure that once Mara had seen all the figures, she would have a very reasonable chance to convince her. She and Carlo had worked hard for that. They had already financially exposed themselves, but they needed a further loan that, without Mara's signature as a guarantee, the bank would have never granted.

"I need my glasses, where are they? Oh, there. Would you pass them to me, please?"

Giulia went to get Mara's reading glasses as she began looking at the documents with poorly concealed disinterest.

"Oh, I don't know, Giulia. These are a lot of documents to go over, and I'm exhausted tonight. Leave them with me, and I'll check them in the morning."

Mara piled up the papers and removed her glasses, a clear sign that she was not open to negotiation.

Giulia stood up abruptly, "Can you not trust me for once? Look at the project. It's the future. Everything we spend on the new construction will be back in our pockets probably doubled and most likely in less than five years. It's all written there. Look at the figures and the estimate. If only you would make an effort to read it instead of discarding the whole thing just because the idea is coming from Carlo and me."

Mara sat there looking at her daughter, and her expression of contempt needed no words.

Giulia was used to that patronising look and could barely

contain her anger; her face was a vivid red. She gathered the documents and threw them back into her briefcase. Her mother was never going to sign for the loan.

"Don't you think I know you had just pretended to leave everything in my hands? The reality is that you think I'm a failure like my father. Roberto is your guard dog, not the manager. I bet you two have a direct secret line so he can inform you of every single move I make." Giulia shouted while walking towards the front door. Her words remained unanswered.

Giulia had never felt Mara's love and even less her trust. Growing up, she got used to it, but it did still hurt.

Mara didn't believe in outbursts, and her daughter should have known better than reacting as she did. Mara didn't attempt to follow her or conciliate her because that would have meant giving in or implying that she would have considered her proposal when, instead, she had no intention of doing so. She let her daughter go. It was only another of their many arguments, and it would pass.

Giulia was no doubt her father's daughter. She liked luxury and felt entitled to a lavish lifestyle only because she was born into a wealthy family. She always accused her mother of being stingy. What she didn't understand was that Mara had to be extra strict, so she would not end up a loser, a victim, or a weakling. The family didn't need another one. Lorna, Mara's sister, had already damaged the family enough in the past. Mara knew that her daughter resented her but took consolation in the fact that if Giulia was not a complete failure, it was only because of her parenting. One day Giulia would understand that everything her mother did was for her own sake.

2

PONTE ALTO - ITALY

The sun was already up and warming the air. Mara had always been a morning person and still was, but since she wasn't expected in the office anymore, she could stay lounging in her dressing gown a bit longer and that morning was no exception.

She got up, tightened her robe around her slim figure, she opened the French door leading to her bedroom balcony and inhaled the scented morning air. Leopold, her old cat, jumped off the bed and started to rub around her ankles purring loudly.

"Yes, yes Leo, it's breakfast time."

Leopold had been with Mara for over ten years; she had found him one night in heavy rain when he was only a little kitten. He was hiding on top of her car tyre, and she only noticed him because she dropped the car keys. When Mara bent to pick them up, she saw something furry on the wheel. At first, she thought it was a rat and screamed, attracting the attention of a few passers-by who came to check if she was ok. She had never felt so stupid in her entire life, a grown woman afraid of a rat. Except it was not a rat and the "meow" that started to be audible from under the car made it immediately manifest. A young guy kneeled and extracted the little creature, wet and terrified. Of course, everybody's heart was melting for the poor kitten, but nobody offered to take him home. Mara had buried her husband not long before and didn't intend to take care of anybody else, not even a cat. She didn't even particularly like animals. Some of her friends tried to convince her to get a pet dog or cat, "They are such a font of joy and company," they used to say. To Mara, they only represented a font of dirt and responsibilities she didn't want. Mara Kopfler didn't need company and liked her life as it was.

On the other hand, Mara Kopfler also treasured her role as a pillar of the community. She was a woman whose principles and morals never failed, at least on the surface. Not wishing to appear heartless, Mara brought the neglected kitten home and gave it to Edda, with strict instructions to bathe him, feed him and make sure he would stay only in the garage or the garden. The kitten was left in the garage for a few days and then freed in the garden, but he kept going back to the patio door and stared inside. One day of nasty weather, he managed to sneak in and made himself at ease on Mara's couch in the sitting room. Edda swore she did not let the kitten in; nevertheless, Mara harshly blamed her for it. The weather was miserable outside, and he surely would have caught pneumonia. In those conditions even the garage was too humid and cold, Mara could do nothing else but keeping him inside, and that evening the two of them watched tv together. Maybe Mara's friends were not that wrong: it was surprisingly pleasant to have furry company. The main character of the movie was called Leopold, and after him, Mara named the one creature who would become her most loyal companion in life. Only to Leopold Mrs Mara Kopfler could confess her more profound thoughts, because she was sure he would have never talked.

Leopold bumping her again, and this time, more urgently

brought Mara back to reality. "Ok," she said, petting him on the head, "let's go eat." Mara and Leopold went downstairs to have breakfast. Salmon croquet for him and coffee and Dutch crisp-breads with butter and jam for her.

"Good morning, Mrs Kopfler. Did you have a good sleep?"

"Indeed, Edda. Thank you."

Edda arrived every morning at 7:30 and began her working day by checking the kitchen. When she could hear the creaking of the shutters opening upstairs, she knew her mistress was up and immediately put the mocha on the hob. By the time Mrs Kopfler was down, the coffee was ready and still hot as she liked it. Leopold would find his bowl filled too. Despite all the years Edda had worked for the Kopfler family, nothing more than a mere employer-employee relationship had ever developed between the two women. Between Edda and Giulia, however, things were different. Edda had known Giulia and her cousin Lola as infants and was like a second mother to the girls, in particular to Giulia. After Lola moved to Malta, and Edda's daughter died in a car accident, the Kopflers were all Edda had left. Even though they had never done anything to make her feel a part of the family, she started to feel that way. Her job of looking after the house and its inhabitants became her only reason for living, with Giulia the centre of her undisguised attentions. As Mara sat at the kitchen table and waited to have her breakfast served, she started to sip her coffee and switched the TV on to check the morning news. She watched the news religiously in the morning, at lunchtime and at dinner time. An old fashioned habit she was not yet ready to give up in favour of the web. Meanwhile, Edda went upstairs continuing her routine so that by the time Mara had finished breakfast and was ready to get dressed, her rooms were clean, refreshed and with the thermostat set according to the season.

The house was too big for only one person, and security had become a worry because of the wave of burglaries and violence in the area. Giulia had tried more than once to talk her mother into downsizing, but Mara was not ready to leave. She loved her house; the long driveway between the gate and the house and the vast garden in the back with its secular chestnut trees and the magnificent rose bushes she grew over the years. No other place would have felt like home.

3

DUBLIN - IRELAND

Before Alex and Philip were born Lola knew nothing about Irish primary schools and the Irish system of education; all she knew was what she remembered from her school days in Italy when you went to the nearest school to your home.

Fergus did not know much more than his wife, as when he was of school age, they lived in a remote area in Kerry where there weren't many choices. The complexity of the Irish school system and especially the common practice to pre-register the children for primary school when they were only a few weeks old, seemed to them like pure madness. A madness that soon swallowed them. When it became evident that Lola was expecting the twins, friends and neighbours started to inquire as to whether the couple had given any thought about schools yet. When they began house hunting, even the estate agents were quick in pointing out the presence of good national schools in the proximity, to make one house more appealing than another.

The memory of that Saturday afternoon when they went to see the three-storey Georgian house that later became their home, still brought a smile on Lola's face. They had seen so many houses, but none were right. They were either too old, too small, or in the wrong part of the city. Lola and Fergus had nearly given up hope and were already thinking about how to fit two cribs in the pitched roof bedroom of their small flat when they walked into number 4 in Sandford Close.

The house had a newly renovated kitchen in the basement overlooking a surprisingly sizeable rear garden whose privacy was provided by trees and the tall hedge that ran along the garden wall. The middle floor had a sitting room and a dining room, plus what was called a drawing-room that soon became the twins' playroom. Upstairs were four double bedrooms, two en-suite and a huge main bathroom with shower and bath. Number 4 Sanford Close was the perfect home. It had everything the young couple was looking for except the price. The listing price exceeded the couple's budget, and they knew it, but now, it was hard to settle for something else.

"Do you like it?" Fergus had asked, looking at his wife's mesmerised expression while following the estate agent around. Before she could answer, he made an offer.

Lola, froze on the spot and pulled her husband by the sleeve, "You are joking, right? We can't afford anything like that."

"Yes, we can. We will have to tighten our belts a little but look around you; this is just perfect for us."

Fergus was right, the house was amazing, and one of the best national primary and secondary schools in the district was literally around the corner.

Unfortunately, Fergus was right about tightening belts too. The first thing they did was to get rid of the second car, but that was not a problem. Bus number 19 to the city centre stopped right in front of their gate. Herbert Park, one of the more beautiful parks in Dublin, was only a 10 minutes walk away. The house also had a granny flat that Fergus could use as an office when he was home. Because of his job, Fergus travelled a lot, but Lola didn't mind because when he was back, he was a most attentive husband and father.

But all that was a long time ago.

* * *

This particular morning Lola had just gotten back home after bringing the twins to school. They were in first class, but she had not dared to let them walk down the road on their own yet. When they left for school, it was only drizzling, but on her way back it started to lash rain. By the time Lola reached home, she was thoroughly drenched and shivering in her wet clothes. She ran upstairs to take a hot shower and change to something warm and dry. Fergus had left early to catch a plane to London to negotiate a new contract with a chain of boutiques. He was a project manager, and when things in the company where he had been working for years started to unravel, Fergus decided to open his own company bringing with him a good docket of his old clients. Starting a business was not easy, but now he had established his name and reputation and a decent clients' portfolio. The house was still slightly over their financial status, and they could not afford the lifestyle of the majority of their neighbours. Still, they were living in reasonable comfort, and they never struggled to pay the mortgage.

Since today was Tuesday, the twins had after school homework club, and to Lola, this meant having a couple of extra hours of freedom before collecting them. After the twins had started school, she thought about going back to work. But her salary as a translator would have barely covered the cost of full time after school care. Besides, she enjoyed being at home, and Fergus was more than happy for her to do so. They had no money to throw out the window, but she could afford to raise her boys herself.

Fergus had always wanted her to take some time for

herself. Lola did not have many friends, and her overprotective husband was afraid she could feel lonely. Over the years, Lola had created a social circle of acquaintances, and that was enough for her. Until she met Fergus and his lovely family, she had been a lonely soul. She had learned to enjoy her own company and was quite comfortable with the arrangement.

The rain was still heavy outside, and there wasn't much she could do with her free time today. Surely it was not a day for outdoor activities. She put the kettle on and prepared herself a hot cup of tea while looking at the local paper. As usual, nothing was interesting, just some dull advertisements and the bio of the just-elected local TD. Lola closed the paper and was about to throw it away, when she noticed, on the back of the last page, an advert about the opening of the new cinema. She remembered hearing about it. It looked good, only a block away, and someone from the school said that in the morning it was quiet and always showed the latest movies.

Fergus didn't like going to a movie. He never understood why people paid to watch other people lying and pretending they were someone else. If he was going to fall for that, then it was better doing it from the comfort of his sitting room and for free. Lola knew it was all nonsense and the only reason he didn't like the cinema, was because he could not stay awake.

She checked the shows, and there was an indie movie with William Dafoe that she found appealing and would pass the hours until pick up time.

Lola left the theatre satisfied with her choice, but as she still had plenty of time before collecting the boys, she decided to have lunch at the cinema cafe. She ordered an English muffin and a cappuccino. As she was paying, the lady behind her, asked in broken English, what she got. The woman had never seen such a muffin before, but it looked yummy. Lola tried to describe the pastry straightforwardly. She understood how it was in a foreign country, trying to understand the locals. Besides, her accent was still far from being Irish or Dubliner itself.

Lola could not help but wonder what the woman's story was. She gathered that the lady was Spanish, probably just on holiday and wanted to test herself with a movie. The tables were all occupied. Lola had to wait a few minutes until a couple left and she grabbed the table as fast as she could. The "Spanish lady" was still standing by the counter looking for a free spot. Lola took pity on her and waved her over to sit with her.

As their conversation continued, Lola finally recognised her accent. She was not Spanish but Italian, and even if she was in Ireland for an English course, the woman seemed very happy that Lola started to talk to her in her native language. They talked about a bit of everything. The Italian lady was probably around her mid-sixties and sounded very well educated. Surprisingly, she confessed to Lola to having dropped out of school, and after going through a very rough patch, decided to go back to her studies. After graduating from high school, she even went to university to study psychology. Lola was indeed fascinated by this stranger and wanted to stay and chat more, but unfortunately, it was time to go.

She checked her watch and stood up, "I am very sorry, but I have to go now. I enjoyed talking to you and good luck with your English."

After a few steps towards the exit, Lola returned and extended her hand to the stranger: "By the way, I'm Lola, very nice to meet you."

The two shook hands, and Lola left.

4

DUBLIN - IRELAND

And so there we were face to face, after all these years.

Of course, Lola could not know who I was. I had to be careful, not to upset her and ruin everything. Lola had made her choices years ago, logical decisions but people change, and I wondered if she believed in second chances.

Social networks are high instruments. Once you are in there, you cannot hide, that is how I found her.

"You can pretend to be happy and that you have no past or you can face it and move on."

Those were Dr Strein's words that I ignored for so long thinking I could leave the past behind, but soon I would not have had any history left. Dementia, they said.

I spent a lifetime trying to get rid of my memories, and now I wanted them all back before it was too late.

5

PONTE ALTO - ITALY

Giulia had rung to see if it was still fine for her to come for dinner that night.

"Of course. I'll wait for you at eight," Mara replied, knowing all too well that behind her daughter's visit there was a reason. Giulia was stubborn and proud; after their last argument, she would have never rung first, but she needed those signatures.

Mara had done some research and talked to Roberto. He shared her opinion about the danger of the investment. He also shared her view on Carlo not being a trustworthy business partner. Mara had learnt to accept her daughter's poor judgement when it came to men. In fairness, she had to admit she had been guilty of the same poor taste with her husband, but at least she never let him interfere with the family business. Not that Renzo ever had any interest! He spent most of his time following his dreams, throwing himself into one catastrophic business adventure after another. Mara's constant refusal to finance her husband didn't spare her from having to pay his debts in the end, but she had learnt her lesson: love can be mischievous. It obscures your clarity and keeps you from seeing the other person for who they are. In the case of Renzo and Carlo, two losers. If only Giulia could see it too.

Mother and her daughter made it through dinner avoiding to talk about business. If there wasn't still some tension between the two of them, the evening together might have been nearly pleasant.

While Mara filled the dishwasher, Giulia poured them both a glass of sherry. They had their drink in silence, and around ten, Giulia left. Mara was relieved to see her daughter go and without mentioning the loan.

Maybe she had given up the idea, or more likely she was plotting something. Mara didn't feel petty towards her daughter; she was just realistic.

With Leopold on her lap, Mara started to do some zapping while indulging in a second glass of sherry. It wasn't long before her eyes began to close.

"Come on Leo, bedtime."

Replacing the balconies with electric shutters was one of her better decisions. A touch of a button and she could shut the house. Mara set the alarm and started climbing the stairs.

"Oh, no, Leo. Is it time to get up already? I'm afraid that I'm growing old and lazy," Mara said more to herself than to her furry companion. The noise of the alarm clock in her ears was incredibly disturbing. Most mornings Mara didn't even need the alarm clock; over the years she had built up her biological clock. She pulled her slim arm out of the light embroidered cotton sheet and pushed the button on the alarm clock to silence it. The noise didn't stop. She pushed it again, and again unsuccessfully. It took a few minutes for Mara to realise it was not the alarm ringing but the phone. She sat up on the bed alarmed, it was 3:00 a.m., and someone was calling. Mara's first thought was that something had happened, maybe to Giulia or the hotel. She grabbed the handset, but as she answered, the line went dead.

6

DUBLIN - IRELAND

After our encounter at the cinema, Lola was the only thing I could think about, day and night.

My head was sore, recurrent thoughts and sleep deprivation had always given me a throbbing headache, but with the help of some pills, I eventually managed to fall asleep.

Those few hours of rest served me well. I woke up covered in sweat but with a clear head.

What foolishness to think it was enough to see her that one time.

I wanted to see her again. I wanted to talk to her again, learn more about her life. I studied her routine for over a week; it was not going to be difficult to fake another "accidental" encounter.

I was excited and impatient. I needed to do something to keep myself busy.

I went into town. Dublin is a beautiful city. Its architecture is not as impressive as the ones you see in some continental Europe capitals, but the vibe that it transmits is terrific. Contrary to most big cities, Dublin is still a place where you can feel safe. I liked it and enjoyed strolling around Grafton Street listening to the music of the buskers. It was most refreshing to see how Dublin was a city for young and old. No distinctions.

My stomach rumbled, and I remembered I hadn't eaten

anything since the previous night. I stepped into Bewley's, the oldest and most famous cafe in town. The queue to be seated was huge but fast. In no time I was comfortably sitting at a little table by the window. The menu included a bewildering variety of hot chocolate and teas, but I needed caffeine and sugar.

"I will have an americano and a carrot cake with cream, thank you," my school-days English still worked.

I don't know how long I sat there, looking at people passing along the street was hypnotising.

The waiters were starting to clean all around me, and one brought me the bill. A very polite sign that it was time for me to leave as they closed for the day.

7

DUBLIN - IRELAND

"Oh, hello again," Lola had just come out of her local coffee shop with a cappuccino in hand when she spotted the nice Italian lady from the cinema.

"What a coincidence, do you remember me? We met at the movie the other day?" Lola added cheerfully and continued, "Are you renting close by? This is surely not a touristic area."

"Oh, no. I mean yes, of course, I remember you but what I meant is that I don't live in the area. I've gotten the wrong bus, and here I'm, lost."

"I know what you mean. When we first moved here, I kept getting the wrong bus and these residential areas they all look the same. The same type of houses, same shopping chains..." Lola consoled her.

"My husband is away with the car. Otherwise, I would have given you a lift, but if you remember the address of where you are staying, I can tell you which bus to take to get there," Lola tried to help.

"Oh, any bus to the city centre would do," the old lady answered not taking her eyes away from the kind young woman.

"OK, then. I still have some spare time before school pick

up and If you like, I can walk into Herbert park with you. It's a lovely park and in particular at this time of the year. It's over there, just across that road. And outside every exit of the park, there is a bus stop," Lola said, pointing in front of her.

This time the lady was less talkative, but she did ask a lot of questions. Lola didn't mind; she was dying for a decent conversation with someone over ten.

Lola enjoyed talking with this fascinating stranger who, for some reason, didn't sound estranged at all, but her time was up. "I'm sorry, but I have to go back now, it's time to pick up my kids from school."

The woman stared at Lola without saying anything, but then like she woke up from a daydream she took both Lola's hands in hers, and said: "Nice to see you again."

Lola was slightly taken aback by the gesture. It was far too personal, but she didn't give it a second thought since she would probably never seen the woman again.

"If you take that path on the right, it is the shortest way to the exit and the bus stop."

Lola excused herself one last time and headed the opposite way.

* * *

It was Friday, and Lola loved Fridays: the end of the week and the beginning of the weekend.

She and Fergus didn't go out that much, but most Fridays, they had a "date night in".

The evening would begin by giving the twins their bath. Once in their PJs, they were allowed pizza in front of the TV. Fergus and Lola always sold this routine as a treat to the boys, who excitedly waited all week for Friday. Actually, the gift was for the parents. They could lock themselves in the kitchen and have wine, cheese and long uninterrupted chats while listening to music.

Fergus had an old record player and a big collection of vinyl. Some were from his younger days, others he had inherited from his father; the rest were all presents from his brother, Dylan. The two siblings started this tradition when they were teenagers: For each other's birthday, Fergus gave Dylan a book of poetry and Dylan would give Fergus a record.

Lola liked Dylan and even more so his wife, Carmen. After Fergus's parents, they were probably the happiest couple she knew. They both quit their job as accountants and used all their money to buy and restore a property in the west of Ireland, that they converted to a B&B. The business picked up quickly and successfully. Unfortunately, with that kind of business, they had to be there year' round. Summer was the busiest season, but tourists showed up at their door throughout the year. The only days they closed was between the 23 and the 27 of December. Then the B&B opened its door only to the family who soon initiated the new tradition of getting together for Christmas.

When things between Lola and Fergus became serious, on the last Christmas they were still in Malta, he asked her to go back home with him to meet his family. Lola still remembered how embarrassed she was as she would have never been able to do that for him. She didn't have a family to introduce, or rather, she didn't have a family that she could call her own. Lola knew it was not her fault, but couldn't help feeling ashamed. Lola had been raised to feel the shame for who she was. She was her mother's daughter, and since Lorna was not there anymore to pay for her sins and all the embarrassment she had caused the family, it was Lola's duty to carry that weight and pay for it.

Lola found it very difficult to talk about her upbringing. It was hard to explain the level of mistreatment she sustained for all the years she had lived with her aunt Mara and uncle Renzo.

Sometimes when she tried to open up to some friends, they could not understand how deep her wounds went. Most of the times, the fact that she had grown up with money, made her look like a whiner. What people didn't understand, or didn't want to understand was that there was not enough money in the world to compensate what she had missed growing up: Love. Besides, what her aunt gave her when she reached the legal age of eighteen and decided to leave, was nothing compared to her mother's part of the inheritance. Lola refused it because the last thing she wanted was the money of a woman who took her own life leaving behind her three-year-old daughter. Of course, Giulia and Mara never argued with her decision. Giulia only saw the chance to enlarge her already conspicuous inheritance and Mara, probably saw it as a payback for saving her and raising her. Despite all her doubts and fears, that first Christmas with the Owen family was the best Christmas she had ever had. For the first time, she felt the warmth of a family around her.

After the twins were born Fergus suggested to have Christmas in their own home. They could have joined the others later, but Lola always refused: she didn't want to miss Christmas with "the family" ever again.

Over the years, Dylan and Fergus began a joke about how their wives wanted to marry the whole family more than them. In a way, this was certainly the case for Lola. She couldn't speak for Carmen, but she had the clear impression that it was the same for her sister-in-law too.

8

DUBLIN - IRELAND

She remembered me, and she even invited me to have a stroll with her. Was Lola friendly to an elderly lady or did she enjoy my company for real?

I know it must sound absurd considering we barely knew each other, but I felt there was a connection and she felt it too. I am sure.

I was not very talkative. I purposely let her talk, thereby learning a good deal about her and her family. I registered her gestures, her delicate features.

9

PONTE ALTO - ITALY

"I know the bank is pressuring you, but the old witch won't sign the papers." Giulia was on the phone with Carlo and desperately trying to calm him down.

"You assured me your mother would agree to invest in the plan. If the project doesn't move forward, we will lose everything we've invested so far; which in my case is everything I had left plus what I borrowed from some Albanian mafia guy. He won't think twice about killing me. Or, in the best-case scenario, he will kneecap me." He was panicking, and now Giulia was too. She risked to lose the man she loved, and she was involved with a band of criminals.

Giulia collapsed on the bed and let herself have a long cry, holding her head in her hands.

Her mother always despised public exposure of feelings.

"I grew up with a mother who used to show her feelings all too well and, believe me, it was not pleasant," Mara used to say to her daughter as a child, and so Giulia was not allowed to show any feelings as it could be a sign of weakness. Mara never talked to her daughter about her mother or her sister Lorna. The little Giulia knew about them, she knew it because she had overheard it. The only person Giulia could be herself with was her father. Renzo was different from his wife. Giulia always wondered how he could have stayed by the side of such a woman for so long. Unfortunately, Renzo had long gone, and Giulia had no time; she needed the money now.

She would have to go and talk to her mother again.

10

PONTE ALTO - ITALY

Mara wasn't home, but Edda told Giulia she would be back for lunchtime. Giulia stayed and waited. She hadn't announced her visit to avoid questions and possible discussion over the phone.

That afternoon, she and Carlo had a meeting with the bank at 4:30, one more reason to pressure Mara to make a decision and with some luck the right one for them.

Giulia had her speech all prepared in her mind, and of course, under no circumstances could she mention Carlo's debt with the Albanian racketeer. That would cause Mara to lose even the little trust she had in her daughter.

Giulia's phone began buzzing. It was Carlo. She rose from the sofa. If Edda was in the corridor dusting, she didn't want her to overhear their conversation.

"Wait on the line for a second," she told him as she entered Mara's study. She closed the door and sat at the desk. Carlo said he rang to apologise for his reaction earlier, but Giulia knew he only wanted to know if there was good news. Giulia found it very hard to hide her annoyance as he was pushing her over the edge and she felt powerless. Giulia honestly didn't know what to expect from this meeting.

"So, we meet the bank in, what, four hours? And still, we don't know if we have the grounds to be approved or not?"

"I told you I'm waiting for her to come home and I'll do my best."

"Your best won't be enough; she has to sign. We need her signature one way or another."

Giulia didn't like Carlo's accusatory tone. He had no right to talk to her that way. These were the times when she regretted the day she agreed on the project and blamed herself for being so naive. The first figures that Carlo gave her were manageable with the capital she could invest without further authorisations, but then they doubled. Her signature was not enough as a guarantee anymore. They needed Mara's.

When she was nervous, Giulia had the habit of scribbling. That was what she was doing at the moment while pretending to listen to a hysterical Carlo. After she terminated the unpleasant conversation with her boyfriend, Giulia realised that the paper she had scribbled on was some official document. Instinctively she turned it over to see what it was.

"Oh, shit," it was a bank statement. Giulia didn't recognise the bank.

A smirk formed on her face, her mother had a secret offshore account. This didn't surprise her; what surprised her, instead, was that she was not aware of it. Giulia went through the statement, and a recurrent payment grabbed her attention. The beneficiary was anonymous, only a bank account number and just when she was about to write it down, the front door shut, and she heard her mother's voice.

She rushed to tidy up the desk and leave the study before Mara saw her. Mara Kopfler didn't like people going into her home office uninvited, and her daughter was no exception.

11

PONTE ALTO - ITALY

Mara opened the gate for her daughter and watched her leaving through the CCTV camera. She always did that with her guests, to be sure they had left, and nobody had the chance to sneak in while the gate was closing.

Giulia turned the corner and pulled over.

Her hands were shaking in anger. She was furious. The old witch had just had it her way once again. Sometimes Giulia wondered if her mother took pleasure in humiliating her. Never mind that she was a grown woman, with a career and financial independence, because all that came from Mara and she didn't hesitate to use it to control her. Tears were running down Giulia's face; her palms were red and sore after she had slapped them violently on the steering wheel. Absorbed in her thoughts, she jumped when her mobile starting to ring. It was Carlo again. Giulia didn't find the courage to answer. That was it; everything was lost: her money, his business and their story because she strongly doubted that their relationship could survive such a downfall. He might not have survived himself, considering the people he went to ask for help.

More tears filled her eyes; she didn't want to lose him. Maybe he was not the most upright of men, and she was the first to admit their relationship might have looked superficial to most. Still, she loved him, and despite what her mother thought, she was sure he loved her too.

"I won't let her win this. She is done ruining my life," Giulia said to her reflection in the car's rearview mirror. She dried her eyes, recomposed herself and took her mobile out of her handbag: "Everything is fine. I will see you at the bank." She didn't give Carlo time to reply and hung up.

Giulia found a parking spot directly opposite the bank's entrance.

She gave her face one last check, took a deep breath and slipped the documents for the loan approval back into her briefcase.

Nobody would have noticed it was not Mara's signature. Giulia had become a master at forging her mother's name in her school days.

The bank had no reason to contact Mara as her signature was just a collateral guarantee, and Mara had no reason to contact the bank. To her, the matter was closed when she denied signing and reinstated her power once more.

The only thing Giulia had to take care of was finding a plausible explanation to justify to her mother and her guard dog, Roberto, that the project could go ahead without further guarantees. She would say Carlo had found some investors.

Only when they left the bank's building, Giulia's heartbeat went back to its regular rhythm. Everything went well.

"I have to go back to the office for an hour, to sort something out but then we can go out for dinner and celebrate. Let's say I will pick you up at 7:30?" Giulia gave Carlo an acquiescent smile, happy to be left alone to calm down and let all the tension go.

She hadn't told him she had forged her mother's signature yet, but she would. She knew she couldn't keep something like that from him, and after all, she did it for them. As he said himself, he was the one risking the most, and she could not let him down.

* * *

The doorbell rang at 7:30 sharp: "Are you ready?"

"Why don't we stay in instead?" Giulia suggested. If she had to tell him the truth about the forged signature, a crowded restaurant was not the best place.

"Ok, I just hope you have a bottle of champagne in the fridge."

"Bollinger."

"That will do honey; you get the glasses while I open the bottle."

Giulia took the crystal wine glasses from the cabinet and waited for Carlo in the living room.

Carlo filled the two glasses and left the bottle in the ice bucket to keep it chilled.

"To my beautiful fiancé and our success," he rose his glass to Giulia.

"Fiancé?" Giulia repeated to make sure she had heard correctly.

"I know, I know, I still have to wait for the divorce, but I can't wait to show the world how much I love you and how much you mean to me."

Giulia swallowed the full content of her glass in one gulp and looked at Carlo in disbelief.

Without saying a word, he took a little box from his pocket and opened it, "Would you marry me?"

Giulia's excitement and happiness were hard to conceal. One more look at her ring finger now adorned with a beautiful sapphire and diamonds band, and then without saying a word, she hugged her future husband and kissed him.

Half an hour later, they were lying naked in bed.

"Now, as much as you are the tastiest thing I know, I'm starting to be a bit hungry," Carlo broke the comfortable silence between them.

"Me too. Carbonara?" Giulia suggested.

"Deal!" Carlo happily agreed, and after a quick shower, they joined forces in the kitchen.

Both still in their bathrobes, they sat down at the kitchen table, and avidly started to eat their spaghetti and drink the leftover champagne.

"You know what I was thinking as well?" Carlo suddenly said.

"I want to hear it only if it's as nice as a marriage proposal," Giulia replied coquettishly, but she never felt happier.

"I think we should live together, even if we won't be able to get officially married for a while. I'm already spending more time here than in my apartment so ....What do you think?" Carlo's self-confidence seemed to shake when Giulia just looked at him without immediately answering, but then she showed him the biggest smile he had ever seen on her pretty face.

"I think it's a great idea." Giulia stood up and went to sit on Carlo's lap, "Go grab your stuff. You are moving in."

The following morning Giulia woke up first and when Carlo got up, she was already in the kitchen making coffee.

"Wow, is this how you are going to spoil me every morning from now on?" he joked, moving her hair aside and kissing her on the neck while stealing her cup of coffee with his free hand.

"Maybe."

Carlo drank his morning infusion of energy, as he used to call his first cup of coffee of the day, and looked at his wristwatch, "Shit, I'm late, sorry love I got to go."

Giulia was still too sleepy to be responsive and blew him a

kiss not getting up. Halfway through the door, he turned: "And by the way, you haven't told me yet how you managed to convince the old witch of signing. I want to hear everything about it tonight," and he was gone.

She still hadn't told him that she had forged Mara's signature, but how could she? Last night's opportunity evaporated after he proposed to her. Telling him the truth would have spoiled everything, but keeping it a secret it would eventually destroy everything.

She had to tell him, no matter what!

12

DUBLIN - IRELAND

I knew it was risky, but I couldn't help it.

I was not going to talk to her this time, and I was not going to let her see me. All I wanted was to watch her. See her again, even if from a distance.

I hid behind the newspaper kiosk on the opposite side of the road from the boys' school. Pick up time was mayhem, all those kids running everywhere and all those parents and au pairs and grand-parents waiting outside. For a fraction of a second, I lost her in the crowd, but I soon spotted her yellow dress with the white roses printed on it.

I crossed the road to have an unobstructed view. The twins' class was the last one to come out.

The image of the two boys running towards their mother and hugging her warmed my heart, but it also brought back so many regrets. If I could only go back in time.

I followed them home until they disappeared behind the green double door of their red brick Georgian house.

When I saw some correspondence sticking out the letterbox, I took it. Why? I still don't know.

All the letters were addressed to Mr Fergus Owen or Mrs Lola Owen. Lola took her husband's name.

"Hey, what are you doing?"

A voice called from behind me. I dropped the envelope I was still holding in my hand, and I ran as fast as I could without turning back.

I was soon out of breath, and I had to stop.

The woman who yelled at me didn't follow me. I was safe, but my heart was galloping, and my legs were shaking.

13

DUBLIN - IRELAND

When the front door opened, Lola had never been happier to see her husband.

Fergus was home earlier and with a big bunch of flowers.

"Mmm, something you need forgiveness for?" Lola said jokingly and threw her arms around her man's neck.

"Maybe... but you will never know," he teased back kissing her.

"Where are the boys?"

"They are upstairs in their bedrooms reading."

"Reading? I've been away a few days, and you managed to transform those rascals into little nerds?"

Alex and Philip had never shared Lola's interest in books. Fergus was also a good reader, but not as greedy as she was. She had pushed the boys for years, but reading had always proved to be very difficult for them. The teacher said not to worry about it as it was quite common in bilingual kids and suggested some extra work to do at home, which Lola had done diligently over the years and it eventually paid off.

"I'm going to take a shower, and I'll be back down in ten, fresh, clean and scented."

What Lola liked most about Fergus was his positive attitude towards life. He helped to lock the shy insecure girl that she once was, in a secret mental drawer, where she kept all the unpleasant memories of "her past life".

Lola carefully arranged the flowers into a Waterford Crystal vase and placed it on the kitchen island.

"Mm, bruschetta, candles and Merlot...." Fergus exclaimed, pulling out one of the stools to sit down and starting to pick at the food sneakily.

"I'm starving," he added with a false guilty face in response to his wife's look. He knew that look and it said not to eat everything before dinner.

"Well, another ten minutes and dinner will be ready. Do you think you will survive?" Lola replied.

"Hey, it's not my fault if I've married an Italian woman with an incredible talent for cooking. Of course, I can't control myself in front of her dishes!"

Lola threw at her husband the kitchen towel she was holding, and they both broke into a deep laugh. She was far from being a good cook.

She had no talent in the kitchen at all, but she had the gift of fantasy. When her gang was sick of eating pasta, she invented easy recipes from scratch using leftovers. Most of the time, the results were open sandwiches or plates of cold cuts and cheese adorned with a salad. Salads were, in fact, her speciality; anything she had in the house was thrown in: walnuts, boiled eggs, tuna, goats cheese, whatever!

* * *

The boys were excited to see their father and Lola had to share her husband. When they eventually went to bed, she had him all to herself.

"Are they settled?" she asked when he was back downstairs after bringing them to bed.

They were old enough to change and wash without any of

their parents' supervision, but they still enjoyed being kissed goodnight.

That was usually Lola's task, but that night Fergus took over, and Lola relaxed on the couch.

Fergus let himself fall beside her and took one of the two glasses of whiskey that Lola had prepared.

He took the first sip while his wife curled up to him.

They stayed there in silence for a while, just enjoying each other's company, until they couldn't hear any more sound coming from upstairs.

"I think they are asleep," Lola said, getting up.

Husband and wife were burning with desire to be together.

They switched off the lights and hand in hand went upstairs to their bedroom.

The following morning Fergus woke up first and went down to make breakfast. He expected Alex and Philip to already be in the playroom watching TV, but surprisingly they were still asleep.

He retrieved the newspaper from the driveway. They had signed for the Irish Times weekend home delivery. Weekends were the only days the couple had time to read the news thoroughly on paper, as they both preferred.

Still sleepy and with her hair sticking out in all possible directions, Lola appeared in the kitchen.

It was June, and the temperature had started to be summery. Her light kimono robe was tight around her waist, showing a bit more curves than she would like. She was not particularly tall, and after the twins, her figure had never gone back to what it once was. She had never been petite, and she had always been generous around her waistline, but she was too lazy to kill herself multiple days a week in a gym. Her Pilates classes were enough. Most of the days, she liked what she saw in the mirror. Of course, there were bad days, she was a woman after all, and no woman wants herself as she is, but she was at ease with her body, and she just tried to dress according to her figure.

There was a time when she was concerned about Fergus not finding her attractive anymore, but he didn't seem to have noticed the extra pounds accumulated on her hips and abdomen. To be honest, he was not the slender guy she had met in La Valletta so many years ago either. Still, he was to her the most attractive man on the planet.

"So, you haven't told me what our dear neighbour Siobhan wanted yesterday while we were on the phone," Fergus asked while presenting his wife a mug of hot black coffee and some toast with butter and jam.

"You are not going to believe it," Lola answered, swallowing a bite of toast.

"Let me guess... with the break-ins that happened in the last six months, she's back on her kick to get a neighbourhood watch up and running again."

"That as well of course, but this time she also caught an old lady going through our mail."

Fergus looked puzzled at his wife, waiting for more details.

"According to Siobhan, this lady was checking out our house and ravaging inside our letterbox, but she ran away when she went after her."

"I thought this was supposed to be a quiet and secure area. And anyway, what would a thief want with our mail?" Fergus asked.

"Bank's information, bills, something to use to steal our identity."

"Well, sure they won't go far with our bank's details. Seriously, that woman has far too much time on her hands, and since the break-ins, she had become paranoid."

"I thought it was a bit ridiculous too, but you know how Siobhan is... I didn't want to contradict her and get trapped in an endless discussion on the subject. "

"Can't blame you, that woman is like a mastiff when she gets something in her mind. I don't know where poor Finn finds the patience to listen to her all the time. Let's hope the Garda will grant us the Neighbourhood Watch Scheme." Fergus finished his coffee and went off for a shower.

Fergus never really liked Siobhan, he thought she was a handful and had a far too extravagant taste in clothes; but Lola had the chance to know her a bit better over the years, and there was much more to that woman than showed. Indeed, she tended to be polemic and not to give up until she got what she wanted, but she proved to Lola, on more than one occasion, to be a good listener and a reliable "friend". Plus her daughter Alahnna, was the only baby sitter she trusted to mind the twins, and they adored her.

14

DUBLIN - IRELAND

The morning was bright; the sun fully up and already warm. The little residential road was busy with mothers and nannies taking the children to school. A small army of men wearing impeccable tailor-made suits was quickstepping carrying their real leather briefcases or, getting into their brand new SUV.

It was perfect; nobody would have paid attention to an elderly lady. I waited patiently outside number 4 Sanford Close until the front door opened. It was just past 8:30 am, Alex and Philip ran out the door with their backpacks swaying from one side to the other on their small backs. Fergus followed a few seconds later. He was wearing a t-shirt that accentuated, even more, his already protuberant belly.

He had let his beard grow since I saw him the first time, and now it was thick and black in contrast to his hair that had many stripes of white already.

Father and sons turned the corner, out of my sight.

I was still there, hoping Lola would leave the house too. I was not planning another "accidental" encounter; I only wanted to take a glance at her.

No luck, Fergus was back, but there was no sign of Lola.

For a second, I thought he had noticed me, but it was more likely paranoia.

I was ready to leave when a car pulled over in front of the house. Fergus opened the double gate, and the car drove in. A couple of approximately my age got out. I moved closer in the attempt to overhear bits of their conversation. The front door swung open, and Lola ran out to greet the elderly couple. Mama Angie and Papa Pat, she called them………

* * *

"Hey you, still around stealing correspondence?"

Siobhan's scream made the entire Owen family turn. Siobhan was sure it was the same woman she had seen previously sneaking around the post box of her friends and neighbours. She had a clear sight of the opposite side of the road from her kitchen window, and she had seen the woman standing there watching, spying on the neighbourhood. Siobhan walked down the street yelling. When she passed in front of Lola and Fergus, they stopped her and asked her what was going on.

"See that woman, that's the one I saw taking your post. I'm sure."

Lola, Fergus, Pat and Angela, all turned their heads towards Siobhan's accusatory finger's target.

The woman on the other side of the road was petrified and didn't dare to move or speak.

"Wait a minute," Lola said," I know that woman. You must be mistaken, Siobhan."

Lola waved at the Italian lady she had met at the cinema. She crossed the road and went to her, followed by Siobhan.

"Hi, lost again?" Lola said with a big smile trying to make sense of the woman's presence in front of her house but not wanting to be rude and ask a direct question.

"I remember you told me where you lived and because I'm

leaving tomorrow, I just wanted to leave a thank you card. You know for your kindness and your help."

"Oh, that is very sweet of you."

It sounded a bit strange and maybe overzealous, but Lola had no reason to doubt the sincerity of the gesture. She had instead plenty of reasons to shoot a killing look at her neighbour.

Against her will, Siobhan apologised and admitted she must have mistaken Laura for someone else.

"Hey, I have an idea, why don't you both come in for a coffee? Fergus's parents have just come back from Portugal, and will be staying with us for the night, before driving home." Lola said to a sceptical Siobhan and Laura.

Laura had just left with the excuse of a plane to catch, and while Pat and Angela had gone to freshen up, Fergus had locked himself in his office.

Only Lola and Siobhan were left in the kitchen. It only took a quick look at Siobhan's expression, for Lola to know something was up.

"I'll put on the kettle, and you shoot whatever you have to say."

"Is it that obvious?"

"Well, apart from the fact that you didn't take your eyes off Laura for a minute as well as giving her a third-degree interrogation, yes, even your face is giving you away," Lola replied sitting down in front of Siobhan with two mugs of tea.

"OK, OK, Mrs Freud. It's just that there is something odd about her. She gives me the creeps. Even if she is not the same woman I saw the other day, and I know what I saw!"

Lola's scepticism was all over her face.

"Oh feck it, you are probably right, and I'm just paranoid with all these burglaries and all," Siobhan added trying to sound as much convincing as she could. She gave a quick look at her watch and stood up, "I have to go now," and she walked towards the door followed by Lola.

"Hey, where is the beautiful pic of the four of you?" Siobhan asked already with her hand on the door handle.

Lola immediately looked at the console table by the door, where she used to keep a lamp and a few silver frames with family pictures. One was visibly missing.

"Oh don't tell me you broke it," Siobhan said, running her finger over the mark in the dust that the removed frame had left, "well, obviously you didn't break it while dusting, did you?" she then laughed gently.

Siobhan was one of those persons who could say the most horrible things but in the sweetest way.

"I told you that you should get a cleaner dear. You cannot possibly do everything yourself. Lucky you, you don't have a mother-in-law like mine. Something like that would make her taunt me for years."

Lola laughed, and for a moment, the image of Finn's mother popped into her head. She had only met her once, and that had been enough.

By the time Siobhan had left, Lola had forgotten about the missing frame. The twins had probably taken it for some school project and forgot to put it back.

15

PONTE ALTO - ITALY

"Hello," Mara picked up the phone, but she knew already she would have just met silence on the other end of the line.

She had been receiving those unnerving phone calls for several days.

"Who are you? What do you want?" she couldn't help but ask.

"You know who I am, and I know what you did." A sharp, angry voice replied before the line went dead.

Mara struggled to gasp for air.

So many years had passed, but she would have recognised that voice among millions.

The next few days Mara continually waited for the phone to ring. She wanted to talk, to explain, to reason and end this nonsense. Every time the landline rang, Mara jumped and ran to the phone, but it was never the voice she was waiting to hear.

She had to tell Giulia. She had no idea how her daughter could react to what her mother had done.

Mara knew that her actions could appear cruel, but she had done it for her family. She did what she had to. Giulia would have probably understood her reasons; after all, she was the one who had benefited the most. Still, Mara was sure that her daughter would be furious for being kept in the dark and for the possible consequences that they could face.

She locked herself in the study to avoid Edda overhearing her on the phone.

"Is it so urgent, Mum? Can it not wait until tomorrow? It's just that I have plans for tonight and ..."

Giulia had planned to tell Carlo everything about the forged signatures that night. He nearly blew everything out the other evening when they were dining at Mara's. Giulia had been quick to change the subject, but she could not go on like that. Carlo was not stupid and would have soon wondered why they couldn't mention the start of the project to Mara.

"No, Giulia, it can't wait. Otherwise, I wouldn't insist. Please, I need to see you and talk to you."

Her mother's despotic attitude would have usually irritated Giulia, but this time was different: something was alarming in Mara's tone. She sounded worried, possibly afraid, as incredible as it could be.

"Ok then, I'll see you in half an hour."

Giulia stepped off the treadmill and texted Carlo: - Sorry, hon. The old witch wants me to report for duty ASAP. I won't be home for dinner. See you later. Love you.-

She took a quick shower, grabbed a pair of leggings and a silk tunic and slipped her feet into a pair of Pretty Ballerina shoes already by the door.

Driving to her mother's place, Giulia kept wondering what could have required such an urgent meeting. The thought that Mara could have found out about the forged signatures had crossed her mind, but in that case, Mara would have been furious, not worried or afraid.

16

DUBLIN - IRELAND

Long days and warm enough to sleep with the windows ajar, the typical Irish summer. Lola always loved this time of the year and loved to look at their back garden as it was an explosion of colours. Lola may have lacked in the kitchen, but her green fingers were something to envy. Her garden was her pride and joy, even at the cost of spending hours kneeled pottering in the dirt. The previous year, Fergus and his father had built a canopy covering half of the patio, so now even on those warm but drizzly days, they could still enjoy the garden.

The boys were jumping on the trampoline, and Lola was sipping some blueberry juice on her swinging chair.

There was one thing she could not get off her mind: what had happened to the silver frame by the door?

She was sure the twins had it, but Alex and Philip had sworn they had not taken it, and she had no reason not to believe them.

The idea of a burglary crossed her mind, but what kind of sloppy robber would go after a silver frame and leave her purse, which was always by the door?

Lola was utterly absorbed by her thoughts and missed the phone ringing.

"Mum, the phone ..." the boys started to shout. Lola was forced to leave wherever the world she had lost herself in and looked at the twins trying to figure out what they wanted.

"The phone.....It keeps ringing," they said in unison.

Lola got up to get the phone, and while trying to remember where she had last left it, she heard knocking at the door.

"What is it today? Can someone not have any peace?" Lola muttered as she went to open the door.

Siobhan, dressed in a emerald and turquoise silk tunic was standing in front of her

"Are you going to let me in or not darling?" the woman said to Lola waking her from her trance.

"Sorry, yes of, course." Lola closed the door behind Siobhan and started to walk back to the rear garden still looking for her phone.

"Do you mind calling my mobile, Siobhan? I can hear it but I can't find it, and I know I missed a few calls. I want to check that everything is OK, you know after Pat's heart attack, I'm always a bit nervous when the phone rings unexpectedly or at an awkward time."

"Sure darling, but apart from the fact that it's four in the afternoon, and I wouldn't exactly qualify it as an odd time, I wouldn't bother too much as it was me calling."

"You? Why?"

Siobhan's right eyebrow arched up.

"I mean, why calling if you are here?" Lola added.

"Yes, I'm here now!" Siobhan said, rolling her eyes and continued, "But before you did me the honour to come to the door, I knocked at your door and rang your phone for fifteen minutes."

"Oh," Lola exclaimed genuinely surprised, "sorry, I was in the garden, a bit lost in my thoughts, I suppose."

"Is there something wrong? Are you OK?" Siobhan asked, suddenly concerned.

If she cared about someone, Siobhan would take their trouble personally and do whatever she could to help. On the other side, she was utterly incapable of hiding her dislike or lack of interest. Siobhan wasn't one of those people universally sympathetic and made no effort to be. A side of her personality, that Lola particularly appreciated as she was sure always to get the truth from her friend.

"You go ahead. I'll grab another glass and the jar of juice from the fridge," Lola said.

Siobhan had made herself comfortable on one of the garden chairs.

On the table, Lola noticed a present. She didn't even realise Siobhan was carrying something when she came in; but now that she thought about it, her hands had been behind her back all the time.

Lola placed the tray on the table and asked whose the gift was.

"Well, honey, that's for you. Open it."

"For me? Why? You are embarrassing me."

Lola didn't like unexpected presents. She didn't like gifts at all.

Every time she received a gift, she felt some obligation to reciprocate. Rationally, she knew it was nonsense, and if someone gives you a present, it's as much to please you, as to satisfy themselves. Still, she could not help it, unless it was Fergus of course. He didn't count; he was her husband.

This little phobia for gifts was another issue Lola blamed on her childhood. Aunt Mara, in fact, never missed a chance to remind her of all the things she had done for her. She raised her under the obligation of gratitude and obedience for her generosity. Anything Lola had received growing up had a price.

Siobhan didn't miss the change of expression on Lola's

face. The last thing she wanted was to embarrass her neighbour and friend. She had seen something and thought about Lola, as simple as that and she explained it: "...Plus, it was on 70% sale. Don't think I spent a fortune," Siobhan added.

Lola relaxed and smiled: It was nothing else than a genuine gesture any friend would do to another. She started to unwrap the parcel with increasing excitement and curiosity, and when she saw the content, she broke out in a big deep laugh followed by Siobhan.

Attracted by the noise of the wrapping paper being crumpled up and by the laughs, the twins ran towards the two women.

"Wow, that is a very fancy pair of flip flops," Alex said.

"They are fit flops, silly. Oliver's mum has them too, and he heard her saying that they do something to your butt, but he's not sure what exactly....Do you know what they do to your butt?" Philip asked his mother, who could not stop laughing.

Discouraged from waiting for an answer, the twins took off and went back to play.

"Who is this Oliver's mum?" Siobhan asked, still giggling, "I must check her out to see if they work."

"Oh, gosh I don't know, but looking at her, she must wear them the wrong way," Lola said.

"Oh, my, Miss Politically Correct has let her tongue unleashed. You naughty girl." Siobhan was laughing out loud and so was Lola, incredulous to have said that and so spontaneously. Well, in fairness, she had never liked Oliver's mum. She was one of those huge matriarchs who think they know everything but the only thing they do is gossiping away.

"Now, honey, try them on. I was not sure about the size, but if they don't fit, I can return them".

Lola started to walk up and down the decking in her new sandals: "They are perfect, thank you so much."

"I got a pair myself, you know. They were selling them

basically for nothing, and as I always see you in flip-flops over the summer I thought you could do with something that wouldn't hurt your back and, as Oliver's mum says, that would massage your butt while you walk too.....If you wear them correctly!" Siobhan replied, squinting her eyes.

"To generous friends" Lola raised her glass inviting Siobhan to toast.

After the first sip of juice, Siobhan's disgusted expression was a clear message to Lola to go to the kitchen and come back with a bottle of Bacardi to add to her neighbour's drink.

Lola did not share the neighbourhood rumours about Siobhan's drinking habits. She had undoubtedly seen Siobhan drinking at some unconventional times of the day, but to call her a functioning alcoholic was far too much.

In the many years Lola had known Siobhan, she had never seen her drunk, or unreliable. She was a woman with an explosive personality and a very colourful taste in clothes. For her misfortune, she was also very wealthy and attractive — all things generating jealousy, envy and false rumours.

"Now, missy, do you want to tell me what's wrong?"

Siobhan had a sixth sense when it came to Lola.

"Nothing really, you know just........." Lola tried to sound reassuring, but the person in front of her was no fool.

"OK then, well, before you came, I was here, and all I could think about was where that photo frame could be."

Siobhan cocked her head and looked at Lola with a puzzled expression.

"You know the one I used to keep by the door with the pic of the four of us. You had noticed it was missing the other day," Lola stated like it was most obvious and Siobhan should have guessed herself.

"Oh, that one. I thought you said the boys took it."

"That was what I thought, but they didn't, or so they said. And frankly, I have no reason not to believe them. Plus, I searched in their bedrooms."

Siobhan said nothing and poured herself some more Bacardi and juice and leaned back in the chair.

Now it was Lola's turn to detect something. "What is it?" she asked.

"Nothing, I was just thinking about that photo frame, and I remembered something from the day we were all here..."

"And......" Lola leaned towards Siobhan, encouraging her to continue.

Siobhan swiftly sat up straight.

"Just promise me not to freak out, OK?"

"OK," Lola said slightly concerned about why she should not freak out.

"Do you remember that morning when we were all in the kitchen and that Italian whatever woman ...."

"Yes, Laura, the one you taunted with scrutinising questions all the time she was here?" Lola interrupted, still feeling annoyed at the memory.

"See, I knew you would freak out..."

"OK, OK. I'm sorry; go on..."

"OK, that's the thing: she asked to go to the toilet, remember?" Siobhan didn't wait for an answer to her rhetorical question and continued, "And she went right when Matthew rang me from school begging me to bring him the soccer bag that he forgot at home like I had nothing better to do," Lola's expression was now obviously impatient for Siobhan to get to the point. Siobhan left her little digression about her spoiled teenage boy and went on, "Anyway, I went into the sitting room to talk because in the kitchen I couldn't hear a damn thing and when I was going back to the kitchen, I saw her coming from the hall. She had her bag with her. The frame could have fit in it."

Siobhan was nearly afraid to look Lola in the eye as she knew how protective she was of the old lady. Lola tended to get attached to parental figures, and Siobhan believed it had to do with the fact that she lost her parents when she was only a child. That also explained her attachment to Fergus's parents.

"Seriously, Siobhan? Again, with this story? What has that poor woman done to you? Was it not enough making yourself ridiculous in front of everybody when you had mistaken her for a vagrant going through my post?"

Lola's tone had been sharper than she intended, and she couldn't miss Siobhan's hurt face.

She wanted to say something, but she didn't know what to say as apologising would have meant admitting Siobhan's delirious theory could be right.

"I told you it was better not telling you," Siobhan said, incapable of disguising her trembling voice, and stood up to leave.

Lola rushed after her and stopped at the front gate, "Sorry, I didn't mean to snap; it's just that... why is everybody so freaking suspicious?"

"Oh, now I am everybody...." Siobhan's turn to snap.

"No, my husband is everybody. He found it very strange that Laura came here to hand me a thank-you card, and even more strange that in the end, she had not even left the card".

Siobhan's face lit up. She knew better than saying anything else, but the fact that Fergus had also sniffed something odd, reinforced her suspicions.

17

PONTE ALTO - ITALY

Giulia was sitting speechless in her mother's sitting room. The woman who had raised her with such an intense discipline and sense of honesty was a liar and the first one to betray those values. But why coming clean now? Something must have happened. Giulia had no doubt. Whoever was capable of such a lie would bring it with them to the grave. She looked straight into her mother's face, her big inscrutable eyes, once emerald green and now of a fading grey, didn't show repentance but fear.

Mara moved closer to her daughter and took Giulia's hands in hers, "Everything I did, I did it for the family and you." There was a time when Giulia craved her mother's sympathy, her physical contact. There was a time when she would have given everything she had for a hug, or Mara to lovingly hold her hands like now, but that time was gone. She didn't want and didn't need her mother's empathy anymore, besides she hardly believed it was sincere.

"Bullshit." Giulia freed her hands from Mara's grip and stood up.

"You did it for yourself! Have you ever thought about the

suffering you have caused? And what if you are found out? What will become of me?"

Giulia's words were full of anger and disappointment, and Mara finally admitted why she decided to tell the truth, "Someone has found out." Mara told her about the phone call and continued, "I have to tell Lola everything, you must understand. At this point, I have no choice. If I do it first, hopefully, the matter will stay inside the family."

"This is insane, mum. We will have someone blackmailing us forever. There must be a way to stop her before she gets to Lola."

"She already got to Lola; only she has not said anything to her yet. She wants me to do it, but if I won't, she will. And that I cannot afford. She will drag our name in the dirt. Don't you see? If I can talk to Lola first, maybe she will understand, maybe they both will and agree to keep it quiet."

Giulia had stopped listening. She was not sure how to tackle this, but she was confident of one thing: her mother will not say anything to anybody. The past had to stay buried no matter what. Her mother was old and would probably never see a day in court, but she had everything to lose.

"Listen to me..." Giulia turned towards her mother and grabbed her by the arms, "You are not going to say or do anything. Not until I think clearly through this. Do you understand me?" Giulia was not asking; she was ordering.

"You are not going to stand here and insult me. My actions did benefit you the most, and it is clear that you have no intention to renounce your privileges, so spare yourself from being pathetic and spare me the lecture." Mara had gone back to her usual sharpness, but before she could finish, Giulia started screaming in her face: "Can you at least listen to yourself? You old fool! It's not only about you anymore. It's about me too, because your shit is going to hit me like a spate."

Mara's outraged expression didn't stop Giulia from continuing, "As your only concern is your precious reputation, you better do as I say. Or I swear to God, I will go to the police myself. They will see me as another victim of your lies and crimes."

For the first time, Giulia felt some power over her mother, but the truth was that neither of them had the whip hand and they needed a plan to stop the only person who now wielded it.

18

DUBLIN - IRELAND

So many years had passed since the last time we spoke, but her voice had not changed. She still had some power over me, but I detected fear in her answers. I cut the phone call short. My emotions were too strong.

One part of me feared that she would trick me, as she had always done, but I tried not to think about it. I had a message to deliver. I wanted her to know that I knew what she had done, and I wanted to be clear what I expected her to do.

I thought about Lola, how she would react when she knew the truth. She would be shocked at first, maybe even disappointed, but she is a clever woman and love always wins. There was only one problem, her neighbour. I was sure Siobhan had not believed for one second to have mistaken me for someone else, but I never imagined her suspiciousness brought her to follow me. I saw her parked outside my place.

She had probably already checked with the school also and discovered I was never a student there. I needed to stop her. I could not afford for her to blow my cover with Lola. It was too early for the truth to come up.

* * *

I called a taxi as I had no time to wait for the bus. I had to be in Sanford Close as soon as possible. With a bit of luck, Siobhan had not talked to Lola yet.

I looked carefully on both side of the road before climbing Siobhan's doorsteps. I didn't want Lola or Fergus to see me as for their concern I had already left the country.

There was no doorbell; just one gold plated lion shape knocker, and it was cumbersome. There was no answer. I discretely took a peek through the front window, and nobody seemed to be home. I couldn't leave without talking to her, but waiting at Siobhan's doorstep was not an option. I was too exposed. I crossed the road and waited behind a big tree.

19

DUBLIN - IRELAND

"Are you not going to answer that? Your phone has been ringing all morning," Fergus said, pointing at his wife's mobile vibrating and ringing on the kitchen counter.

"Nah, it's Siobhan. She probably wants to go for a walk, but I want to spend the entire day with my husband today. I'm happy you took a day off. Maybe we can do something as the boys are in school longer at homework club?"

"Well, if that's your desire, I sure don't want to disappoint you, madam," and Fergus hugged Lola from behind gently starting to unbutton her shirt. Lola turned around to face him: "Well, I was more thinking about a movie or something, but if you have other suggestions," she gave him a naughty smile.

Passion was never a problem in their relationship, but the arrival of the twins made it challenging to find the time to enjoy each other's company intimately.

"You should take a day off more often," Lola said to her husband, both still naked and cuddling. The bedroom window was open; the sun was high and warm; the breeze smelled of summer and felt like a gentle caress on their faces.

"You know what I would like now?" Lola said after her

tummy rumbled and distracted them both from their imaginary trip.

"I want coffee and a ham omelette," she continued.

"Let's say ham and courgette, and I'll have one with you," Fergus agreed.

* * *

"This is lovely; we are so lucky," Lola ate the last piece of her eggs, leaned her head back and lifted her bare feet to rest them on her husband's lap. Their peaceful moment was interrupted by a text message coming in.

Lola went to check concerned it could be the school. It was not.

"I'm afraid I have to ring Siobhan back," she said, sitting back on her deck chair and handing the phone to Fergus so that he could read the text she had just received:-Jeez, woman where are you? I urgently need to talk to you. It's serious-

"I hope it's not another of her theories about Laura," Lola said.

"What do you mean?" Fergus's attention was not on the phone's screen anymore but his wife.

"I thought I told you..., anyway, the other day when she came to bring me the flip flops, she went on again about the fact that we know nothing about Laura and about how strange it was that she came all the way here for a thank- you card and then the picture frame's story..."

"Wait a minute, what picture frame?" Fergus looked at his wife, having no idea of what she was talking about.

"You know, the one that was in the hall. The one that I can't find anymore. Do you remember? I'm sure I told you."

"Oh, that one!" everything was now clear to Fergus, "But you also told me the boys took it for a school project."

"Well, that's what I thought, but they swore they didn't."

"And what would Siobhan have to say about It? Who does

she think took it? A ghost?" Fergus concluded laughing, but the grin on his wife's face told him she didn't find the situation funny at all.

"Apparently, to her, the most obvious explanation is that Laura took it."

"That's ridiculous. I admit I find the woman a bit odd and she gives me a bit of the creeps but thinking that she had come into our house to steal a picture frame is far too much."

Lola was relieved that Fergus didn't support Siobhan's theory.

"And this is not all," Lola continued, "I made a mistake to tell her you didn't trust Laura either..."

"It's not that I don't trust her," Fergus interrupted to justify himself, but Lola silenced him with her hand and kept talking, "You don't like her whatever. The fact is that you should have seen the sparkle in Siobhan's eyes. I'm surprised she had not called you instead of me. You know, to discuss strategy against the enemy."

"Well, maybe now you are a bit too harsh on the poor woman. You always say it yourself that she tends to be protective with the people she cares for and you are one of them," Fergus said, taking his wife's hand in his.

"I know, and you know how much I like Siobhan, but still I can't help but be slightly annoyed with her."

Fergus could not help but smile as his wife, who reminded him of a child who had just fought with her best friend.

"I tell you what. We are going to forget about this entire matter for what is left of our kids free time, and then I'll go to collect the boys, and you will pop into our over-imaginative neighbour's to see what the emergency is."

Lola lifted her shades and kissed her husband. He was good at finding solutions and fixing problems, and she loved this side of him; it always made her feel safe.

20

DUBLIN - IRELAND

I nearly had a heart attack when the neighbour saw me again. And then all those questions she asked. I was sure she suspected something, but that was not what I had in mind. The only thing I could think about was Lola's words when I asked about her parents. She said she was an orphan and had never met her father, and her mother took her own life when she was only three. It was as someone had stabbed me in the heart.

If I was not sure what to do when I first arrived in Dublin, now I knew. I was going to make the one person responsible for all this to pay for it. I wanted revenge, and I wanted the truth to come out.

My sister had turned me into a ghost, but she should know that spirits always come back to haunt.

I looked one more time at the frame I took from the house. It was a beautiful picture of the four of them. A happy family, a family of which I should have been a part of.

Rage rose inside me.

21

DUBLIN - IRELAND

Siobhan came home alone. My prayers had been heard.

I watched her go inside. I carefully looked around me to be sure nobody saw me, and I climbed the doorsteps for the second time.

She opened the door. On her heavily lipsticked lips, there was a big smile that faded away as soon she saw who it was.

"You! What are you doing here?"

I felt Siobhan's surprise but sensed no fear in her voice.

"I just want to talk," I said, keeping my voice as low as possible not to attract any attention.

"I don't think there is much you can say. I know you lied to my friend and I'm going to tell her everything. I knew I was right about you. There is just one thing you can clarify for me, why? What do you want from her?" she spat at me.

The fact that she had not spoken to Lola yet was the only thing I cared about, all the rest I could handle.

"I can explain everything, and I swear I don't intend any harm to Lola. Just let me explain. Please, let me in, and I'll tell you everything. The whole truth." I was nearly begging, but she remained untouched. She stood there, staring at me. I understood she had no intention to hear my side of the story.

"I don't think so, you weirdo. Do you want to talk? Let's go next door to Lola. Then you can explain and tell your truth."

She reached for her keys, and she was about to step out the door. She heard no reason. She wanted us to go to Lola. I panicked, and from there on, everything is blurry in my mind.

I must have pushed my way in, and she must have fought back, and that would also explain the scratches on my arms. I pushed her, she tripped. Everything had happened so fast, too fast: one minute we were talking by the door and the next one she was lying on the floor senseless. I kneeled to check on her, and I saw the blood coming from the back of her head.

I felt sick, but I made it out the door and ran to the path before emptying my stomach.

I didn't mean for any of this to happen. I just wanted to talk to Siobhan, to tell her the truth and ask her not to say anything to Lola before I had the chance to speak with her. She was still breathing when I left, at least I knew I didn't kill her, but what will happen when she wakes up? She will tell, and for me, it will be the end.

Back in my room, I couldn't find any rest. I stayed awake all night, waiting for the police to knock at my door and arrest me, but nobody came.

Then I had an even bigger worry than Siobhan reporting me. What if she had not made it? What if she had died?

I could be a murderer.

22

DUBLIN - IRELAND

"When you are enjoying yourself, time always passes too fast, doesn't it?" Lola said, retracting her legs from Fergus's lap, "I'm afraid it's time to go and get the boys."

"Already?"

"Yep...Welcome to my world!"

The couple left home together then split right outside their gate. While Fergus turned the corner to go to the school, Lola just went next door to see Siobhan.

The little pedestrian gate was open, and Lola immediately thought it was strange. Since all the robberies in the area, Siobhan always kept it closed. She climbed the steps up to the entrance of the house only to realise that the door was ajar. Lola knocked, but no sound came from inside the house.

"Hello, Siobhan? Are you there?" Still no answer.

Something was not right! Lola let herself in, "Siobhan? The door was open, so I'm just coming in," Lola didn't finish her sentence before a deep scream came out of her throat. Siobhan was lying on the floor in a pool of blood.

The ambulance didn't take long to arrive. Straight after

999, Lola called Finn. He came as the paramedics were bringing his wife out on the stretcher.

"I don't know. I can't say what happened; when I arrived, the front door was open. I just walked in and there she was on the floor in a puddle of blood. She must have tripped and banged her head; I mean what else could have happened?" Lola gave him the same version she had given the paramedics.

* * *

The following day, after dropping the kids to school, Lola went to the hospital to see how her neighbour and friend was. Finn was there, and so were Alahnna and Matthew.

"The doc says she will be fine. But at the moment, they are keeping her in an induced coma. Until the internal bleeding in her brain stops, and the bruise is absorbed completely" Finn updated her.

"I'm so sorry; if only I had popped in earlier...." Lola's eyes began to fill with tears. If only she had answered her damn phone, none of this would have happened.

"Are you joking Lola? You saved her life, and we'll be grateful to you forever."

And for the first time after years of acquaintance, the reticent Dr Finn Drake hugged her revealing all his vulnerability.

The nurse came in to let them know visiting hours were over. Only the closest family members were allowed to stay now.

"I'll be back tomorrow. But if there is anything you need, please let me know." Lola gave a last glance at the bed where her friend was lying immobile like she was sleeping and left.

She had nearly reached the elevator when she heard someone calling her from behind: "Mrs Owen, please wait".

The voice was not familiar to Lola; she stopped and turned to see a man walking towards her. His facial features were robust and angular, and his being over 6 feet in height made him look intimidating. But a head full of wild ginger curls gave him somehow a gentle expression.

"Detective Enda McCarthey, nice to meet you," the officer showed his badge and shook Lola's hand.

"They told me you are the one who found Mrs Drake." Detective McCarthey didn't wait for Lola to respond; after all, it was not a question but a fact, "I would like to ask you a few questions if you don't mind, Mrs Owen?" This one was a question, but his tone made it clear that she could only answer "yes".

"Of course," Lola replied.

"After you found your neighbour lying on the floor, what did you do exactly? Can you try to recall your actions as precisely as you can?"

"Yes, but I already said it to the paramedics. I don't know what else I can add…"

"Please, Mrs Owen. I need to hear it from you, and any small detail could be crucial."

"Ok, then, "Lola said, not sure what all this was about, "I went in, I saw her, I kneeled to feel her pulse, and then I called 999 and her husband and my husband."

"Did you touch her head, where she was bleeding, I mean."

"No, I'm pretty sure about that, I don't do well with blood. It took all my bravery and a hard stomach to wait for the ambulance inside." Lola felt slightly ashamed, but ever since she remembered blood scared her. Even when she had a blood test done, she had to look elsewhere as the syringe filled with the thick red liquid.

"So, you didn't go out after finding her? And your hands were not dirty with blood?" Detective McCarthey asked with a frown.

"Just a little. The blood was running from Siobhan's head down to her hand, where I touched to feel her pulse."

"Did you touch anything inside or outside the house? The door handle or the handrail, maybe?" he continued.

"No," Lola answered short. Lola would never use any handrail anywhere as her aunt Mara raised her with the phobia that they are dirty and full of other people's germs. She wanted to tell McCarthey, but maybe it was not the right time for such a comment.

"If you don't mind coming down to the Donnybrook station, we would like to take your fingerprints anyway. We can also arrange to come to you with a kit if you prefer," the detective asked, again with a tone that didn't leave many choices of answers.

"Of course, I can't force you if you don't want. You are not a suspect," McCarthey then added in front of Lola's lack of response and with a softened tone.

"I don't care to have my fingerprints taken, I have nothing to hide, but can I at least know why? I thought it was an accident." Lola felt under scrutiny, but most of all, she felt McCarthey owed her an explanation.

The detective hesitated: "It seemed to be an accident, at first, ma'am. But the paramedics spotted some bloody prints on the door and the handrail outside, that showed there was someone else present at the scene. Of course, Mrs Drake will be able to tell us what happened as soon as she wakes up, but for now, I have to investigate the accident as an assault."

Lola was aware that her mouth was wide open, and her expression was probably the most idiotic the detective had ever seen. Maybe Siobhan's security paranoia was not groundless.

"Do you think she surprised someone breaking in? There have been a lot of break-ins in the area recently." Lola asked.

"It's a possibility, but nothing is missing. Of course, whoever had broken in might have got startled and run." Detective McCarthey's words hung in the air. It was not what he believed had happened.

23

DUBLIN - IRELAND

The journey to the airport was the longest of my life. Every time I heard a siren, I turned my head by instinct, to see if they were after me.

I was taking my passport from my handbag when my eyes fell on the TV opposite the gate. I usually don't like to watch the news; I don't need a reminder of how perverse human beings can be. But that night, I couldn't ignore it.

They were talking about a vicious attack which occurred in one of the most prominent areas of the city. Siobhan's face soon appeared on the screen. They showed the paramedics taking her away and Lola looking on.

I went closer to the TV to hear what they were saying. I needed to know what had happened to Siobhan. Was she alive? And if so, did she already talk with the authorities? Did Lola know?

Of course, I was aware the news wouldn't answer all my questions, but at least it would tell me if I was a murderer or a wanted person.

Siobhan was alive, they said. They were keeping her in an induced coma, but she would fully recover.

The police were looking for witnesses of a burglary gone wrong.

That, plus Siobhan's unconsciousness gave me enough time to go ahead with my plan and sort things out in Italy first. Then Lola could know, and even if Siobhan reported me, it wouldn't matter.

Time was ticking, and before I boarded the plane, I dialled my sister's number. I wanted to let her know I was coming for her.

I was not going to let her get away with what she had done, and I wanted her to know.

24

PONTE ALTO - ITALY

"You thought you could get away with that, didn't you? And why wouldn't you? You did get away with what you have done for so long, that I bet you thought to be off the hook forever. Well, I'm sorry, but it's over now."

It took Mara all the energy she had to hide the shock mixed with fear in her voice." What do you want?" she asked in the end as sharply as she could.

"I simply want back what is mine, and I want you to pay for what you have done."

"There is nothing left for you here. You had made your choice, and we had made a pact. You are as guilty as me."

"Don't you dare, you evil bitch. You lied to me."

The voice on the phone was angry and full of rage.

"How did you look at yourself in the mirror all these years without feeling disgusted with yourself?"

"If it's money that you want, I can give you more," Mara knew far too well the problem was not the money. She knew her sister was not going to fall for it, but it was worth the try, at least to gain time to think about the next move.

"You can't buy me this time, Mara."

"Easy to say now, isn't it?" Mara was slowly regaining her strength and confidence.

"You had become like dad, only he killed mother, and you killed me." Lorna was starting to be overwhelmed by the emotions.

"Mother killed herself. She was weak, and she didn't care enough for us to survive. She was as selfish as you have been, or you have forgotten that both you and your daughter have only to thank me for being alive?"

Mara was fully back in control; her voice sharp and resolute; her words like stabs. A painful silence fell, Mara had scored a point.

"I know, I made mistakes, but they were nothing compared to yours. I'll deal with my responsibilities. I'm willing to take the risk, and whatever will happen, it will be worth it because that's the only way to make you take responsibility for everything you have done and pay for it."

"All I did was clean up your mess, as usual," Mara shouted over the phone.

"Maybe, but in doing that you made more mess. And this time it's your mess."

Mara didn't expect such strength and determination. She had lost her power over her sister, and it scared her. For the first time in her life, things were slipping out of her control, and there was nothing she could do about it.

How could she have been so naive to think that the past wouldn't have come back?

* * *

The door of the study was ajar, and Edda popped her head inside to see if she could get in and clean. Mara's blank look didn't register her presence, "Is it everything alright, Mrs Kopfler?"

"Yes, of course," Mara answered as she had just returned

from a parallel world. Her eyes were red in fear and discomfort for what was inevitably to come.

"What about knocking Edda? Have you ever heard of that? Now I would appreciate some privacy if you don't mind."

Edda instinctively stepped back, mouth open and speechless. She was about to leave when her employer called from behind: "Were you spying on me?"

The old woman blushed and muttered some apologies, "No. The door was ajar, and I thought I'd come in to see if I could clean the study."

Mara didn't have anything against poor Edda, but she could not afford anyone to stick their nose in this business.

"Now I'm done, you can go in and clean. And by the way Edda, I saw you the other day consoling Giulia. She's not a little girl anymore. I think you spent enough time spoiling her. Maybe if I hadn't allowed you to do so all these years, she would be less weak, " Mara coldly said.

Edda stiffened but still didn't dare to make eye contact.

"She's not your daughter, and I don't appreciate that you are getting in between our arguments," Mara added and left.

Edda rushed inside the study, closed the door and allowed herself to cry. It was no news Mara could treat her housekeeper like that, just sometimes Edda felt it was far too much and today when she had mentioned her daughter, she thought that it was too low even for Mara Kopfler.

If only she had the bravery to rebel.

25

DUBLIN - IRELAND

Lola kissed the twins goodbye, she waited for them to enter the school gate and continued walking in the direction of the local Garda station. She knew where it was, but had never stepped foot inside.

When they first moved into the neighbourhood, she remembered Fergus showed her where the Garda station was, "In case anything ever happens," he said.

Donnybrook Garda station was in an old historic building squeezed between a nail bar and a fishmonger. Lola pushed open the little pedestrian gate and walked through a wholly paved garden, where there had once been a lawn. She pushed the heavy black door in front of her, but it was locked. On the sidewall, there was a small sign with the opening hours. Below it there was a bell to ring in case of emergencies.

Lola was not sure if her reason to be there qualified as an emergency, but she didn't want to return another time. Also, that detective at the hospital had asked her to go.

Even if she had no emergencies to report, she felt more than entitled to ring the bell.

She didn't have to wait long before a young Garda came to the door.

"Good morning, what can I do for you, ma'am?"

Lola had just introduced herself when someone shouted from inside, "Let her in Kevin. I asked Mrs Owen to come down."

The young guard stepped aside and politely gestured to Lola to go in while he locked the door behind her.

"Good morning, Mrs Owen, and thanks for coming so soon," Detective Enda McCarthey said, extending his arm to shake her hand.

"The sooner, the better, they say, right?" Lola answered back, even if she did not think so at all. If it were for her, she would have come down in the afternoon. Who wants to waste their kids' free time in a police station?

It had been Fergus that suggested she would go first thing in the morning.

"Better not to let the Garda wait," he had said. Since she had met him, Fergus always got nervous around the police and far too much concerned about helping. Lola only understood later in their relationship why, after he confessed that in his teens he was caught smoking a joint in a park. The local sergeant, who happened to be also a family friend, had brought him in and kept him in a cell for a few hours as to show how he could end up if he kept going down that road.

Fergus believed he was exaggerating; after all, it was only a bloody innocuous joint, but he learnt his lesson. After that episode, he had always been respectful of the law when at his best. Exception made for the occasional joint he still shared with his brother on the odd times when they got together.

"Kevin, would you get the fingerprint set ready please?" the detective ordered.

Lola felt the young guard's eyes on her. He didn't know if he should treat her as a suspect or a witness.

"Please follow me, Mrs Owen," Detective McCarthey opened his office door, and Lola followed him in. He took a seat behind a desk and gestured for her to sit on the opposite side.

Lola was nervous, she didn't know why, but her foot tapping rhythmically on the floor betrayed her.

"Before we proceed with the fingerprints, I have a few questions for you if you don't mind. Also, I need you to sign a consent form agreeing to have the prints taken willingly."

Detective McCarthey's tone was professional, but not cold. Detached maybe, but there was nothing in his voice that made Lola think that he doubted her account of the events. The previous evening, she had convinced herself that the only reason they wanted to fingerprint her; it was to prove her involvement in the attack rather than exclude it.

Fergus had as usually found the way to dismiss his wife's absurd rumination, "These things happen only in the movies and to those who have something to hide. And that's not you," he said.

Lola replayed her husband's words in her head and relaxed in the artificial leather chair. If that office needed something, it was a restyle. Thankfully she was wearing a pair of long wide linen trousers preventing the skin of her legs from sticking to the seat.

"Mr Drake told me that a few days before his wife's attack, she had a run-in with someone on the street, and she was quite upset about it. Someone who was searching in your letterbox. Were you aware of it?"

McCarthey already knew the answer, but he was verifying if Lola's account coincided with Finn Drake's'.

"Yes, she told me. We had a few burglaries in the area, and she was quite upset about it..." Lola gave the full account but tried to leave Laura out as much as she could. It's not that she wanted to keep anything from the police and even less she wanted to make Siobhan look paranoid, but at the same time, she believed Laura had nothing to do with any of this, and it was all a big misunderstanding.

"We are ready, detective," Kevin popped his head into the room and waited for orders.

"Oh, perfect, we are coming, Kevin."

McCarthey stood up, and so did Lola. She exited the room first, impatient to have her prints taken and leave the station.

"Just one more finger and we are done," the young Garda was not seeing much action these days as protector of the law and fingerprinting someone was probably the most exciting task of his day.

It took Lola several washes and half a bottle of hand soap to scrape the horrible black ink thoroughly away from her fingers. The last thing she wanted was going around like a listed criminal of some sort.

That evening, Lola waited for Fergus to arrive home and after she filled him in with the details of her visit to the Garda station, she let him put the boys to bed and went to the hospital.

When she arrived, Finn and the kids were leaving; she met them at the parking lot.

They told her there were no changes in her state, but she went up anyway.

She had to admit that what happened to Siobhan made her realise she had more feeling for the woman than she thought. It was so strange to see her there, with no makeup, no colourful outfits or extravagant accessories. Lola told her briefly about her day, gently caressing her hand. She kissed her on the forehead and left.

It had been a long day, and Lola was looking forward to a quiet evening. She was glad that Fergus was home and could handle the boys for a while. Since the attack, they were tormenting her with questions about what had happened to Mrs Drake. They wanted to know what she had seen, how she had found her, if there was a lot of blood and, ultimately, after they heard their mother had her fingerprints taken, they could not stop talking about how cool it was to do the same stuff they do in the movies.

Lola understood their concern and excitement. They were eight years old, what else would you expect! But still she wanted them to shut up, and now she craved some peace. Maybe, her finding Siobhan as she did had affected her more than she wanted to show. What she didn't know was that it was just the tip of the iceberg.

26

PONTE ALTO - ITALY

It had passed a long time since the last time I flew to Venice. The view was mesmerising. The day was sunny and bright; it had been like landing on the water. The group of students that were on the plane started to take pictures with their phones. They were incredulous of the vision, making them excited and noisy. Unfortunately, the flight attendants spoiled their enthusiasm, forcing them all back to their seats.

I purposely packed only a cabin bag not to waste time at the belt. Once out of the airport, I went straight to ask for the bus to Ponte Alto.

It would have been quicker and easier to drive, but I didn't want to rent a car. I wanted to stay anonymous.

I had twenty-five minutes to wait before my bus left. I ate something and bought a couple of bottles of water as the heat was more overwhelming than I expected.

As soon as the bus left, the driver informed us that we would have stopped twice to use the restroom, stretch our legs and grab something to eat or drink if we wanted, but we could not stay over fifteen minutes at each stop.

The coach had every comfort, from wifi to air conditioning.

We left the motorway and took the old road up to the Dolomites.

The fresh air of the mountains was most welcoming compared to the sticky and humid atmosphere of Venice.

Except for a couple of tunnels dug into the mountain, that made the way exceptionally shorter than I remembered, nothing much had changed in the landscape. The wild urbanisation that had plagued Italy in the last 40 years had somehow left these territories untouched.

From the bus station to the B&B I planned to stay, it was only a brief walk.

By the activity in the streets, it was evident that the tourist season had already started.

When I arrived at the guesthouse and asked for a room, Mr and Mrs Schwartze didn't notice the coincidence of me showing up just after Mrs Martin had called to cancel her booking.

I never actually thought they would, and anyway, it was a risk I had to take. I couldn't afford to wander around with the chance that someone would recognise me. For the same reason, I couldn't leave my documents with the Schwartzes for the moment; I faked a migraine attack and went straight to my room.

If everything were going as planned, I would have provided them with my identity the following day.

27

PONTE ALTO - ITALY

Giulia hadn't spoken to her mother since their last argument.

She knew Mara was too proud to reach out first.

Giulia could be stubborn but was not the over-proud type, how could she be with a mother like hers! There had always been only space for Mara's pride in their house.

Giulia knew she had to engage first. She couldn't keep hoping that something would happen and that her mother would fix this as she had always fixed every problem before. She knew she was only postponing the inevitable.

Carlo didn't know anything about Lorna yet. Giulia hadn't told him. Not because she didn't trust him enough, but because she didn't want to answer the millions of questions he certainly would have asked. So now she was keeping two secrets from him. She hadn't told him about the forged signatures either. Again, not because of a lack of trust, but because it was never the right time. Now, what Giulia started to wonder was if the right time would ever come, or if she was procrastinating out of cowardice.

Maybe her mother was right after all. Giulia was weak and incapable of facing reality. Tears started to fill her eyes.

She wanted a magic potion to get out this bundle of lies and secrets with no hassle and no harm.

She stood there in the kitchen, incapable of moving. Her look lost in the emptiness, and her hands closed in a tight fist on the table. She was trying to control her nerves and at the same time holding herself to stand still. The tears started to flow down her face; her mascara smudged all over her face.

"Hey, are you OK?" Carlo's voice woke her from her trance.

Incapable of speaking, Giulia turned towards him and buried her face in his broad chest sobbing.

He didn't say a word but gently kept stroking her hair until she had let it all out and found the strength to detach herself from him.

"I think we better talk," Giulia said in a whisper and sat down at the kitchen table, exhausted but already feeling lighter.

Carlo filled a glass of water from the sink and sat down opposite her.

They talked in a way they had never before. It was as if for the first time, they had allowed themselves to show their deepest feelings. Giulia unveiled her fragility and Carlo his sweetness. Giulia told him everything about the fight she had with her mother and the reason behind it. It was a weight far too heavy for her to carry alone. It would have been the right time to confess she had forged Mara's signature also, but Carlo's worried expression stopped her. He had received enough bad news for one day, that would be far too much to process.

"Oh, boy……Fuck…" that was all Carlo had been saying for the last ten minutes. Giulia followed him with her wide eyes going up and down the kitchen.

She was supposed to be the one in distress, but the roles had now reversed. Carlo was panicking. He had not built his career in construction without dirtying his hands on the edge of illegality, but what his future mother-in-law had done was beyond imagination. Giulia grabbed one of Carlo's hand and made him look her straight in the eye.

"Do you still love me? Do you still want to marry me?"

The question took Carlo entirely by surprise. Of course, he did, and so he said to Giulia. That was not what he was upset about; the point was what was going to change financially for them. Carlo was only thinking about the consequences for the business if what Mara had done became public.

"Listen to me; this has nothing to do with you, or me, or us. I love you, and I want to marry you. I picked you, not your family. You are you, and you have nothing to do with your mother. She is a fucking bitch."

Giulia looked at him raising one of her eyebrows, and he went on, "I mean, no offence, but you must agree that it takes some stomach to do what Mara did."

Giulia nodded, and without having any control over her words, she said, "But I'm not like that, am I?"

Carlo broke into a loud and too artificial laugh: "Are you joking with me? Hey, you were in tears because of all this. Your mother happily lived through her actions for nearly forty years without a hint of remorse." Carlo lifted Giulia's chin and continued to speak to her in an even softer voice, "Honey, you are nothing like her, and thankfully because otherwise, I would be afraid you might stab me in my sleep."

Now it was Giulia's turn to let out a laugh.

"But we can't ignore the situation, and we need to know what this means for us and our plans. I mean, if everything comes to light will your mother's inheritance stay intact? Will her signatures still be accountable as a guarantee for our loan?"

Carlo had a point. Giulia needed to know where she stood and what were the real risks for the family and the business, forged signatures aside.

"You know what? I'm damn tired of being treated like an

untrustworthy child. It wasn't me to mess it all up this time. I'm going to talk to her. She owes me more explanations, and she owes me answers about my future, our future, the business's future. And she needs to fix this or else I'll do it."

The distress in Giulia's voice had become a rage.

She kissed Carlo's thin line that was his lips and headed for the door.

"Where are you going?" he asked with a wary expression.

"I'm going to talk to the old witch, and this time she better listen to me."

Giulia closed the door behind her and walked straight into the lift where a big full-size mirror reflected the image of a determined young woman. She liked that reflection, maybe for the first time in her life.

"And you know what? I can get used to this," she said to herself.

After tonight, there was no going back for Giulia. From now on, she was going to lead the game.

28

DUBLIN - IRELAND

"Damn it!" The swearing was coming from the downstairs bathroom.

Fergus met the twins' look; they lifted their shoulders and hands: "Women...who understands them?" they exclaimed in unison and walked off to go back to the garden.

Fergus couldn't resist a smile, but after looking at his wife's face when she got out of the bathroom, he immediately changed expression.

She had been crying, her eyes were puffy and her nose red after being blown too much.

"The residues of this damn ink won't come off." Lola had a sponge and a towel in her hands that were red because of all the rubbing.

"Hey hey hey," Fergus said, gently taking the cleaning items from his wife's hands and throwing them in the bathroom sink. He led her to the sitting room and made her sit on the sofa.

Lola was silent, she was tired, and her eyes were filling with more tears.

"What's up? Talk to me."

Lola eventually let all her pain out. She was a river in

flood.

Fergus said nothing; he held her in his arms until she stopped sobbing and started to speak of all those feelings she was holding.

"What if Siobhan doesn't wake up?"

"She will honey, the doctors themselves had said she is not in a life-threatening situation. It's just a matter of days until the haematoma in the brain will dry out, and they will let her out of the induced coma."

"I know what they said," Lola's words came out sharp, but both of them ignored her tone, "but what if they are wrong, what if the haematoma doesn't dry out? It happens all the time." Lola was on the verge of starting to cry again. Fergus put two fingers on her lips, "Shhh, that's nonsense. She'll be OK."

"I ignored her calls, and last time we talked, I told her she was a paranoid looper. And now she is in a coma; those could be my last words to her. If only I had bothered to answer her calls, none of this would have happened......" Lola heard no reasons.

"There was no way you could have known what she wanted or what was going to happen," Fergus's purposive words didn't sink in his wife, who completely ignored them, and eventually let out what had been torturing her for days.

"And you know what the worst is? Finn and the guys keep thanking me. They are treating me like a hero, like I saved her life when, instead, I caused all this because I should have gone to her much sooner..."

"You did save her life, Lola. God knows how long she would have stayed like that and with what kind of damages or consequences if you had not called over." Fergus couldn't see where Lola was going with all this, why she was blaming herself.

"No Fergus, I nearly killed her because if I had listened to her messages and took her calls, I would have been there, or she would have been here. I don't know, but surely she wouldn't have been attacked."

Fergus believed her words were all nonsense, but he also understood why she was upset, "Honey, if you are guilty of that, then I am too. I kept you at home with me."

"That's ridiculous, you can't blame yourself," Lola said, looking her husband in the eye.

"Then neither can you. That's my point. It happened, and it's nobody's fault except for the villain who assaulted her. You have no responsibilities except one: You saved her life. If Siobhan is alive, it's only because of you. Because you arrived when you did, and you called 999. This is the only truth, and she's going to be OK as the doctors said."

Lola's more serene look gave Fergus some relief.

The couple was soon interrupted by the boys barging into the room.

"Why is mum crying?" Alex asked, stepping closer, while Philip stayed behind.

"Mum has a bad headache. She needs to rest a little before dinner."

"Is it because of what happened to Mrs Drake?"

Lola looked at Fergus, begging for help with her eyes. She had no energy to get involved in such a talk with her sons.

"I'll handle this; you go upstairs, take a shower and lie down for a while," he whispered to his wife and left the room with the boys.

* * *

Lola threw herself under the shower and stood there for a while as the hot water hitting her skin felt incredibly soothing.

Fergus's words kept resonating inside her head, and she slowly convinced herself that he was right.

Feeling much better, she turned the water off and stepped

out of the shower reaching for her bathrobe. She tightened it around her waist and started to towel dry her long hair. The weather was unusually warm for Ireland, but she still could not get away without using the hairdryer as her hair was too long and too thick.

She had to admit that the cry made her feel good but left her with swollen eyes and an uncomfortable feeling of emptiness in her stomach.

Still, in her bathrobe, Lola lay in bed, "only ten minutes," she said to herself but fell asleep for over two hours.

After she woke up, she stayed in the room a little longer. She was so tired, and it all showed on her face. She applied some anti-black circle under her eyes, some mascara and a bit of blush on her cheeks and went to pick something comfortable to wear. She slipped into a knee-length tunic and grabbed a cardigan; in case they were going to have dinner in the garden. If the weather was good, the boys loved to have their meals outside.

Over summer, the boys were allowed to bring their dinner up to their treehouse. Fergus and his father had built it together. There was nothing Pat could not make with his hands. Inside it was big enough to contain two bean bags and a little IKEA coffee table. Gradually the boys had brought up a few of their board games and a couple of boxes of Lego and Playmobil. Angela had sewn curtains for the two little windows in the front and Lola was making sure to give it a clean once a week.

Lola went downstairs and could hear her husband whistling in the kitchen.

Outside was very quiet, and the boys were nowhere to be seen or heard.

She entered the kitchen and hugged Fergus from behind, "Thank you," Lola whispered in his ear.

"Yes, you are a lucky woman, now if you want to excuse me, I have to go back slaving away, or my wife will beat me."

29

PONTE ALTO - ITALY

I hung the "do not disturb" sign outside my room and sneaked out unseen.

I had no intention to hide for much longer, but for now, it was the best solution. I couldn't wait to be able to come to light with my truth; to get back what they had taken from me. My old life was only a step away, but I had to be patient and not rush things. I learned my lesson after what happened in Dublin.

It was late in the afternoon but still hot, the refreshing evening breeze from the Dolomites hadn't arrived yet to bring relief.

The house was still the same: Huge, well-kept and intimidating. The Kopfler Grand Hotel and the Kopfler Residence were both built with the only purpose of displaying power.

I took out a handkerchief from my handbag and dried some sweat that ran down my neck and temples. I rang the bell on the side of the gate. I asked to speak to Mrs Kopfler. I said I was an old friend. Walking along the driveway, I bet whoever the housekeeper was these days, she would be in big trouble for having let a stranger in.

To my surprise, Edda was still working there, and she was waiting for me at the door. She was old, and I wondered if she was still there out of loyalty or necessity.

"Come this way, please. Mrs Kopfler will be with you shortly."

Edda's voice distracted me from my thoughts. She hadn't recognised me. I suppose I was much older as well, and my figure was not slender anymore.

Even inside the house had not changed much. Mara had kept most of the antique family pieces of furniture: dark and heavy like the atmosphere I remembered from growing up.

Edda escorted me into the sitting room and gestured for me to take a seat before leaving the room and closing the door behind her.

I started to be nervous, too nervous to sit down and stay still.

After a few minutes, I heard steps in the corridor, and a voice outside in the hallway, "Thank you, Edda. You can go for the day now."

I prepared myself and faced the door, but nobody came in for another few minutes until the front door had closed shut.

Mara had waited for Edda to leave. She knew I was there and wanted no witness to our meeting.

30

PONTE ALTO - ITALY

When she heard the bell, Mara immediately checked the monitors to see who it was.

She was expecting this visit but not so soon. She ordered Edda to let the visitor in.

Despite Mara's effort to keep calm, her nervousness hadn't gone unnoticed, and neither had the fact that the woman at the door had been adamant not to reveal her identity. Mara managed to discourage any possible questions her house-keeper might have had. Edda obeyed, and when dismissed for the day, in a rush and with no explanation, she left without saying a word.

Mara didn't move from the corridor until she saw Edda closing the front door behind her. Edda didn't recognise Lorna, and this was playing at Mara's advantage. The fewer people who knew, the better. At least until she had worked out how to handle the situation and contain the collateral damages.

Mara stopped outside the sitting room. She took a deep breath and opened the door with forced confidence which only seemed to Lorna's eyes like arrogance.

Mara hadn't changed over the years: everything in the

way she acted showed boldness and a willingness to fight, but Lorna was prepared to fight back this time.

"How could you have done this to me?" the words came out of Lorna's mouth with no fear.

Mara had thought about how to answer that question since their conversation over the phone: "You did it to yourself," attacking was always the best defence.

"Come on, did you ever question yourself? A mother who wants to get her child back would do anything. Have you?" Mara added, with the clear intent to send her rival to the corner.

Lorna had always been fragile and weak in her mind. Since they were kids, Mara didn't have to make an effort to overpower her sister.

Lorna stood there paralysed. Those words had stabbed her in the heart. She wanted to react, but couldn't. It was as her strength had suddenly vanished and she was back to that weak, fragile girl she once was.

"The truth hurts, doesn't it? Why are you here? To make yourself feel better by blaming everything on me?" Mara had no mercy. Her entire world was at stake, and she needed to protect it, but she went too far.

The rage Lorna had felt when she had heard Lola saying her parents were dead was back, and it gave her the strength to do and say what she was there for.

"You know I looked for her after I got better. I only disappeared from her life and let her alone because I thought that was what she wanted. I thought she hated me for what I tried to do to her."

Mara didn't back off, "And she did," she spat out, cold and sharp.

"No, she didn't. She thought I was dead," the anger disfigured Lorna's face. She was like a feral animal and started to walk towards her prey.

Mara took a few steps back. For the first time in her life,

she felt threatened. She tried to avoid Lorna's gaze. It was a look that could kill. Her sister was not only seeking justice but revenge as well.

"I will ruin you. You and your daughter are going to suffer as much as Lola and I did, but because I'm not a monster like you, I am going to give you one more day to fix things. After that, I will, and I can assure you it won't be pleasant."

Lorna walked out of the room and left.

31

PONTE ALTO - ITALY

Giulia drove to her mother's place. She opened the glove compartment and took the gate's remote Mara had given her in case of an emergency, along with a pair of the house keys.

Her brand new Volvo SUV headlights were illuminating the gate while it slowly opened. Giulia was absorbed in her thoughts, going through what she wanted to tell Mara when she saw a figure leaving. She had no time to look at her thoroughly, but she hadn't recognised her as one of her mother's friends. Not that she knew all the old witch's friends of course, but still she thought it was weird that she was walking. The house was not far from the town centre but yet a good twenty minutes on foot. Anyway, whoever the woman was and whatever reason she had to be there, it was the least of Giulia's concerns at the moment. The gate was now fully open, and Giulia drove in hoping there were no other guests inside. Tonight, she needed her mother's full attention.

She walked straight in, calling for her mother.

The house was silent, but the lights were on. In the kitchen, the dinner was still in the oven half cooked.

"Mother" Giulia called one more time, and again nobody answered.

She checked the study first and then she went to the sitting room.

Mara looked like a caricature of a 13th-century portrait, sitting still like a statue with Leopold on her lap purring.

"Mum, are you OK?" Giulia asked, walking toward the woman, who only vaguely resembled her mother and kneeled in front of her.

Mara lifted her head, making Giulia jump back when she saw her mother's expression. Her eyes were different; they were wide open and lost; the eyes of a trapped animal.

It didn't take long for Giulia to connect the dots: the stranger leaving the house, the state her mother was in: "Was she here? Is she here in Ponte Alto? What did she want?"

Mara still had not said a single word.

Giulia's concern was now turning to anger. Anger at her mother, at her aunt, at her cousin, at everybody involved in this "thing" that was turning her world upside down.

"Mum. Look at me. Pull yourself together and tell me what happened."

Giulia was standing still, cold, resolute; a woman who both the women struggled to recognise.

Mara eventually awoke from her comatose state, straightened her back and spoke calmly, telling Giulia everything that had happened. Mother and daughter stayed silent for a few minutes, processing the facts.

"We need to talk to her," Giulia said.

"We?" Mara jumped to her feet and went to the drinks cabinet to pour two glasses of scotch. Her voice was back to her usual controlled tone.

"Yes, WE. Because it seems quite obvious to me that this is not your shit anymore, but it's also mine. Isn't it, Mother?"

Mara was in no doubt that Giulia was not an ally, and

whatever she had in mind to do it was not to help her out, it was exclusively to save her own ass.

"Do you know where she is staying?" Giulia asked.

"She didn't say, but not at our hotel. I'm sure." Mara answered before emptying her glass in one gulp and refill it.

"I saw her leave on foot. She must be staying in town somewhere," Giulia looked at her watch, "it's not late, I'm going to do a few phone calls, and then maybe I will go into town to see if I can find out something. You better put that bottle down, make yourself some chamomile instead and go to bed. I want your mind bright and working tomorrow."

Giulia stormed out of the house before Mara could even reply.

She climbed back into the car and drove off. Just around the corner from the house, she stopped and took her phone from her bag. She rang the first number on her speed dial list.

"Hello."

"Good. I'm glad to hear you managed to recompose yourself, or at least to pretend you have."

Mara couldn't make any sense of Giulia's phone call. Why did she ring? She had just left! Was it a tactic? Or did she want to blame her further?

Mara had no time to say or ask anything before Giulia went on: "I just called to say, do not answer your phone or the door for the rest of the evening. Avoid any contact with anyone. In particular her!"

Giulia hung up and dialled the second number on her speed dial list.

"Hey, it's me."

Carlo's voice was sleepy; he must have fallen asleep in front of the TV as soon as she had left.

"Hey hon..." he managed to say in between yawns.

She imagined him scratching his head and getting into some sitting position on the couch. A wave of love and sweetness transfixed her and then more anger.

Why was all this happening right now, in the happiest time of her life; just when everything was going so perfectly?

She told him everything Mara had told her and asked him to help her make a few calls around B&Bs and hotels.

"Well, honey, it's not easy to look for someone we can't describe and whose name we don't know, because she would not have used her real name, would she?"

"No, I don't think so. Lorna might be a lunatic, but she's clever. She has always been, according to my mother, just unstable. They spoke on the phone early this morning, and mum thinks her sister was at the airport; she had heard airport announcements in the background. My aunt must have checked in late this morning or early in the afternoon. Let's focus on that, and let's call everywhere central. She came by foot, and with this heat and at her age, I don't think she was coming from far."

* * *

Giulia drove to the hotel, parked in her reserved space right in front of the entrance and locked herself in her office. She rang the kitchen to get something to eat. She had barely eaten anything all day, and now her stomach was gurgling.

Just the time for a couple of calls and a young waiter knocked at the door and brought in a silver tray with a plate of cold cuts, cheese and olives and a glass of chilled Traminer.

"Do you need anything else, Miss?" he asked.

Giulia smiled and waved him away.

All her phone calls were of no help until she remembered The Schwartze Guesthouse. What better place for someone who wanted to remain hidden.

"Bingo!" Giulia nearly screamed after hanging up the phone. She immediately called Carlo, "I got her."

"What are you going to do?"

"I don't know. I haven't decided yet. I'm not sure I can wait until tomorrow to talk to her. Anyway, see you at home in a while."

At the reception desk of the Guesthouse, there was nobody. One of the guests, Mr Derrik, explained to Giulia that the owners had just left and wouldn't be back until the following morning to serve breakfast. Of course, in case of an emergency, they were reachable by phone. They were living in the house too, only in the other wing. Mr Derrik was a little Austrian guy around seventy and spoke excellent Italian. He had been a regular guest of the Schwartzes' for over ten years as he loved to hike around the valley. Giulia had no interest in his tales, and she was about to abruptly dismiss him when she thought that he could be of use to her. She asked if he had noticed a new guest arriving today and he confirmed that a lady had indeed arrived. She had been resting in her bedroom all day because of a terrible headache.

"Of course, it's not that I make other people's business mine," Mr Derrik urged to point out before he continued, "it merely happened that when she checked in, I was passing by the reception desk and I overheard her conversation with Mrs Schwartze."

"Of course," Giulia replied, blessing Mr Derrik's compulsion for gossip and encouraging him to keep talking, "She looked like a nice woman, but she must have been exhausted as the "do not disturb" sign was still on her door when I left for dinner tonight. It's a real pity I'm going tomorrow. We could become friends. We also have the rooms one opposite the other, eight and nine. You know after my wife died, I'm trying to find some company, but these days it's so hard......."

Giulia had learned enough. She let the man blather a bit longer and then, excusing herself, she parted his company.

32

PONTE ALTO - ITALY

I didn't want to leave like I was running away, but emotions started to overpower me. I felt my eyes filling with tears, and I didn't want my sister to see even the slightest hint of weakness in me or then it would be the end.

It always took a little spot of weakness for Mara Kopfler to embed her final and fatal blow. But this time, things were going to be different. This time she was the prey, and I was the hunter. That sparkle in her eyes when I left was nothing but fear.

I was sure nobody saw me leaving or coming back to the guest house. As far as everybody was concerned, I was still resting in my bedroom.

The shower I took after being back didn't refresh me for long. The room had no air conditioning, and I could not open the window because it overlooked the garden, and I didn't want any other guest to see me. I lay down, staring at the ceiling for a moment, thinking of my next move, guessing at when I was eventually able to have my life back.

I had almost fallen asleep when a knock at the door made me jump.

Who could it be? The "do not disturb" sign was still on the door, and it was getting late.

I didn't answer, but then there was another knock and another one. Whoever it was, they weren't going away.

I opened the door and when I saw who it was, I tried to remain calm.

Why was she here? How did she know where I was staying and more importantly, did she know who I was?

I had a bad feeling and felt vulnerable.

"I have nothing to say to you or anybody else. I told my sister everything I had to say. Now leave, please." My tone was purposely contemptuous. I hated everybody connected to Mara. To me, they were all accessories to her crimes.

I tried to close the door, but something stopped it, and when I looked down to see what it was, my body was pushed inside the room. I was unsteady on my legs and stumbled backwards. I turned my back for a second to hold the grip of something and keep the balance, and then I felt it — a blow to the base of my head.

The pain was sharp, excruciating. I fell on the floor. I instinctively touched the back of my head with one hand, and when I brought it back in front of me, it was soaked in blood. Everything went blurry around me.

The room was hushed. The only noise was my moans, but after the last blow on my face, they stopped too. Now the only audible sound was coming from the bones in my face being smashed.

33

DUBLIN - IRELAND

The heatwave that had hit Ireland in the last few days had reached its end. The temperatures had dropped to those of an average Irish summer.

Lola was doing some washing up in the kitchen while distractedly looking out of the little window over her sink. From there she had a complete view of her front garden and the main street.

Her attention fell on a car pulling over and parking on the road between her house and the Drakes'.

Since what had happened to Siobhan, she was more careful and watched out for unknown or suspicious vehicles or persons in the neighbourhood.

The wind had risen, and the kitchen's French door banged shut.

"Damn it," Lola said to herself. Shortly after they moved in, the same thing happened, and the door's glass smashed. After that accident, Fergus had screwed a latch to the outside wall upon which to hook the door and keep it open, but most of the time Lola forgot to secure the door. She left her surveillance spot and ran to the door to close it with the handle.

The sky had darkened, and the weather had suddenly turned dreadful, she quickly moved the garden furniture under the canopy and called the boys, who were utterly oblivious to the atmospheric mayhem, back inside.

"Mum, it's not even raining yet. Why can't we stay outside a bit longer?"

Alex and Philip came in whining and stamping their feet, but as soon as they had removed their crocks by the doormat, thunders roared, and torrential rain started to pour. That was why they couldn't stay out any longer.

The two boys were looking outside the window with a startled expression like they had never seen so much rain at once.

Lola went to switch on the lights. Even if it was only 4:30 pm, the room got dark with the onset of evening.

Alex and Philip had goosebumps on their arms and legs. They were both very skinny and had very fair skin, but their hair was dark — obviously inherited from the Italian side of the family.

Lola herself had coal-black hair that she loved and was proud of, mostly for the fact that she had no grey hair yet. The only disadvantage was that her body hairs were pretty dark too. Not having her facial, legs and bikini wax done regularly was not an option for her. The good thing was that despite her winter pallor, it only took a tepid ray of sun on her to get some tan.

"Boys go change into something warmer please," off she sent them upstairs, but before they stepped out of the kitchen, and after they threw to each other a look of conspiracy, they went, "But if it's cold, that means we can have hot chocolate?"

Lola didn't reply but took out of the cupboard their favourite Spiderman mugs. A clear sign that the hot chocolate was on its way. Little heavy feet were noisily climbing the stairs.

After a few minutes of peace and quiet, the same little feet were noisily running down and rushing into the kitchen.

Lola set the two steaming mugs on the table along with a plate containing some marshmallows and two slices of toasted bread with strawberry jam, then went back to watch the road.

The car was still there, but she had not seen who got out of it. Lola decided to wait by the window for a little longer, hoping to see someone going back to it. She also thought of taking down the car registration number, but that meant going outside, and in those weather conditions, she wouldn't dream of it.

The boys were done with their snack, and they went to watch a movie.

The car was still there, and nobody had returned to it yet. Lola had wasted far too much time watching the neighbourhood; she had things to do. She collected the boys' mugs and plates, put them in the dishwasher and just when she was ready to give up her surveillance mission for good, the car's lights flashed. Someone had opened it from a distance with the remote.

That made sense she thought, if it were her, she would have done the same in that weather. She waited, and after a second or two, she recognised Detective McCarthey. Most likely, he had gone to the Drakes' house. Maybe there were some updates. She was dying to know, but she felt it would have been far too invasive to ring Finn immediately after the police had left.

The rain eventually stopped, and the wind calmed down. The sun was back up and shining in the sky. Lola could feel its warmth coming in from the windows.

"Mum, it's sunny again, can we go back out?"

Lola looked at her watch; she hadn't realised it was

already nearly 7 o'clock. The chores around the house had kept her busy for longer than she thought, and the brightness of the evening outside made her lose her perception of time.

Fergus was not coming home till late as he was working on a chain of boutiques up in Co. Monaghan. Initially, he was supposed to stay overnight, but he felt it was too soon after the attack to leave his wife overnight. Of course, Lola had never said anything or complained about it, and frankly believed her husband's worries were far too exaggerated, but she appreciated the gesture.

"Boys, come here," she called, "you know what? Mum got very delayed, so how about you go and put your jammies on while I order a pizza?"

"Yeaaaaaa"

Alex and Philip rushed upstairs while Lola scrolled Domino's app on her phone. They confirmed three ham and cheese pizzas would be on the way in 15 minutes. She set the table and poured herself a glass of wine.

34

PONTE ALTO - ITALY

Giulia walked back to her car. The adrenaline was still violently pumping inside her body. She felt powerful, invincible. It was like she had just discovered how strong she could be.

She was too excited to go straight home. She drove around aimlessly, for how long she couldn't say.

When Giulia got home, the lights were all off. She was sure to make as little noise as she could. She drank some water and went straight to the bedroom. Carlo was fast asleep, snoring.

She looked at his body, lying naked on the bed. He was still a handsome man. His sallow skin turned golden with the moonlight coming in from the window. He always forgot to shut the blinds. Giulia left them up as she was afraid of waking him up with the noise.

She tiptoed into the en-suite. She could do with a shower. The tension of the evening made her sweat but then she would have woken Carlo for sure, and he would have asked questions, and she was too tired to answer. She just washed her underarms and her feet before slipping into her nightgown and join her lover in bed. Or to be precise, her fiancé. That word was still a dream in Giulia's head.

They had had an affair for years, and there was a time when she thought he was only fooling her around and that he would never leave his wife. But he did, he left his wife to be with her. He chose her, and he did it for what she was.

Giulia was not stupid, and she knew Carlo liked money as much as she did. If she weren't coming with that asset, he probably never would have fallen for her. On the other hand, it was the same for herself. She liked him and his power.

They matched each other, in a good and in a bad way, but the main thing was that they could be their real selves when together. They didn't have to pretend to be someone else.

Giulia went to bed, and despite the heat, she went close to Carlo so that their bodies could touch. She fell asleep dreaming of their life together. A life that nobody would have ruined. Not her mother, not her aunt, nobody.

* * *

The morning light blinded her eyes; Giulia took Carlo's pillow and covered her face.

She could hear noises coming from the kitchen, and soon, the smell of coffee reached the room.

The alarm clock on the bedside table said 8:30 am. She had overslept, but maybe that was a good thing. It was going to be a busy day, and she had to be well-rested. She thought about the previous night. She was nervous in the beginning, but then, after she knocked at Lorna's door, she realised to have all the strength necessary to face her. Now the adrenaline had gone, but her confidence stayed.

Giulia got up, her bladder pushing. She barely made it to the bathroom.

She took a shower and applied only some mascara.

Giulia's face, like the rest of her body, was tanned and needed no makeup.

She picked a blue sleeveless knee-length dress and joined Carlo in the kitchen. "Good morning," she greeted him.

Carlo didn't turn as he was busy putting the coffee and some croissants on a tray.

"I set the table on the balcony," he chirped carrying the tray outside, "it's still lovely out there, but they are forecasting dense temperatures again for the rest of the day. Maybe some rain overnight."

Giulia sat down and voraciously took the first bite of her croissant.

"You got home pretty late last night, I was worried, but then I must have fallen asleep, and I didn't even hear you," Carlo said expecting to hear the details of his fiancé's evening.

"You were snoring like a bear," Giulia answered, not volunteering any further talk.

"Are you going to tell me what had happened last night or not?" Carlo openly asked in front of Giulia's reticence.

Giulia wolfed down the last piece of the croissant with some coffee and with her mouth half full started to talk: "There is not much to say."

Carlo looked at her and waited for more.

He was not going to drop it.

35

DUBLIN - IRELAND

It was past midnight when Fergus arrived home. He sat on the edge of his side of the bed and started to get undressed when he felt a caress on his back.

He turned and saw his wife retracting her arm and smiling at him.

"Are you still awake?" Fergus asked, kissing her on the forehead.

"I woke up when I heard your car on the gravel. But I suppose I wasn't in a deep sleep yet. The silence of the night amplifies every little noise."

Fergus smiled back at his wife." I'm going to take a shower," and he disappeared into the bathroom.

Lola turned on her back, closed her eyes and by the time Fergus was back in bed, she was already asleep. Fast asleep this time, safe in the knowledge he was at home with her and the boys.

Lola's alarm rang at seven, like on every school day. Fergus was still asleep. She knew he had no appointments until twelve and left him in bed. She got ready trying to make the least noise possible and to make sure the boys would make no unnecessary noise either, starting with not running down the stairs to have their breakfast.

The boys were eating their cereal while Lola packed their lunches and checked the temperature outside with one hand out the window. The sun struggled to stay out as the sky was overcrowded with passing clouds, but it was not cold. On the contrary, it was one of those cloudy but warm and humid days.

"Grab your hoodies and your bags. It's time to go."

Lola threw a cardigan over her t-shirt and started going toward the front door followed by the twins.

* * *

"Love you, have a nice day in school."

She kissed them both on the forehead, and after watching them walk through the school gate, she walked back home.

Fergus opened the front door for her.

"Are you up already? I thought you were going to sleep a bit longer this morning."

"I'm fine. Besides, I have a few calls to make before heading to the meeting in town."

"Have you already had breakfast?" Lola asked.

"Nope, I was hoping you would make me some while I'm getting dressed."

"Like I never do, right?" Lola jokingly rolled her eyes and pinched her husband on the arm.

The scent of cologne arrived in the kitchen before Fergus.

Lola laid two mugs of coffee on the table and a bowl of porridge with some grapes and strawberries and sat opposite her husband. Neither of them had yet the chance to start a conversation when the doorbell interrupted their complicit silence.

"Are you expecting someone?" Fergus asked.

"No," Lola replied, "unless it's the postman," she added and automatically looked through the kitchen window overlooking the front of the house.

"I don't see anybody at the little gate, and the postman always buzzes from there, he never comes up to the front door, unless I open it for him."

Fergus felt Lola's nervousness and stood up to go to the door.

Lola could hear him talking to someone and stretched her neck in the attempt to overhear bits of the conversation and find out who it was. When the voices eventually started to approach the kitchen, she recognised Finn Drake's.

Lola was quite surprised by that visit and so early in the morning, but most of all she wondered if it was good or bad news. Whatever it was, Lola was sure it had something to do with the detective's visit from yesterday.

"Finn has something happened?"

Her tone was far too alarmed; Fergus didn't miss it, and neither did Finn most likely.

Fergus caught his wife's look, and she realised that the poor man didn't need her to bring more drama into his life.

"Sorry, Finn, where are my manners. Can I make you a coffee?" Lola offered, trying to make up for the moment of embarrassment her words had caused in the room.

"Please have a seat, man," Fergus said, pulling a chair from the table and gesturing for Finn to sit down. Maybe now they were a bit too adamant about making him feel at ease.

Finn Drake cleared his throat playing with the coaster, and teaspoon Lola had just brought to him and started to talk.

"I won't stay long. I have to show my face at the surgery today." Finn said, but his body language suggested otherwise. He was not in a rush to leave. He looked like someone who needed a place to stay hidden for a while.

"I wanted to thank Lola for going to the station to have her fingerprints taken," he continued, "you already have a lot on your hands with the boys and everything, and after they took mine and the kids, I know what an awful experience it is. They say it's to exclude your involvement, but what you feel it's the exact opposite. I felt under suspicion...."

Fergus and Lola looked at each other: Finn was on the verge of crying.

The whole situation was becoming too much for him, and he was struggling to maintain control, that was clear.

"You know, I always used to complain about what such a pain in the arse Siobhan is, but now that she is not around, I feel lost. In her odd way, she kept everything together, me included." Finn Drake spoke, keeping his eyes on the mug of coffee like the black liquid had some hypnotic power.

Lola and Fergus didn't know what to say. Maybe they didn't have to say anything, but just let him get it all out.

He dried his eyes and threw an embarrassed and apologetic look at the couple who were staring at him speechless.

Lola took his hand in hers: "She will be back soon Finn, you heard the doctors. She's not in any life-threatening danger."

Fergus stood up and squeezed Finn's shoulder in a sign of affection and solidarity on his way to the counter. He went back to the table with a fresh pot of coffee and refilled everybody's mug. The trio sat in silence for a few minutes, until Finn spoke again, but this time his voice was more in control. He felt lighter, better, reassured.

The poor man only needed to talk and show his feelings for once.

"Anyway, I also came because that detective, McCarthey, came over yesterday..."

"Oh yes, I saw his car parked on the street," Lola blurted out interrupting Finn.

The two men both turned their eyes to her: her husband with an expression enquiring if it was indispensable for her to interrupt Finn's account; her neighbour, instead, wondering if she had any info to add.

"Yes, since the robberies and the attack she spends hours patrolling the road from the kitchen window and checking on possible suspicious movements," Fergus said trying to justify his wife who blushed, feeling embarrassed but also annoyed by the comment.

"Oh," Finn commented before continuing, "so, anyway, he came over to inform me that apart from the fingerprints of us four, yours and Melinda's, they found a set of unknown prints, possibly from the attacker. Unfortunately, they found no match in the database, but they will keep searching. I don't think they will ever find who did this unless Siobhan will be able to say who it was."

"We can only hope she will be able to remember," Lola said and then enquired about Melinda. Melinda was the Drakes' cleaner since forever, and over the years she became nearly a member of the family. Lola had great sympathy for the woman. Melinda was in her seventies, and not as able as before, but Siobhan refused to let her go. She, instead, hired someone younger to help her here and there. Melinda was aware of the special treatment and profoundly grateful for it.

"Ah, the poor woman, nearly had a heart attack when we told her. In the chaos, we forgot to tell her, and when she came the morning after the attack, she found the police yellow tape still on the door and the handrail to welcome her. I gave her the week off because it's hard enough to deal with the kids. I didn't need her around too. If you know what I mean."

"Totally." Fergus was quick to answer.

"Right, I better go now," Finn stood up and went towards the hall.

Fergus opened the door for him and hugged him, "Listen, whenever you need us, we are here. Even just for a chat."

"I know, and I appreciate it. Really."

That was probably the first time in many years that Lola saw her husband and their neighbour being so friendly. They looked closer than ever.

How sad it is that only when you risk losing someone, you do realise how much you care about them, she thought.

36

PONTE ALTO - ITALY

It was a beautiful morning, a light breeze from the lake was making it particularly pleasant for the Schwartzes' guests to enjoy their breakfast in the garden.

Mrs and Mr Schwartze had been busy serving their customers and taking care of the arrivals and departures. It was only when Mr Schwartze took the register to notify the Police the new visitors, following the Italian law, that he realised the lady staying in room nine, had not yet brought down her documents.

"Honey, have you seen the lady staying in room nine this morning? She hasn't come back with her documents yet."

"I thought she dropped them off to you earlier on," Mrs Schwartze replied and kept cleaning the tables.

"Nope, she didn't," Mr Schwartze announced solemnly.

"Was she down for breakfast?" he then asked.

"No. She wasn't. Maybe she's still unwell," Mrs Schwartze dismissed her husband and went to water the garden plants before the sun reached that side of the garden too.

"Poor woman. Anyway, I need her papers so maybe tell Zoe to start remaking the bedrooms beginning with hers, so she can ask her to come down immediately. Then she can go back to bed as long as she wants."

Mr Schwartze showed a slight annoyance. He wanted to bring the name of the new arrivals to the Police before it was too hot to walk around town. Those few extra pounds he was carrying made it even more challenging to cope with the heat.

"Don't worry. Zoe already started her rounds, and I told her to leave the checkouts last as the rooms won't be occupied until afternoon. An hour at the latest and she will be in number 9." Mrs Schwartze tried to reassure her husband, but unsuccessfully, "I was hoping to get this thing done before midday. You know how I hate to be out around midday, too bloody hot," he replied with a mix of annoyance and disappointment in his tone.

By 11:00 am, the day had already turned sultry. Arnold and Petra Schwartze were outside in the garden, refreshing themselves with cold tea and reading the newspaper.

They were on the opposite side of the lake from the Kopfler Grand Hotel and had a perfect view of it. Even if the large building made all the little houses and chalets around the lake look minuscule, it didn't ruin the landscape at all. On the contrary, its 20's style made it something beautiful to look at, and despite its mastodontic structure, it appeared light and classy.

Mrs Schwartze loved peeping at the guests arriving with their extravagant cars and indulging themselves on the deck in outfits fit for a movie.

Along the lake, there were pedal boats to rent for as long as you wanted. The lake was big enough to contain dozens of those at the same time, without risking a collision.

The Schwartze, instead, had four rowboats, which their guests could use free of charge.

Their maintenance was one of Mr Schwartze's hobbies. He spent most of the winter varnishing them, and the results were well visible.

In between those ugly plastic pedalos, Mr Schwartze's shiny wood boats stood out. Often it happened that tourists came to enquire about them, but he was not keen to place them in the hands of anyone but his most trustworthy guests. Not even for a fee.

Mrs Schwartze was lost in thoughts staring at the lake when a scream coming from inside the house brought her back to reality. She instinctively looked at her husband, who put down the paper and stood up to go and check. Neither of them had time to say or do anything before a hysterical Zoe appeared in the garden.

The couple couldn't calm her down and neither could they make sense of what she was saying. She was shaking and mumbling something about room number 9.

The elderly couple exchanged a suspicious look. That was the room of the still unknown guest.

"I'm going to have a look, you look after her and try to calm her down. See if you can make sense of what she is saying."

Mrs Schwartze had Zoe sitting down on one of the deck chairs. The poor girl was in such a state of shock that when Mr Schwartze came back, she had still not been able to explain what had happened.

Mr Schwartze's pallor made his wife jump.

"Call the police!" he said.

The first thing that Mrs Schwartze thought was that the woman had left unseen and without paying her bill, but when her husband sat down unable to stop his legs from shaking, she knew it was something more serious.

Mr Schwartze covered his ghostly white face with his hands, and it was then that the traces of blood became visible.

37

PONTE ALTO - ITALY

Inspector Furio Zamparelli waved at the young uniformed officer guarding the entrance to the guest house.

It was originally a private residence, and the owners had done an excellent job in restoring it without losing the beauty and the charm of the Austro-Hungarian architecture that distinguished most of the buildings in Ponte Alto.

"Inspector, this way," Deputy Inspector Piva led the way to the bedroom where the maid had found the body.

"Piva, I saw the Carabinieri too. Why are we both here?"

"They called me, out of courtesy," Deputy Inspector Luca Piva explained and before adding anything else he waited for his boss's reaction.

Zamparelli's nostrils opened like he was about to breath fire. He had been transferred two years ago, and still, the commander of the Carabinieri, the other police force operating in the territory didn't trust him. Inspector Furio Zamparelli didn't want to say it openly, but he was sure it was because he came from the South. The misconception that people from the south of the country were work-wise far less trustworthy than their peers from the North was still alive among many around the north of the peninsula, and a remote location at the feet of the Dolomites, like Ponte Alto, was surely no exception. Ponte Alto was a beautiful little town that hordes of tourists invaded every summer. Winter could be busy too as it was not too far from some well-known ski resorts and for those who didn't like the high altitude or didn't want to drive long distances far up into the mountains, it was a nice compromise. Unfortunately, the locals, despite their constant interaction with strangers, were still highly diffident of any foreigner.

"The maid found her this morning, and Mr and Mrs Schwartze, the owners of the place, called 118. When the Carabinieri arrived and saw the body, they decided to call us. Based on the modus operandi, they are convinced the killing is related to drug trafficking. Since they know we are investigating the local cartel, they thought it would be something of more interest to us," Deputy Inspector Luca Piva explained.

"Mmm...." Zamparelli said while taking out a pair of latex gloves and shoe protectors from his pockets.

The inspector walked around the body and stopped, "Or they were a bit too impressionable," he said, pointing to some vomit close to the window.

"Shit. I hadn't seen that," Piva said, feeling mortified by his lack of observation, and promptly tried to fix it, "or it might even be from the killer."

"I doubt that someone who commits such a crime is that queasy. But it worth a shot to send it to the lab."

"Are we taking the investigation then, Inspector?" Deputy Piva could barely hide the excitement in his voice.

"Well, it looks like it could be related to the case we are already investigating and, besides that, I don't see anybody else interested here, Piva," Zamparelli said looking at the two Carabinieri's patrol cars leaving the scene.

"Good day gentlemen, what do we have here?" Paola Montalto had just arrived in the room with her team of crime scene investigators, "OK then, everybody out and let us work. Anything you touched that I should know?" She inquired.

The inspector and his deputy moved their head side to side with an outraged expression: they were not beginners!

"And that is not ours," Piva added, pointing below the window.

* * *

"This is Mr and Mrs Schwartze, the owners of the guest-house," Deputy Piva introduced the inspector to the couple that was peeping in from the corridor.

Inspector Zamparelli shook their hands with a hint of fascination at their peculiar appearance. Arnold Schwartze looked like he had jumped out a Tolkien book. Long white beard, red bowtie with little yellow spots on a short sleeve shirt that could have been ironed with more care.

His trousers were kept in position by a pair of red braces, most likely because no belt was long enough to go around his waistline, rather than for a sense of style. Petra Schwartze was tall enough to be a good match for her husband but slim. Her body was like a long stick, and every time she moved her hands or adjusted her body position the pendant she was wearing on a long golden chain around her neck, created a little metallic concert together with the bangles that adorned both her wrists.

"Can we just go and talk in our private rooms?" Mrs Schwartze suggested, "Some of the other guests already saw the police going in and out, and we would like not to upset them nor feed their curiosity. Of course, we will have to tell them what has happened but......" Mrs Schwartze's voice started to shake; her husband wrapped his arm around her and finished the sentence for her, "Inspectors, we don't even know what exactly has happened. In the beginning, I thought the lady had just flown without paying the bill, but when I came to the room, and I saw her on the floor and all that blood ..."

"Had she fallen? What had happened?" Mrs Schwartze started to talk again, but Inspector Zamparelli ignored her questions and instead locked eyes with Mr Schwartze. He hadn't told his wife about the condition of the body. Anybody who knew the state of the victim could guess that it had not been a fall that had killed her.

Only when they were all sitting on an old fashion green velvet couch, the inspector informed the elderly couple about what had presumably happened according to the evidence and information they had so far.

Mr and Mrs Schwartze were genuinely shocked.

"And did the lady have a name? Of course, you have her documents registered," Deputy Piva asked, taking out his notebook.

The couple looked at each other and went paler than they were already.

"She arrived yesterday, around midday. She had no reservation, but luckily enough, one of our guests had just cancelled her booking, and so we had a free room to give her. She asked to go straight to her bedroom because she was not feeling well and promised to come back down with her documents to check-in properly later." Arnold Schwartze explained.

Zamparelli and Piva had no reason to doubt Mrs Schwartze's words, it was plausible, and in fairness, the couple looked naive enough to trust strangers in anything they would say.

"So, she arrived, went to her bedroom and you had not seen her since?" Zamparelli summed up.

"No, because we don't provide dinner, we only see our guests at breakfast. During the day they are free to come and go as they please. We waited for her to come down, but when by seven o'clock she was not back down yet, we just decided to let her rest and wait to speak to her in the morning," Mrs Schwartze spoke to justify their failure in following procedures.

"So you are not physically in the guest house all day and not at all at night, right?" Zamparelli asked, and after the couple nodded with their heads, he went on, "So she could have left or received a visitor at some point without you noticing? "

"Pretty much, yes," Mr Schwartze said, but his wife patted him on the hand, as she had suddenly remembered something, and spoke up, "Actually shortly after 10:00 pm I saw someone leaving the guest house. It's not that I spend my evening checking out the window, but the gate creaks and the noise attracted my attention."

"And how are you so sure about the time?" Piva interrupted the woman's account, continuing to scribble on his notepad.

"Because when I heard the noise of the gate, I had just switched off the TV. See, on Thursdays, they show inspector George Gently, and I never miss an episode. It starts at 9:00 pm and finishes at around 10:00 pm."

"I never watch it. I find it extremely boring..." Mr Schwartze felt the urge to add, but neither Piva nor Zamparelli were interested in his cinematographic taste at the moment. They were interested in what his wife had seen.

"And you saw someone?" Zamparelli asked, trying to hide his impatience.

"No, just a shadow. I couldn't recognise who it was. It could have been anybody and to be honest, I didn't pay much attention." Mrs Schwartze was sorry not to be of more help.

Zamparelli and Piva looked at each other: it could have been anybody, or it could have been the culprit.

"I think we are done for today. Thank you for your time. Now we need to speak to Zoe, your maid," Zamparelli said, getting up.

"Of course. The poor girl was in such a shock that I sent her to rest while waiting for you," said Mrs Schwartze, and continued, "you wait here, I'll go and get her for you, then Arnold and I will go outside in the garden so you can talk to her here in peace."

Zamparelli thanked her and sat back on the couch that Piva never attempted to leave, as though it might have been old fashioned, it was also one of the most comfortable sofas the young man had ever sat on.

38

PONTE ALTO-ITALY

When Mrs Schwartze came back with Zoe, the two officers were standing by the window looking at the lake.

As soon they heard the two women coming in, they turned and unable to conceal their astonishment, they both let a few seconds of silence pass before greeting Ms Falck.

It was evident that they both expected someone much older and shabbier. Zoe Falck was probably around 25, tall, slender and incredibly pretty.

"Thank you, Mrs Schwartze," Zamparelli cut it short and walked to the door to close it.

Unfortunately, the young maid had not much to add to what they already knew.

Even if the "do not disturb" sign was still on the door, she knocked as instructed by Mrs Schwartze. When nobody answered, she tried to open the door with the skeleton key, but it would not go into the padlock because there was a key on the inside. At that point, she knocked again, and when she still didn't get an answer, she tried the handle and realised the door wasn't locked. She went in, but before she could go any further in the room, she saw the body and ran.

* * *

"So, what you think?" Deputy Piva asked his superior as soon as they were in the car heading back to the station.

"I don't know Piva. The MO screams drug-related payback, but the more I learn about our victim, the more I have my doubts."

Piva looked at Zamparelli waiting for more because if he knew his boss, the inspector already had some theory in his head.

"Think about it," Zamparelli continued as expected, "she arrived and locked herself in the bedroom with an alleged headache. She promised to go back down with her papers, but she didn't."

"Or maybe she was going to, but someone stopped her before she had a chance," Piva interrupted, keeping his eyes on the road.

"And took her papers? No ID has been found in the room, and the content of her handbag was scattered on the floor. So obviously someone searched through it. Nah, I don't buy it."

"What if she was a mule and had decided to keep a little bonus for herself? She has been given exemplary punishment for everybody to see. They took her papers to delay the recognition and not to leave any trace behind." Deputy Piva objected. He had still not ruled out a possible connection with the other drug trafficking-related murders they had investigated in the last few months.

"But why smash her face like that? I mean, we already don't know who she was because she had not given her name for the check-in, and they left no papers to confirm her identity. What the cartel would do in these cases is burn the fingerprints."

"Maybe they didn't have to because she is not in the system," Piva replied.

"Maybe..." Zamparelli agreed, but he didn't sound convinced. To him, something didn't add up.

To the inspector, this murder looked like something personal, a crime of passion, not business. The victim had been battered to death; it was not just a deal gone wrong. That was a fury hiding personal reasons. There were pure hate and deep feelings in that crime scene.

The two officers drove in silence to the station, but Piva knew that the inspector was a man used to following his instinct rather than the evidence, and he had the feeling that he wouldn't let it go so smoothly.

If Zamparelli suspected there was something more behind this murder, than he would pursue that trail.

* * *

"Piva," Zamparelli called with his hoarse voice from the door of his office.

Piva went in and sat opposite the inspector, hidden behind the smoke of his electronic cigarette.

"I just spoke to superintendent Di Fazio. The investigation of the B&B murder is officially ours. For the moment, I prefer to let her believe it's related to the drug cartel we are after."

"Let her believe?" Piva asked letting the words hang in the air.

"Yes, Piva. Because not even you are convinced about it, right?"

Piva said nothing, he didn't find the whole thing so suspicious, and his face gave him away.

"No, seriously Piva you have no doubt? Don't you smell anything fishy? Seriously? Well, this is why you are still a deputy!"

Piva swallowed his saliva and pride. That did hurt, but by now, he had learned that Zamparelli was not a sensitive soul.

39

PONTE ALTO - ITALY

Giulia still felt a strength she had never experienced before.

-Maybe this is what they call a survival instinct- she thought.

She drove to the hotel and went straight to her office. A couple of calls to the bank and then she would finish what she had left unresolved the previous night.

The frenzy of people, cars and sirens going on and off on the other side of the lake captured her attention. A chill shiver ran through her body.

Giulia cut the phone call short with an excuse and picked up her iPad to google the latest local news. There was nothing online yet, but still, with that chaos, it could have been too risky now to go ahead with her plan.

The hotel's foyer was much busier than usual, and the receptionists were struggling to calm people down.

"Have you heard what happened?" Roberto asked as he appeared from behind Giulia, who had just exited the lift. She had not heard him coming. The noiseless way he moved around reminded her of a snake.

"Jesus, you scared me," she told him in annoyance, "No, what has happened and what's this chaos?"

"They found a woman beaten to death at the Schwartzes'. The police don't know who she is. She had no ID with her. Rumour has it the murder might be related to drug trafficking. And now people are panicking. Our guests are enquiring about what happened and questioning the safety of their stay here. Some of the Schwartzes' guests, instead, want to move here because they don't want to sleep in a place where people get murdered. It's pure mayhem."

Giulia opened her mouth to speak, but no sound came out. All the events of the previous night started to pass in front of her.

Did she leave any traces? Would there be anyone able to place her over there? Would anybody be able to identify the victim? She had to know.

"I heard the inspector would do a press conference this evening. I suppose then we'll know a bit more," Roberto went on.

Giulia tried to look calm, but her heart was racing. This could be a potential disaster, or it could be the end of all her troubles without any damage. She had to talk to her mother.

Mara was in the garden, sitting on a bench she had bought at an antique auction when Giulia was just a child. It was one of those steel engraved benches so popular for gardens in the twenties. Mara was impeccably dressed as always, but there was nothing pretty in her look today. Her eyes were nearly transparent and lost in the void. For the first time, Giulia realised how much her mother had aged.

When Giulia approached her, Mara instinctively straightened her back, to regain a composure she had allowed herself to lose when unseen.

"You know, right?" Giulia spoke first. For some reason, nothing happened in town without Mara Kopfler being informed.

Mara raised her eyes to her daughter; Giulia took a step back like those eyes were physically and painfully transfixing her. Neither of them spoke for a few seconds until Giulia eventually made sense of her mother's expression and silence.

"You don't think I had anything to do with it, do you?"

Giulia took another step back. She wanted to shout all her outrage at her mother, but instead she let herself drop onto one of the garden chairs.

Mara spoke first, "Do you?"

Giulia sank a bit further on her seat.

"No!" It was the only thing she managed to say.

Mara extended her hand and squeezed her daughter's. A simple gesture of affection, but so out of character for her. Instinctively, Giulia retracted her hand and looked her mother straight in the eye.

"I had to ask. You must understand," Mara said, seeing the pain in her daughter's eyes.

"You know what, Mum? I don't. You are my mother. You shouldn't even be thinking something like that. And then what? Just because I said I didn't do it, all of a sudden your doubts would disappear? Do you know what I think? I think you don't give a fuck if I did it or not, even because, let's face it, if I did, I only made your problem go away. The truth is that you want to hear me say I didn't, so you have no responsibility and no weight on your conscience."

Giulia got up, and so did Mara.

"Don't be ridiculous. It's just you were so upset last night......"

"Well, so were you, Mum. Maybe I should ask you the same question. Because you know what? I don't think you give a damn about the death of your sister. After all, you already killed her once. The only thing you care about is not having your precious name dragged through the mud."

Mara ignored her daughter's words and replied with a simple statement: "We need to go to the police."

"What?" Giulia could not believe her ears.

"We need to identify her," Mara added like it was the simplest thing in the world to do and would have no further implications.

"No, don't you see? Then we will be the first the police will suspect. They don't know who she is, and they have no way of linking her to us. With her gone, all our troubles are gone too, and your secret is safe." Giulia was desperate to make her mother change her mind.

"They will find out who she is sooner or later, and when they do, we will look even guiltier. Don't you understand? Don't you see it's time to come clean? It's for the best, and it's the only way to contain the damage."

Mara was determined, but so was Giulia and she was furious. First, her mother had accused her of murder, and now she wanted to give herself up and drag her along.

"Are you stupid or what? The police found no ID in her bedroom, and as far as everybody is concerned, Lorna died a long time ago. Why would you crucify both of us?" Giulia's face was livid. Her anger and desperation were taking over.

"What about Lola?"

"What about her? Have you ever stopped for one minute to think about in the last forty years? About what you have done to her? I don't think so. You made us all live a lie, so why bring the truth up now? When the only other person who knew is out of the way, forever?"

Giulia was shouting.

"Would you please lower your voice?" Mara said quickly checking if Edda was anywhere nearby.

Mara watched Giulia leaving still in full rage.

It was no news for she and Giulia to argue, even violently, but today they both passed a point of no return.

Mara felt ashamed to have believed her daughter could be involved in Lorna's murder, but she did think it, so she had to ask. She only wished all her suspicions and doubts were gone.

40

PONTE ALTO - ITALY

When the morning light started to enter the bedroom, Mara felt some comfort as a new day was beginning.

She had barely closed her eyes for the whole night. She had lain in bed, staring at the ceiling and thinking about what to do. The recent events had been a consequence of what she did 40 years ago. Her sister's murder was her fault. Giulia was right; she had killed her twice.

Since when they were children, the sisters' personalities were like night and day. Mara was steadfast, determined, capable, and their father's favourite; Lorna was insecure and mentally fragile, like their mother. Their parents had grown apart over the years, and while their mother was retracting into her little exclusive world more and more every day, their father was making sure to defend the family name.

Till the day he died, Mr Kopfler maintained the version that his late wife had accidentally drowned in the lake, and that was the only version of the facts they were allowed to talk about in the house. However, there was no accident.

Mara and Lorna were there, and neither of them had ever forgotten that day. The old Mrs Kopfler went to her daughters' bedrooms and hugged them both never like before, and then she left without saying a single word.

Her eyes were different; Mara would never forget them. After she heard the house door opening and closing, she called Lorna, and they followed their mother. For Lorna, it was like a game, but Mara knew something odd was going to happen.

It was a cold January afternoon. In those days no tourists visited Ponte Alto during winter. Most of the locals shut down their activities for the season and went to work in the nearby ski resorts.

The girls hid behind some trees and watched their mother walking into the water. The two sisters stayed there, waiting for a few minutes and then ran to the hotel to call for their father.

By the time they got back to the lake, Ester Kopfler's green raincoat with its white spots was floating on the surface of the lake.

There was no enquiry, and the only version the newspaper ever published was that Mrs Kopfler must have fallen into the water while having her daily stroll and tragically drowned.

From that day, it was like Mrs Ester Kopfler had never existed. Mara kept being her father's daughter, and Lorna ended up being nobody's daughter.

Now Mara could see how things could have been different for her sister, but at the time she was just a liability for the whole family.

When their father died, Lorna only got what the law entitled her to, while Mara inherited the rest of the family assets. At the time, it was the most practical thing to do as Lorna had developed mental issues and soon after addiction to both drugs and alcohol, disgracing the entire family. Ultimately, she got pregnant and married her dealer. Their marriage didn't last long as he died of an overdose.

What could have been Lorna's chance to get clean and

rebuild her life, it brought her instead further down into a spiral of depression and neglect. In the beginning, Mara tried to help, if not for her sister's sake then for her niece's, but soon she gave up. You can't help someone who doesn't want to be rescued. They were sisters but had nothing to do with one another. Mara had her own family to look after as well as the business. She lost contact with her sister and her niece until one afternoon when she received a phone call from the social services. Mara could not pretend any longer not to have a sister: reality came knocking at her door and in the worst way possible.

Mara and Renzo went to Lorna's house. The front door was open, but there was nobody inside. All of a sudden Mara knew why her sister had not shown up for her meeting at the family support centre. She knew where to find her.

Like mother like daughter, as their father used to say not wasting any chance to condemn the daughter that, like his wife, only brought trouble and shame to the family.

Mara and Renzo rushed to the lake's shore.

It was one of those cloudy winter days when it looks like the light will never make it through. The grey of the sky and the water were one thing. There was no horizon line.

In the mist, they could see a figure walking into the water: Lorna. Her walk was awkward as she was struggling to keep going. Mara and Renzo looked at each other in shock: she was carrying something substantial in her arms. Lorna had her child with her.

Mara wanted to run after her sister, but her legs didn't move.

Memories started to fill her head, her mother in her green spotted coat was now walking alongside her sister. It was like she was in a trance until Renzo's voice brought her back to reality. He had rescued mother and daughter.

The rest was history.

Mara and Renzo had the chance to get rid of all their troubles. The lake was deserted. There were no witnesses to what had really happened. Mara and Renzo practised their version for the police over and over again. In the end, they nearly believed it themselves. But Lorna hadn't drowned, they locked her into a psychiatric hospital in Switzerland.

The entire town cried over the coincidence of a daughter sharing the same unfortunate destiny with her mother.

What Mara had not realised, was that pretending her sister didn't exist was not enough to erase her from her life. Twenty years had passed, and the day arrived when Lorna was back on her feet and ready to come back. Mara had never told Lorna she had declared her dead. Mara knew that the only reason Lorna wanted to go back was her daughter, and so she took it away from her. Mara told Lorna that Lola didn't want to have anything do with her. It was plausible after all, Lorna was the mother who tried to kill her. To Lola, instead, like to anyone else, Lorna had drowned.

Once again, Mara had been lucky but naive: people cannot be erased at our pleasure only because they represent an inconvenience in our lives.

She had made that mistake, and now she was afraid that her daughter had made it too.

41

DUBLIN - IRELAND

"That's fantastic, Finn. Thanks for calling. I'll come straight after school drop-off."

Lola threw her mobile on the still unmade bed and ran into the bathroom where Fergus was still in the shower.

"Hey, missus, do you have morning plans for us?" he winked at his wife after she wide opened the shower glass door.

"Siobhan is awake," Lola shouted in joy and hugged her husband without caring about getting wet all over.

"And to answer your question no, I don't, but only because I have no time. You will have to wait until tonight...."

That phone call had made Lola's day.

She knew the doctor had said Siobhan was going to be all right, but as long as her friend was unconscious, she found it difficult not to worry.

When Fergus came down to the kitchen, his wife had her back to the door still busy making the kids' lunches.

Fergus took a mug, poured himself some coffee and sat at the table joining the twins in their giggles at the sight of Lola whistling and discreetly dancing.

"Mrs Drake is feeling much better, that's why mum is so happy this morning," Alex whispered in his father's ear.

When Lola eventually turned and saw the expression of all three boys in front of her, she blushed.

"It's nice to see you like this again," Fergus said delicately placing his hand on top of his wife's as she sat beside him. Lola smiled at him and brought a mug of coffee to her lips.

"Listen, I've plenty of time to drop the boys to school and bring you to the hospital, before heading off. At least you won't have to get the bus at this time in the morning. God knows what time it might show up."

"Thank you, that would be great."

* * *

"Come on, guys, or you'll be late."

"Mum is still upstairs getting ready," Philip protested while his father brusquely waved them into the car.

The three of them were sitting inside the car, and Fergus was thumping his fingers on the steering wheel. He said he had plenty of time but not that much time.

"Here I am, sorry." Lola eventually joined them.

"Have you changed your mind about staying over in Longford tonight?" she inquired when they were about to exit the driveway.

"No," Fergus looked at his wife puzzled by her question.

"Your bag is in the bedroom. I just thought you changed your mind," Lola candidly said, but the implication in her tone was all but innocent, "and then you are always the one complaining about me being late, eh? Of course, you are the first to get ready. You forget half of what you have to do."

"Damn it!" Fergus reversed and quickly went back to the house to get his overnight bag; Lola and the kids could hear him mumbling something to the door.

Eventually, they made it to the school, and they were now on their way to the hospital.

The St. Vincent University Hospital was one of the most advanced in Ireland. Over the years they added units and refurbished it completely. Quite close to where they lived, it was unfortunately on one of the busiest roads, in particular during rush hours.

Lola could see Fergus getting impatient; they'd already been stuck in Sandy Mount Road for fifteen minutes. If they didn't start to move soon, he was going to be late for his meeting.

"I'm sorry, honey," Lola apologised feeling guilty about delaying her husband, even though he had offered to drive her.

"It's OK, darling. It's not you. It's that damn traffic light at the end of the road. Seven roads are converging in one, unbelievable. I don't even know why they haven't thought of another solution for that crossroad. Maybe it was OK thirty years ago but now...." Fergus started to beep the horn angrily.

"Listen, drop me here. The hospital is not far. I will be faster on foot, and you can reverse and go back. The traffic will be in the opposite direction, and you'll be on the motorway in no time."

"Are you sure? " Fergus liked that proposal and wanted to get himself out of that traffic jam as soon as he could, but at the same time felt like he was dumping his wife after he had suggested helping her.

"Yeah. We are both wasting our time and getting stressed here. "

Lola got out of the car, and five minutes later, Fergus was back on the N4. He was on his way to the motorway when his mobile beeped with an incoming text message of his wife thanking him for the lift and saying how much she loved him.

He smiled at the phone screen and sent his wife a love

heart emoji; the only thing he could manage while driving. He had tried to use Siri a few times, but it had been a disaster.

42

DUBLIN - IRELAND

When the lift door opened on the fourth floor, the silence that permanently inhabited the ICU curbed Lola's enthusiasm at the prospect of seeing her friend awake.

She went straight to Siobhan's room, but when she saw a woman she had never seen before coming out in tears, she stopped. There were no familiar faces in the corridor: No Finn, no Alahnna, no Matthew and no Melinda either. She didn't dare to knock on the door, let alone walk in.

Thankfully a nurse was coming towards her. Lola had seen her before.

"Good morning," the nurse greeted Lola, obviously recognising her too.

"If you are looking for your friend she's been moved to another room. She doesn't need the ICU anymore."

A wave of relief shook Lola's entire body. The nurse gave her Siobhan's new room number and the floor she was on, and Lola turned back to the lift at a pace.

From outside the room, she could hear many voices. She knocked and went in.

"Lola," Siobhan exclaimed opening her arms wide, and

with her typical pompous tone, that was so familiar and so nice to hear again. When Lola managed to free herself from Siobhan's thigh embrace, Finn hugged her too, and Detective McCarthey extended his hand and gave her a firm handshake. The moment of embarrassed silence was interrupted by someone opening the door. A nurse with a pointy nose and a loud voice barged in.

"Ladies and gentlemen, I think Mrs Drake needs to rest now. We have already broken the rules enough for one day by allowing you all here outside of visiting hours."

"But my friend just arrived, and she saved my life. Well, that's what they said because I don't remember a thing," Siobhan tried to protest, but the nurse was incorruptible and didn't move until she saw them all leaving the room.

"I'll come back tomorrow, love you," Lola whispered from the door.

Lola, Finn and the detective took the lift together.

"Did you drive?" Finn asked Lola, more to break the ice than out of real interest.

"Fergus dropped me. I'll take the bus home."

"I would give you a lift, but I'm already late for an appointment at the surgery, sorry," Finn added, and Lola was genuinely OK with that as she was well used to public transport.

As soon as they were out of the building, Finn waved good-bye and walked quickly to his car. Lola and McCarthey kept walking in silence until the detective offered to drive her home.

"Oh, thank you. You are very kind, but it's not necessary. I'll wait for the bus." Lola had no desire to be stuck in a car with McCarthey and talk about the investigation because, in total honesty, she could not see any other subject they could talk about.

"Don't be silly; we are going in the same direction."

Detective McCarthey was a man who didn't take "no" for an answer.

Lola wondered what he was like in private life if he had one. The majority of law enforcement officers were unable to keep stable relationships, according to the crime books she had read. But the multicoloured Loom band bracelets on his wrist told another story. Lola guessed he had kids, girls to be precise: daddy's girls.

Lola loved her boys but always wondered how nice it would have been to have a girl as well. A girl who grew up to make her father proud and jealous at the same time. A girl who could confide in her mother and share secrets with her; a daughter who could be everything she had never been allowed to be in her childhood and youth.

"Mrs Owen? Are you OK?" Detective McCarthey voice and his large, heavy hand on her arm awoke Lola from her daydream.

"Yes, sorry, just lost in my little world for a moment."

That was the effect that her past caused every time she recalled it. That was the reason why she had fought so hard to leave it behind.

43

DUBLIN - IRELAND

Reluctantly Lola got into McCarthey's unmarked car, and the fact that the detective had his handgun on his belt, made her feel even more uneasy. Garda officers usually do not carry guns unless they are of high ranks, like sergeants or detectives.

"Are you uncomfortable around weapons or just around guards, Mrs Owen?"

Detective Enda McCarthey's comment took Lola by surprise and made her realise how odd her behaviour must have looked. Still not weird enough to justify the detective's seemingly innocent remark.

Lola's reaction must have made McCarthey realise he had pushed his sarcasm too far and so he tried to apologise, "Sorry, I didn't mean to sound unmannered, but you look like I'm holding you hostage."

The problem was that she did feel like a hostage. McCarthey had forced her to accept a lift, and now he was only waiting for the right moment to ask his questions.

Lola candidly answered those she knew how to respond to. The detective was interested in the Drakes' marriage, and soon Lola realised the implications of those questions and became more and more reticent. She couldn't even imagine any possible involvement of Finn in his wife's attack. When Detective McCarthey's car finally pulled over in front of her house, Lola felt immensely grateful that her time under scrutiny was over.

Lola already had her hand on the door handle to open it and get out of the car as fast as possible when the detective stopped her.

"You do understand I'm not the bad person here. The bad person is whoever viciously attacked your neighbour and friend, and he or she is still out there. So anything you know you should tell me. No matter how small or insignificant it might sound. Any little detail might help at this stage, no matter who it might be about. Then it will be up to me to prove innocence or guilt, but to do that, I need facts and to be honest, in this story, there are plenty missing," McCarthey said as he pushed back a rebel ginger curl from his forehead and then released Lola's arm. Lola managed to get out of the car, she thanked him for the lift and still feeling his piercing green eyes on her, she walked toward her house. She opened the front door but didn't dare to turn in case the detective's Hyundai was still there.

Enda McCarthey waited in the car for a few minutes wondering what the Owens were doing in such a neighbourhood. Those houses, unaffordable for most, were the residences of the ones coming from money or that had skilfully ridden the Celtic Tiger and managed not to get blasted by the recession. He had made a background check on everyone involved in the case, and if the Drakes perfectly fitted the stereotype, Lola and Fergus did not. They neither came from money nor had any. The Owens had simply made their pact with the devil in the form of a humongous mortgage.

Enda McCarthey lived in a beautiful area in the Goatstown district. He had bought a decent size semi-detached house and bound himself to a considerable mortgage for the next thirty years, but nothing like the one the Owens must have had. The thought of the pressure the couple must be under every end of the month horrified him.

* * *

Detective McCarthey's words kept echoing in Lola's head. She took off her shoes and kicked them to one side of the hallway. She went straight to the sitting room and let herself collapse on the large corner sofa. She grabbed one of the cushions that she meticulously scattered upon it every morning after tidying up, and covered her face with it.

She felt exhausted, and she felt sudden hate for the poor detective. She knew he was only doing his job, but he was also making everybody feel bad.

When Fergus wasn't at home for dinner, Lola and the boys always had easy meals. She sold them to Alex and Philip as a treat, but the truth was that she was glad to defrost something or improvise some scrambled eggs and beans.

On these solitary evenings, Lola missed conversing with her husband but, at the same time, she liked having some alone time. She enjoyed the freedom to wear her PJ's while ready to eat cross-legged on the couch watching some old episode of Columbo. Fergus hated Columbo, but to Lola, it reminded her of when she and her cousin along with her aunt and uncle, used to watch it all together on Sunday afternoons.

She was only a kid and missed most of the connections but enjoyed the fact that for a couple of hours, it was like having a healthy family, maybe even a happy and loving one. Unfortunately, that was only in her imagination.

It was 8:30 pm, and the sun was still up.

"Mum, close the curtains properly, OK? Or the light will blind us tomorrow morning." Philip liked to sleep in total darkness, while Alex preferred the comfort of a night light. Because they still wanted to share the bedroom, they compromised by putting some glow-in-the-dark stars all over their bedroom ceiling.

"Goodnight, boys, sleep tight."

When the boys were smaller, they refused to go to sleep if it was still daylight outside, but over time they got used to having light until late in the evening during summer and darkness from four in the afternoon in winter. The time of their tantrums had long gone.

Lola was tired, but it was too early for her to go to sleep. She sat in the garden with a glass of wine, trying to distract herself browsing through the pages of a magazine. When the evening breeze started to chill her bare shoulders, she went inside.

The television wasn't of any comfort or distraction as there was nothing interesting to watch. In the end, not even Columbo had shown up that evening, Lola switched to the skybox set and looked for some TV drama that didn't require much attention or concentration. Criminal Minds was perfect for spending an hour. She had already seen the episode multiple times, and before they captured the psychopath of the day, she decided to go to bed. This night was one of the warm ones but being at home alone, she didn't like to have her window open. Besides, without Fergus in bed with her, it wouldn't be that warm. She always joked that he was like a radiator, his body temperature was consistently high, and his skin was burning, plus he always rolled onto her side of the bed. It was like having a human electric blanket.

They had not spoken all day, but she knew he had one meeting after another, and he was supposed to dine out with his potential client.

She sent him a goodnight text message and then switched the mobile to night mode. She turned the bedside lamp off, and in a matter of seconds, she was fast asleep.

44

PONTE ALTO - ITALY

"Father, forgive me for all my sins......."

Mara knew that Father Nello could not betray the seal of confession, but she would have trusted him, nonetheless. He was a good man besides being an excellent priest. Mara and Nello knew each other since they were kids and had grown up together. Back in the school days, he was the most handsome of the boys, and when he announced his decision to become a priest, he left a trail of broken hearts behind, Mara's included. His vocation arrived only in his early twenties. Until then, Father Nello and Mara had been very close friends. She wouldn't have minded their relationship developing into something more romantic, but he kept playing the part of a friend. Of course, the announcement of his going into priesthood explained his behaviour, but still, it was a disappointment.

Mara had always carried him in her heart, and when he came back to the local parish after years in the Vatican, to her, it was like a sign. Their friendship had never faded. He knew everything about her family, and if there was someone who could understand the reasons behind her actions, it was him. Father Nello listened in silence to Mara's confession and then, still not speaking, he left the confessional. He gently went around to his old friend and delicately holding her by one arm helped her getting up. It was just the two of them in church, nearly no-one confesses anymore nowadays.

Mara's knees were aching, and with the pretence of massaging them, she avoided looking him in the eyes. She wondered what he was thinking, not as a priest but as a man.

"Let's go have a cup of coffee in the rectory. You need a friend now, not a priest."

They talked for most of the afternoon. Nello struggled to hide his shock when she told him the truth about what had happened to Lorna but years of wearing the cassock had taught him not to be surprised by any revelation.

Nello was no fool, and he knew Mara talked to him as a priest first, to be sure he couldn't say anything. His old friend was not there to clear her conscience but to figure out what to do.

He held Mara's hands, and she allowed him because speaking to him had brought her a certain lightness. It felt good to tell the truth and reveal her feelings. Mara also confessed her worries about Giulia, but once father Nello started to ask further questions, she abruptly retracted her hands and changed the subject. She was exposing herself and her daughter far too much.

"Listen, Mara. I'm not here to judge you. My role as a priest is to promote forgiveness. God is forgiveness, "Qui sine peccato est vestrum, primus lapidem mittat," Nello took his old friend's hand back in his and continued, "but the forgiveness you are looking for, nobody can give it to you. You must forgive yourself, and the only way is to tell the truth to those who need to know. You need to repent your sins."

"And what about Giulia? What if she is involved?" No matter what Giulia might have done, she was still her daughter and Mara had to protect her.

Nello walked to the window overlooking the small, well-kept garden of the rectory. That view inspired most of his Sunday sermons, but today it was of no help in finding the right words that he needed. How could he tell his longtime friend that she had to find the courage to look into her daughter's soul and decide whether she was capable of killing someone and, if necessary, go to the police?

In all the years of knowing Mara Kopfler, that was the only time Nello saw a defeated look on her face.

Mara left the rectory knowing what she had to do, but the initial lightness and relief Mara had felt after confessing everything had vanished. She now felt like she was up against the wall hopelessly waiting for the firing squad to shoot.

45

PONTE ALTO - ITALY

"Are you not going to answer?" Carlo eventually said after Giulia's mobile rang for the third time in 20 minutes, displaying Mara's number as the caller.

"The last thing I need right now is to talk to her," Giulia snapped.

Carlo knew that when his fiancé was that upset, it was best to leave her alone and so with an excuse, he went to the balcony.

"I'm sorry, I didn't mean to snap at you," Giulia said with a genuinely apologetic tone and carrying two ice creams.

Carlo smiled back at her and patted the space beside him on the swing seat, inviting her to sit down.

They ate their ice creams in silence, enjoying the evening breeze that, even in the hottest evenings, always blew on the balcony of the penthouse. Giulia's flat was in the tallest building of Ponte Alto, a modern tower built by Carlo's company.

The project had been approved thanks to the political influence of the Kopfler family and the economic incentive that Carlo had dropped on the Mayor's desk. When the construction works started, the town split into two opposing factions. One against it, in the name of tradition; and the other that would only have to benefit from the project.

Once the building was finished, even the most hostile had to admit that it didn't ruin the landscape at all. Ultimately, as promised, it attracted wealthy investors who bought most of the apartments mainly to be occupied during the summer and winter holidays season.

Giulia's penthouse was her reward for her role in making the building possible. She loved that place. The entire town was visible from up there as well as the lake in all its vast beauty.

"You must admit she is right," Carlo spoke with an uncertain tone, breaking the peaceful moment, "I mean when she said you must go to the police," he quickly added after Giulia shot him a look that could kill.

"And say what?" she snapped again, but this time there was no apologies to follow.

"I mean, you were there, at the Schwartze Guest House, people saw you, and you know who she is. The police will find out sooner or later......"

Giulia was enraged; she felt like the only person who should support her was turning against her too. She stormed away.

"Damn it!" Carlo said to himself.

He followed her inside only to find her by the kitchen sink, splashing water on her face to wash away the tears that she couldn't control.

Carlo pulled her into his arms, and as much as she wanted to pull away from him, instead she just surrendered herself.

"I'm sorry," he whispered.

"I swear, I was there, but I didn't see her. I knocked, and nobody answered, so I left. I drove around to calm my nerves and then I came home."

"I know," Carlo said calmly, "and I didn't think even for a

split second that you had anything to do with the murder. What I meant was that if the police are going to find out who she was and that you were there, it might not look good that you had kept it from them."

"Why can't things ever go smoothly for once?" Giulia had now freed herself from Carlo and was walking up and down the kitchen.

"My head is exploding. Everything is so overwhelming, and it's all my mother's fault. If she had not been so hostile and selfish, none of this would have ever happened. First the signatures, then my aunt..."

Carlo still didn't know she had forged her mother's signature on the bank's papers and Giulia immediately regretted her words. She could not tell him now. It would give her even a stronger motive, in everybody's eyes, his included.

"Well, like you, in the end, had convinced her to sign those damn papers, I'm sure you will persuade her to do what's best for everybody in this matter too. We only need to decide what's best. Keep our mouths shut or tell the police what we know?"

Carlo was right. She needed to reason and recall the events minute by minute.

Carlo and Giulia went through the night of the murder over and over again. Every time some new detail emerged, but the conclusion was always the same: except for Mr Derrik, who had left the following day and was now presumably miles away, nobody had seen her at the Schwartze Guest House.

Furthermore, when she phoned around to check where Lorna was staying, she had never introduced herself.

"OK, that's good, Hon!" Carlo was halfway between patronising and consoling, "Now the only thing you must make sure of, is that the encounter between your mother and your aunt had happened as discretely."

Giulia nodded.

"Take a sleeping pill, have a good rest and tomorrow first thing you'll go to your mother and see what she has to say."

46

PONTE ALTO - ITALY

"Piva," Zamparelli barked from his office, "Any word from forensics or the pathologist? They showed up with their big flashy new lab-van, but their speed is still more akin to a tortoise than a hare."

Piva stood by the door and let his boss finish, "See my desk? Not one bloody report yet!"

Zamparelli had the tact of a bull in a china shop, but he was not prone to lose his temper. He could be harsh but not choleric. His mood told deputy Piva only one thing: the inspector had a call from Belluno.

Belluno, was where Superintendent Luisa Di Fazio was based. She was a driven woman who had climbed the ranks of police quickly, and she expected all her officers to solve cases just as quick.

"I'll ring Doctor Ferrari again," Piva said in the end.

"I'll ring him. You get out all the statements from the case. Someone must have seen or heard something," Zamparelli ordered picking up the phone.

"Zamparelli, I just told Di Fazio this morning, I'll have the complete report ready by tonight. Tomorrow morning at the latest. So that you know, your victim is not the only one on my table! I have three hikers who ventured off-trail to illegally pick alpine stars and guess what? The Divine punishment descended upon them, and here they are, zipped in a bag with me." The loud laugh of the pathologist to his own joke didn't have any effect on Zamparelli.

"Jeez, inspector, I thought you men from the South had a bit more sense of humour." Even this last attempt at easing Zamparelli's mood failed, and so the coroner waited in silence for the inspector to say something.

"Di Fazio is breathing down my neck. She is busting my balls for results, and I don't even know exactly how the woman died or who the fuck she is, never mind who killed her. Excuse me if I'm not in the mood for jokes," Zamparelli lashed out, finding nothing but support on the other end of the line.

"Don't tell me! That woman is more bitter than limes. Anyway, one thing I can tell you already, and it's that the broken silver photo frame found at the scene is most likely what they used to beat her up. The tip of one corner was stuck in her temple. The blows were applied with force".

"So, you gather it was a man who did it?" Zamparelli asked.

"Or a furious woman. Judging by the trajectory of the blows, whoever hit her was not taller than 170 cm. The object was not heavy, but presumably, the first blow went straight to her temple diagonally, causing her most likely to lose her balance and possibly her senses as well. The killer used the frame to smash her face when she was already on the ground. The cuts are consistent with the broken glass. The fragments are stuck all over under the skin of her face. Or what's left of it anyway, "Dr Ferrari concluded.

"Fuck me, slaughtered with a silver photo frame."

In all his years in the force, Zamparelli had never seen

something as brutal, "So what do you think?" he asked the coroner, trusting his professionalism.

"Of course, this is just my opinion. A guess let's say until I have all the results..."

Doctor Steno Ferrari didn't like to guess, but the way Zamparelli always involved him in his investigations showing to rely on his opinions, intrigued him.

" . . . I think whoever killed her also wanted to make her unrecognisable, but I don't think it's a drug-related crime. The murder weapon was an object of chance and all those blows, even after the victim was dead. It's a crime of hate, and it's personal. Otherwise, why bother removing the picture from the frame?" Ferrari had just confirmed Zamparelli's theory, "I think so too, doc. Here is my theory so far: She was hiding from something or someone, and she was here with a purpose. She knew her attacker, she opened the door, but things got out of control. The killer panicked, tried to hide his or her traces but not being an expert criminal did not think about the possibility of identification through fingerprints or dental records. "

"Very plausible, Inspector Zamparelli. But don't confide in dental records. With the skull in these conditions, even the teeth are irremediably compromised. "

* * *

Piva came into the inspector's office and laid the pile of statements on the desk.

"Sit Piva, help me go through this, and hopefully we will have something to report back to Di Fazio."

Two hours later, Deputy Inspector Piva closed the last file, crossed his arms behind his head and with a defeated tone said: "Inspector there is nothing here, this is a waste of time."

"On the contrary," Zamparelli replied with a vibe of excitement, "see, Piva, they all say the same thing: Our victim arrived and locked herself in her bedroom avoiding any contact with whoever was around, and this confirms our hypothesis that she wanted to keep her anonymity. But there is more. She took the chance of showing up without a reservation. A bit of a hazard at this time of the year, don't you think?"

Zamparelli waited for his deputy to nod, and went on, "You know what I think, Piva? I think she didn't need a reservation because she knew there would be a free room. The one she had just cancelled that very same morning. She booked it and then cancelled it and pretended to be there by chance."

Before the inspector could carry on, Piva interrupted him, "OK, but why not keep the reservation?"

"Because she had booked it under a fake name and once she checked in, they would have checked her documents."

"Yes, but why not use the excuse of the headache as she did to avoid the check-in…"

"Because sooner or later, she would have to provide her ID and wouldn't have matched with the name on the booking. Our victim was not going to run away, Piva. She came to stay, but first, she had something to do. After that, she would have been able to show herself for who she was."

Piva started to see the inspector's point, and it made sense, "So if we find out who she was and why she was here, we will know who killed her."

"Yes, Piva. She said she came from Switzerland by plane, but no flights from either Zurich or Geneva were scheduled to arrive in Venice that day. She lied about it. But why? And why was it so important for people not to know who she was?"

"Well, obviously someone had found out, and it did cost her life."

"Indeed, Piva. Her identity is the key."

"And that is why they savagely smashed her face and took

her documents. This crime has nothing to do with drug trafficking. Inspector, you were right. "

"Glad you eventually agree with me, Piva. Now, I'll see if Ferrari has some time to attempt a face reconstruction and, in the meantime, you run her fingerprints through Interpol."

47

DUBLIN - IRELAND

"You should have heard him...with his inquisitive tone like we are all hiding something, or we are all part of some big conspiracy....And the way he forced me to get into the car with him," Lola complained, moving erratically around the kitchen.

"Maybe he was just nice, he's a police officer after all, and he is supposed to help people in need," Fergus said raising his eyebrow at his wife who was already on her third glass of wine.

"Do I look in need?"

"Surely not in need of more wine! "

Lola emptied her glass of cabernet pretending to be offended and then attacked the cheese and the relish left on her plate.

"I'm serious, Fergus, how can McCarthey even think that there is someone among us hiding the truth about what happened and that Finn has something to do with it? He should be out there looking for the real culprit instead of harassing us," Lola lashed out, with her mouth still half full of food.

"I'm with you. I don't see poor Finn doing something like

that, no matter how much that woman got on his nerves, and if you ask me, that can be a lot."

Lola threw a piece of cracker at her husband, "Don't dare to say that in front of the detective or else it will be used against you." Lola's tone was full of sarcasm and contempt.

"But you must admit that he's right in a way, though. The whole attack is a bit strange. I mean it happened in broad daylight, she opened the door to the assailant, and he didn't even steal anything?" Fergus said, pouring his wife some more wine but not daring to look at her straight.

"Well, I suppose if you put it that way," Lola had to admit that, rationally, for someone who didn't know them or the Drakes, the reality of the events could raise more than one question.

"Maybe you should tell the detective you actually know the woman Siobhan had the run-in with on the street."

That was where Fergus wanted to go, and Lola didn't like it at all. What he was implying was even more absurd than McCarthey's half-spoken theories.

"First of all, Laura has nothing to do with this. She didn't even know Siobhan before that morning. And second of all, Siobhan didn't have a run-in with her. She had just mistaken her for someone else."

"Yes, that someone who was sneaking around our letterbox and, according to Siobhan, she made no mistake at all," Fergus pointed out.

"Jesus, this again?" Lola started to be annoyed but mainly because deep down, she knew there were a few things that didn't add up.

"The woman left the very same day, and frankly, I don't see why she would want to attack Siobhan."

"Still, I think you should mention the whole story to the detective. Just tell him everything you know; that's it."

Fergus's patronising tone annoyed Lola even more, "Unless someone already did it on my behalf, and that is why

McCarthey was so pushy on me saying everything I know, even the smallest detail," her tone was sharp. She was accusing her husband of sneakily talking behind her back.

It took all the will in the world for Fergus to stay calm, "Do you think I said something only to get you or your Italian friend in trouble?"

Lola knew she had crossed the line. What she had said not only was untrue, but it had also hurt her husband's feelings.

"I'm sorry. I'm just so upset. I don't know why I said that."

"I think you said it because you are angry, and I happen to be the perfect punching bag."

Fergus's tone softened. Lola didn't mean to doubt him or hurt him; he knew that now.

"Do you think he believes I'm holding something back? Because I'm not. At least not on purpose. I honestly don't see how the two things can be related..."

Now Lola's voice was a tone too high. That meant she was agitated, anxious.

"Listen to me," Fergus started to speak to his wife softly, "now you are overthinking and making a big deal out of nothing. Detective McCarthey is only doing his job. I don't think he suspects you of anything as much as I don't think he seriously suspects Finn, but he has to check all the leads. Now, you know I share Siobhan's opinion about that Laura woman being a bit weird, but as you said she was gone before the attack and had nothing to do with it. I'm sorry, maybe I should have never brought it up."

That night Lola struggled to fall asleep. She still couldn't keep the conversations with the detective and her husband out of her mind. She hadn't given a second thought to what had happened between Laura and Siobhan, but now that Fergus had mentioned it, it was hard to ignore. Lola kept turning over in bed: Laura, Siobhan, Fergus, McCarthey, Finn and her picture frame. All images that she couldn't send away.

* * *

The school was closed that day because of teachers' training.

A blessing for Lola, as she had no time for overthinking or merely thinking about anything but how to rescue her ears from Alex and Philip pretending to be knights of some magical world.

Because the day was warm but wet, the boys' imaginary kingdom and battlefield spread across the entire house; except for the kitchen where she was hiding, doing the ironing.

After two hours lost in the steam, she happily closed the ironing board, and it was only then that Lola realised she had not heard from Fergus all day. Actually, not only her husband but no one else had either called or sent her text messages or emails, and that was very strange.

Her eyes went instinctively to the top of the cupboard, where she usually left her mobile. It was not there.

Lola went upstairs to her bedroom and found her mobile still on her bedside table.

Fergus had called, but after she didn't answer, he eventually sent her a text. He didn't sound worried at all, just assumed she was busy with the boys or had her phone at the bottom of her bag as usual.

Lola scrolled through the last missed calls, and found three calls from an unsaved number, probably a scam, she thought but then noticed there were four voicemail messages left on the day.

Curiosity got the better of her. She dialled the voicemail and listened: the first was Fergus's attempt to get his wife, the second and the third were empty, but in the fourth message, someone spoke.

48

DUBLIN - IRELAND

"So, shall I file the Drake case under unsolved home invasion, for the moment?" the young Garda asked daring only to step one foot into the detective's office. The fact that he had just stopped shouting on the phone with the forensics at the Phoenix Park lab was not a good sign.

"Should we?" Detective Enda McCarthey replied.

Kevin pondered his answer. For sure, the detective was not asking him what to do with the case. Indeed he wished he was, but the truth was that the only thing he had been allowed to deal with was collecting fingerprints. Was McCarthey sarcastic? That would not have surprised the young guard who was still thinking of the most appropriate answer when his boss told him to come in.

In silence, Kevin obeyed because McCarthey's words sounded more like a command than an invitation. Usually, everything that McCarthey asked sounded like an order, regardless of who was in front of him.

Kevin was used to the detective's attitude and learned over time that it was not his intention to sound intimidating. McCarthey, on his side, was oblivious to the way he was perceived. He was aware his physicality made people think twice before crossing him but had no knowledge of the terror most of the officers at the station felt when addressed by their superior.

To the detective, the fact that Kevin was the only one really and adequately interacting with him was purely coincidental. And it was also the reason why he picked him as his unofficial deputy, the one he could confide in and share thoughts with during investigations. Kevin was also the one he usually brought with him if he needed a backup.

"There is something that doesn't add up. Just, I can't put my finger on what it is," McCarthey said, still going through some statements.

To Kevin, the case was pretty square and straightforward: someone went in for burglary, but it went wrong; they panicked, and they left in a hurry without taking anything. There were plenty of such cases around Dublin, every day. And that road had been the target of a series of burglaries lately. Kevin couldn't understand why his boss was so stubborn.

"Well, Sir, as you said, the husband can be excluded, and there is no evidence that Mrs Drake had an affair or some secret life on the side. We have nothing to look like a possible motive. Still, it's a fact that there had been a few burglaries in the area around the same time as the attack. Maybe for once, the most obvious and simple conclusion is also the right one. In this case, a simple burglary went wrong."

Ignoring the young officer's words, Detective Enda McCarthey kept moving papers around the desk.

"Here it is!" he exclaimed rotating the piece of paper towards Kevin and pointing with his chubby fingers at a few lines.

Kevin read the deposition of a Lelia Doolan, living on the opposite side of the road, and that should have told him something, but still, no bulb appeared above his head.

"Come on, Kevin. You are smarter than this," McCarthey

shouted, making a couple of heads outside in the corridor to turn. Kevin blushed and regretted his boss's habit of always keeping the door open; unless he had to discuss something confidential.

Kevin read Miss Doolan's statement a second time, and a flash of understanding went through his eyes, "The woman Mrs Drake had the run-in the days before the attack was the same she accused of snooping around the Owens' mailbox a few days earlier."

"Exactly, Kevin."

"Then why did nobody bother to mention it?"

"That's what we are going to find out, Kevin. We need to fingerprint the Owens' letterbox too, and I want to talk to Lola Owen again. There might be more than a mistake of identity behind that run-in."

49

PONTE ALTO - ITALY

The talk with Nello put things into a different perspective. A perspective Mara never thought existed.

The regained peace and a clear mind made her oversleep. Mara was still getting dressed when she heard the gate bell ringing, but let Edda deal with whoever it was. When the sound of tyres in the driveway reached the bedroom, she peeped through the window. She was sure it was Giulia. Her daughter could not ignore her calls forever. Usually, Mara would have been upset with her daughter's childish behaviour but not this time.

Mara had made up her mind, she was at peace with herself, and she had taken every possible step to make sure things were going the right way. She would talk to Giulia out of courtesy, only to inform her of her decisions. There was nothing her daughter could say or do to change the course of events.

Leopold jumped onto the windowsill and looked with his owner out of the window. Surprised, Mara didn't see Giulia's car driving in but Father Nello's.

When Mara arrived downstairs, followed by a loyal

Leopold who rarely left her side these days, Edda had already invited father Nello in and had him wait outside in the back garden.

"Should I make coffee for you, Mrs Kopfler? Or do you want some iced tea too?" Edda asked.

"Whatever you're bringing to the Father, Edda. Thank you," Mara answered without even looking at her housekeeper and joined her guest, "Nello, what a surprise."

Mara tried to sound as detached as possible. Her tone revealed the usual coldness she reserved for everybody, and Nello didn't miss it.

He gently touched her arm, "It's OK, Mara. I just wanted to see how you were."

Mara's shoulders relaxed and just when she was about to speak, Edda showed up.

"Thank you, Edda."

The brusque way Mara dismissed the poor woman grabbing the tray from her hands, made Nello look at the housekeeper as if he wanted to apologise on behalf of his friend.

"I've not talked to Giulia yet, but I did ring Lola," Mara began to talk, oblivious to the way she had mistreated Edda.

"I'm proud of you!" the priest's words filled Mara's eyes with tears, that soon gleamed upon her cheeks.

Mara hid her head in her hands, and when she eventually lifted it, she saw Edda at the kitchen window, who quickly turned away.

When Giulia got up, Carlo was already gone. Sometimes it was nice to have the whole house to herself, like before he moved in.

She indulged herself in shuffling from one room to the other and then had her coffee on the balcony. After taking a long shower, she slipped into a sleeveless tight red dress and a pair of high heeled sandals. Since she began dating Carlo, she only wore high heels when she wasn't with him. Carlo was slightly shorter than she was and out of delicacy, she always wore flat shoes when they were together.

Giulia had planned to pay a visit to her mother, but first, she was going to stop by the hotel.

Even if she had nothing physically to do in the office, she had made it a rule to stop by the hotel every day. Show her face around the place, do a general check and, most of all, annoy Roberto by showing him that she was the boss. He felt powerful because of the trust Mara placed in him. Still, if Giulia was there, he had to succumb to the hierarchy. Something that never failed to provide her with extreme satisfaction.

Giulia was walking through the hotel's hall when she heard her name being called. She recognised Roberto's voice and kept walking. After a few steps, she hesitated a second and then stopped waiting for him to catch up with her.

"Am I correct in saying that I heard we are proceeding with the works, starting this autumn?"

Giulia hated his theatrical way of speaking, going around in circles of unnecessary talk before getting to the point. Even more so, she hated when he spoke as "WE" like he owned a share of the hotel or had some voice in the decisions.

The big shades she was wearing hid her rolling eyes. Giulia's first instinct was to remind him that it was none of his business, but then she was sure he would have gone straight to Mara.

"I'm afraid you have been misinformed. We are still discussing options," Giulia replied.

"But from what I heard, and my source is well informed, it seemed quite certain. I'm surprised that Mara hadn't told me anything," Roberto was not giving up, and his arrogance made Giulia's blood boil. She tried to stay calm and not sound snappy. She needed to give him a decent explanation that left no doubt or scope to enquire further.

"I don't know who your source is, but I'm telling you that it's not very well informed. As for my mother, I was not aware she had to keep you in the loop of every family matter. Because this is a family business if you haven't noticed."

Giulia turned around and walked towards her car with just one thought on her mind: The deal they had just sealed with the bank was confidential. Only someone from the bank could have spilt the beans and if Roberto knew, Mara would soon too. Giulia had to stop this right now.

She stopped by the side of the car, and called after Roberto, "Maybe you want to tell your friend at the bank that passing confidential information, whether true or not, is still illegal and enough for me to file a complaint and have her fired."

The expression on Roberto's face confirmed Giulia's suspicions. It was the bank manager who had told him. It was no secret they had been having an affair for months, but this time they had crossed the line and put themselves in a dangerous position. Giulia could only hope her threat had been received loud and clear.

50

DUBLIN - IRELAND

"Mum, are you listening?"

"Yes, of course, keep telling me...."

The truth was that Lola's head was elsewhere since she had heard the message on her voicemail. Aunt Mara had been vague about the reason she wanted to speak to her. That phone call had upset her as much as it had piqued her curiosity. Why her aunt had called after so many years of silence? Lola was impatient to know. Still, the courage to ring Mara back had not come yet.

Lola decided to wait for Fergus to come home. She didn't want advice from him, as she already knew what to do, but he had to be there when she did it.

The voice of her aunt on the voice mail was not the voice she remembered; it was sweeter, her tone more indulgent, and this only increased Lola's anxiety. That woman had never had a word of compassion for her niece, only snide remarks.

A sudden fire had lit inside Lola, a fire fuelled by rage and hatred. All feelings that she thought she had buried forever, and instead, it only took a few words to bring everything back.

* * *

Husband and wife were sitting next to each other on the sofa. The TV was on but with the volume muted.

"So when are you going to call her back? " Fergus asked.

Lola just buried her face in his chest, like a child who doesn't want to face something because it's not going to be pleasant.

"Will you be with me when I do?" Lola asked back, perfectly aware of how childish she sounded but also confident that Fergus would understand. Fergus had only met Mara once, and it had been enough.

Lola had been quite open about the situation she had grown up in, and he always felt very protective of her. His wife was an amazing woman, a fantastic mother, and a brilliant and vibrant human being, but when it came to her family, she became insecure, fragile and impractical. The damage they had done to her was so grave that nothing could fix it.

"Of course, even if I don't think you need anybody to give you the strength to face the old witch because you are the strongest person I know," Fergus kissed his wife, passionately.

They made love on the couch in the sitting room. Neither of them could remember the last time they felt such desire for one another.

"Well, I suppose we'll have to wait until tomorrow for that call," Fergus said with a malicious laugh looking at his watch.

Lola laughed back and covered their naked bodies with the tartan blanket decorating the footstool.

"Maybe I should tell her to ring me more often if this is the effect it has on us."

. . .

The following morning, Lola, realised all the anxiety of the previous day was gone. It was a pleasant feeling.

She rolled over in the bed and hugged her husband, smelling his hair and kissing his neck. He turned and kissed her back.

"You stay in bed a little longer, I'll get the boys up and make breakfast," said Lola.

It was Friday, and Fergus was working from home that morning. She knew he was not in any rush, and she knew he could do with a lay-in considering the mad hours he had worked lately.

Maybe, deep down inside her, despite her lack of anxiety, she was also trying to delay the dreaded phone call. She stepped into the shower, then afterwards she went downstairs to switch the percolator on and then she went to wake the boys up.

Alex and Philip refused to get up. School was finishing up in a couple of weeks, and she could see how tired they were becoming. She was tired of the school routine herself and was looking forward to those two months of freedom from homework and school runs. Late PJ mornings, walks in the park or at the beach — meals in the garden, and on rainy days, cinema or Dublinia. The boys couldn't get enough of the Viking museum.

Fergus had eventually materialised in the kitchen, fully dressed and leaving a trail of cologne after him. He was not a PJs type of guy; he didn't even like tracksuits unless he was up to some athletic activity, and lately, that was a rare event.

The Owens family was about to finish their breakfast when the doorbell rang.

"I'll go," Fergus said, receiving a smile of gratitude from his wife who was still in her house kimono and without her makeup.

51

PONTE ALTO - ITALY

Edda had opened the door and told Giulia her mother was in the garden with Father Nello. Giulia couldn't hide her disappointment. She wanted to talk to her mother alone and as soon as possible, plus the last thing she was in the mood for was the priest's morsels of advice.

Since she was young, Father Nello had always been part of her mother's social circle and for some reason, always felt entitled to advise Giulia about how to live her life.

Giulia stopped at the garden door. From that distance, she couldn't hear what Mara and Nello were saying. The conversation looked to be intimate, and the fact that they immediately stopped talking when they saw her, didn't bode well for anything.

"A bucolic confession?" Giulia exclaimed sarcastically.

"I better go now, nice to see you again, Giulia." Nello stood up, embarrassed.

"No please, you don't have to go," Mara said also standing up attempting to apologise for her daughter's disrespectful behaviour.

"It's fine. I have to go anyway, and I better leave you two to talk, alone."

"I'll walk you out," Mara offered and started to go.

Father Nello didn't follow her immediately like he was pondering his next move and then said, "In the end, a lie is always a lie. It might look easier, but it's not real. The truth, instead, always is. God be with you, Giulia."

Then Giulia knew her mother told him everything.

How could she have been so stupid? She had endangered everybody.

"What have you told the priest?" Giulia bitterly asked as soon her mother was back.

"The priest is my friend, and he has a name," Mara snapped back, realising how naive she had been to think her daughter would understand what she had decided to do.

Mara had now realised it was a bitter pill Giulia would have to swallow. Giulia listened to her mother's words, and the more her mother talked, the more a blind fury built inside her.

Mara had made her decision: The truth would be told. She was not asking for her daughter's blessing, nor was she interested in her advice or opinion.

"You are a fucking stupid, selfish bitch. You don't care about anybody but yourself. I hope you rot in hell," Giulia's nostrils dilated as if smoke was ready to come out. Her eyes filled with tears of rage; she could not control herself any longer and then she felt a sudden pain in her face. Both women took a step back from each other. Mara, incredulous of her act, brought the hand she had just used to slap her daughter to her mouth; Giulia, still in shock, instinctively covered her right cheek with her right hand.

"I'm sorry. I didn't mean to, but you can't speak to me like that," Mara said, letting herself fall on one of the garden chairs and feeling exhausted and emotionally drained.

"You know Mum. I don't think you are sorry, the same way I don't think you believe I had nothing to do with

Lorna's death. But I can tell you one thing: your days are over, and you will regret your decisions."

Giulia stormed out towards the house where she spotted Edda by the garden door. The old housekeeper had probably witnessed the entire scene and heard everything. Giulia didn't care; it was not her who was going to lose everything. Her mother would not drag her down into the mud which she herself was about to sink into.

Giulia got into her car, and once at the gate, she started to beep the horn hoping Edda would be smart enough to check the camera and open it for her. A few seconds later, she was driving away and calling Carlo.

As usual, he managed to calm her down but then he suggested Giulia would go back and apologise. She couldn't believe her ears, but he had a point: they still needed Mara. The loan was at the final stage of its approval, a delicate stage at which Mara was still able to withdraw the guarantor signatures. Except she couldn't, because she never signed, only Carlo didn't know, yet.

Giulia was furious with him, after what she had told him, after the way Mara had treated her, the only thing he could think of was that bloody loan.

She wanted to shout at him that those fucking signatures were safe and so was his loan because she made them so!

"I'm going home now; will I meet you there?" Carlo realised his timing had not been the best and attempted to make up for his lack of sensibility.

"Later, I've something else to do first," Giulia swerved the car and made a U-turn.

52

DUBLIN - IRELAND

When Fergus came back to the kitchen followed by Detective Enda McCarthey, Lola's jaw dropped.

Fergus looked at his wife apologetically, as the detective didn't give him any other choice but to let him in.

"Darling, Detective McCarthey has a few questions for you," Fergus broke the uncomfortable silence that filled the room since the two men had entered.

"As you are here, I'd like a couple of words with you too, Mr Owen. If you don't mind."

"Sure."

"Lovely, maybe I can start with you then? While Mrs Owen goes to get dressed," McCarthey took a chair and made himself comfortable.

Lola and Fergus locked eyes for a second. It was evident that the detective didn't want to talk to them together. Husband and wife had nothing to hide, but still, they felt extraordinarily uncomfortable.

Lola left the room and went upstairs to get dressed.

The weather had turned lovely again and looking at the

sky the day promised to be a proper summer day. She opened the windows; the air was still crispy being that early in the morning and so she put on a cotton cardigan over her sleeveless dress. Just some makeup on her eyes, as her skin already had that glowing gold colour, she usually got during the summer months, and Lola was now ready to go downstairs and face her third-degree interrogation.

The boys were ready at the door with the backpacks on their shoulders, "Aren't you bringing us to school? We need to be there early today, remember? We are going to the park for the bear picnic."

Not only had Lola forgotten about the school picnic, but she had also forgotten the boys were still in the house.

She blamed McCarthey.

"Of course, give me five minutes. Make sure you have everything and your teddies too."

The boys waved the two Harrods Teddy Bears their parents bought for them a few months earlier, while on a romantic kids-free weekend in London. Lola smiled and started to walk to the kitchen, but after a few steps, she felt her dress pulled back. Philip had always had a habit of pulling her by her skirts or sleeves to claim her attention. She turned to see an anxious little face.

"Are you in trouble?" Philip asked. He was a few seconds older than Alex and this, in his opinion, gave him the right and duty to act as the big brother.

"No darling, the detective is here because of Mrs Drake. He wants to ask daddy and me a few more question to help him catch the person who hurt her."

Lola kissed the child on the forehead and stomped into the kitchen even more annoyed than when she had left. She had had enough of that detective and his way of behaving like a bully. It was her home; neither she nor her husband had done anything wrong and had been very cooperative since the beginning. He had no right to barge in there and upset her family.

"Thank you very much for your time, Mr Owen," McCarthey said when he saw Lola coming into the kitchen.

"Not a bother, happy to help," Fergus replied, to the utmost annoyance of his wife.

Why did he have to be so condescending?

Even more annoying was the look the detective threw her as if she had just popped out from an episode of Operation Transformation, and that goofy smile of approval for the way she looked got on her nerves.

"The boys have to go to school," Lola said with a tone clearly stating she was cross with both the men in front of her.

"I'm sorry, to show up at such an inconvenient time," McCarthey said not sounding convincing, and he continued, "If I can suggest, as I already finished with Mr Owen, maybe he can drop the kids while we talk Mrs Owen? What do you think?"

Why did he even bother to put a question mark at the end of his sentence when it was evident to everybody the detective didn't ask a question but gave an order.

"That's perfect," Fergus promptly responded already standing from the chair and smiling like the situation was perfectly healthy and he had his wife in the company of an old friend.

Lola was so annoyed she couldn't even bring herself to wave her husband goodbye.

"Do you think I could bother you for a cup of coffee, Mrs Owen?" the detective asked when Lola was just about to sit at the table in front of him.

"Of course," she answered following the script and went to fill a mug for him.

"Thank you very much, Mrs Owen, you are a star. I didn't have much sleep last night and with a very early rise this morning had no time at all for breakfast."

There was something in the detective's tone that took Lola entirely off guard. It was genuine and gentle. For the first time, she felt he was saying it as it was and with no agenda. Enda McCarthey started to sip his coffee like it was some magic potion.

"Can I make you some toast?" Lola offered.

"Oh no, that would be too much to ask..."

"But it would be lovely." The rest of the sentence the detective didn't dare to finish, but Lola had heard it loud and clear. She went to the fridge to get some bread, butter and jam.

The atmosphere in the kitchen relaxed.

"So, what did you want to ask? I don't think you came over just for breakfast?" Lola intended to make a joke, but unfortunately, it sounded more like a remark, and all the previous tension came back.

Detective McCarthey moved the plate away from him, thanked Mrs Owen and switched back to his usual professional attitude with its hint of a bully.

Lola felt the change far too much, but she only had herself and her big mouth to blame.

"I was curious to know why you had never mentioned that the woman Mrs Drake had an altercation with, was the same she accused of stealing your mail?"

Lola felt her face going red like a child just discovered in a lie or hiding the truth.

Detective Enda McCarthey never thought the Owens had anything to do with the assault of their neighbour and friend. Still, the more the investigation proceeded, the more he instinctively knew that Mrs Owen had more pieces of information than she said she had.

Lola didn't know what to say or where to start.

McCarthey got up and went to refill their mugs with more coffee. A gesture that somehow put Lola at ease.

She told him everything she knew and recalled the

episode involving Laura and Siobhan. Lola also mentioned Siobhan's theory about Laura stealing the photo frame.

"Fine, well if that's all, I think I've already taken too much of your time."

The detective stood up and extended his hand to Lola who took it and shook it feeling slightly guilty for the mean thoughts she'd had about McCarthey. In the end, it was not as bad as she thought.

She escorted the policeman to the door, but before she could open it for him, the detective had stopped by the console table with the photo frames.

"And this is where the picture frame that had disappeared was, right?" the detective asked, pointing at a space between two frames.

"I wouldn't say it disappeared. Most likely it has been misplaced and probably by me. I just don't remember." Lola was aware that she sounded like she was making up an excuse to hide something, but It was too late to take it back.

"Maybe," McCarthey said and left giving the woman a suspicious look.

Lola closed the door behind the detective with extreme relief, and after checking the time she realised Fergus had been gone for an hour now.

She was wondering if giving him a call or not when she heard voices outside.

Fergus and Finn were talking on the road, and when they saw McCarthey approaching, they immediately turned towards the detective, greeting him.

"Detective, I was coming to see you," an excited Finn then shouted.

"Well, Mr Drake, it's usually me saying that."

Lola, also hearing everything that was going on, went out to find out what had happened.

"The hospital just rung me. Siobhan remembers something."

Finn could barely contain his excitement.

"That's fantastic," Lola exclaimed all excited too.

Detective Enda McCarthey said nothing, but a gleam passed through his eyes.

53

PONTE ALTO - ITALY

Even if she knew her daughter would not answer her calls, Mara tried to make contact anyway. Mara also knew Giulia had her reasons. Confessing what she had done was going to affect her daughter as much as herself, but unfortunately, it was destiny: children always have to pay for their parents' sins, even if it's unfair.

Mara also wondered why Lola had not rung her back. Maybe she had not listened to her voice mail. Some people don't.

She tried to call her again, but the phone went straight to the voice mail, and she had to leave yet another message.

Mara now had to make the most challenging call, and she had to make it in person. She had seen on the TV that the inspector in charge of Lorna's murder was someone called Zamparelli. She knew the superintendent in Belluno personally. Going through her would have made things easier, but this time, even Mara Kopfler had to follow the rules and face the consequences of her actions without using her influence.

"Can I talk to Inspector Zamparelli, please? It's important," Mara asked on the phone.

The police officer who answered told her that the

inspector was not at the station at the moment. He was due back in the afternoon. Mara hung up before she was asked to leave her name.

Suddenly the enormity of what she was going to do became overwhelming. A wave of fear overcame her courage.

Even if it was only midday, she poured herself a glass of Prosecco, and then another, and then she turned the air conditioning on and collapsed exhausted on the couch.

Her firmness in coming clean with the past was fading, but then there was Nello. He knew everything. He was bound to secrecy but not regarding the suspicions about Giulia's involvement in the murder. He could identify the victim without breaking any vows.

She poured herself another glass and rang him. Her voice was a tremor; the alcohol had made her mind blurry and dubious:

"Listen to me, Mara; you have to do it."

"Will you come with me? There is no way I can do it without you by my side."

Nello set her mind at peace. Mara would take a shower, eat something, rest for a couple of hours and then Nello would pick her up and together they would go to the police.

"Can I serve lunch?" Edda asked, popping her head into the sitting room.

Mara nearly flipped on the chair; at this stage, she didn't even care if Edda had overheard anything. Everything would be in the public domain soon.

"Thank you, Edda. Leave it in the kitchen, and then you can go for today."

* * *

The shower had helped to rinse away the idleness of the alcohol. When Mara went back to the kitchen, she was starving as the acids in her stomach begged for solid food. The cold roast beef was delicious, and it went perfectly with the potato salad on the side. Mara felt her strength gradually coming back. No matter what Giulia said, she was going to do the right thing, and her daughter would realise it, sooner or later.

She was still in her bathrobe. She had not gotten dressed with the sole purpose to go for a nap after lunch. She needed her head rested and clear, Nello was right. Once in front of the inspector, she would have to answer a lot of questions, and it would be a very long day.

She partially rolled down the blinds but left the window open to let some air pass. The day was hot but with a bit of breeze. Mara had no air conditioning in the bedroom as the walls were so thick that it never got too warm in there, not even during the hot Italian summers.

She fell asleep more rapidly than ever.

Leopold, who was sleeping at the foot of the bed, suddenly jumped down and meowing started to scratch the door.

Mara could hear him, but it was like the noise was far away, and she was too tired to get up and check what was upsetting him so much.

"Come, Leo, come back here, what did you hear? It's nothing," she said still half asleep and attempted to attract the cat back to the bed with a subtle finger gesture.

She raised her head from the pillow but dropped it back as it was too heavy.

Leopold was not giving up until he suddenly stopped when the door opened and ran out.

A figure stood by the door without speaking. Mara widened her eyes astonished: What was she doing there?

Before Mara had time to ask, a pillow was pressed over her face.

She tried to fight back, but her limbs were too heavy to lift.

54

PONTE ALTO - ITALY

Giulia erased from her phone all the missed calls from Mara. A symbolic act, like she had deleted her mother too.

Carlo had also tried to call her, but she had no time nor will to talk to him either. Her number one priority at the moment was speeding up the loan process before the whole mess blew up in her face. She needed all the papers approved before Mara Kopfler's signatures, fake or real, would lose all their worth.

Giulia barged into the bank branch and requested an urgent meeting with the manager. The conversation she had with Roberto that morning gave her an idea.

"I'm sorry, Miss Kopfler, but Mrs Panto can't see you today. She is very busy," the bank manager's secretary said after checking with her boss.

"That's too bad. I was hoping to sort out this matter with Mrs Panto. But of course, if she is too busy, I'll have to take my complaint about a breach of privacy directly to the board."

Giulia knew that the words "privacy" and "breach" in the same sentence would have made any bank employee shake. She also knew that once the secretary reported it to Panto, she would have found time for her. Adriana Panto was an adulteress, but she was not stupid, and by now she had probably already spoken to Roberto and knew he had said what he was not supposed to.

Giulia was sure she had confided in him because of his involvement with the hotel, but she would bet she had also asked him not to let that slip under any circumstances. Thankfully for Giulia, Roberto couldn't resist the temptation to cause her trouble, and now she had an ace up her sleeve.

"Maybe if you can wait here, I'll see if she can make time for you," this time the secretary didn't phone but jumped on her feet and went straight to knock on the manager's office door.

A few minutes later, Adriana Panto was walking towards Giulia.

"Miss Kopfler, sorry for keeping you. I have a very tight schedule today, but Anna told me you have an urgent matter you want to discuss with me?"

Once in Panto's office, Giulia went straight to the point, "I'm not here to discuss anything actually, but I'm here to tell you exactly what I want you to do for me. This, of course, if you want to keep your job and your husband who, I suppose, is not aware of your rendezvous with my hotel manager."

* * *

The breeze that had alleviated the heat during the morning was gone. Giulia liked summers but hated this oppressive weather. She got into her car as quickly as she could, and while still drying the sweat from her forehead and her neck, she switched on the engine and the air conditioning.

She was victorious. Her first instinct was to ring Carlo to tell him their problem had gone away. Her mother wouldn't be a problem anymore, and the money would probably be in his company account by morning. She was ready to ring him when she suddenly thought of the downside to the whole thing: His questions.

First, he would have asked how she had persuaded the bank manager to speed up the process with such urgency. Then he would have wondered why she was so concerned about the rumours around the start of the building work and what she meant by her mother not being a problem anymore. He still didn't know the reality of the situation. She rested her head on the seat with her mobile in her hand. A car pulled up beside her with the explicit intention of taking her parking space. Despite having the engine on, Giulia was not leaving. She needed more time to think about her next move, and so she tried to gesture that she was not going, but they kept waiting. She had no intention of lowering the window and exposing herself to the heat. So, in total annoyance, she fastened her seatbelt and drove off.

Giulia returned to her office. She had a few documents to go through, and afterwards, she planned to relax in the spa. She deserved it.

A couple of hours later, she was about to leave the office when one of the receptionists called saying someone wanted to see her, and it was urgent.

"Who is it?"

"It is a priest," Nicoletta, the receptionist, said.

The only priest she knew and who could show up at the hotel was Father Nello.

"Ok, send him up," Giulia said, wondering what he could want.

"If you are here for some spiritual guidance, I'm not interested. You got the wrong Kopfler. If instead, it's my mother who sent you, well you can turn around and leave right now. I'm not interested in what either of you has to say," Giulia's tone was harsh, and she already had her arm stretched out, indicating to the man the way out.

"Listen, this has nothing to do with you," the priest

started, but Giulia stopped him, "I already told you. I'm not interested in anything you have to say to me. And now if you excuse me, father," Giulia stepped in front of Nello and forced him out of the room.

She locked the door behind her and walked to the lifts.

Nello didn't move, but when the lift door opened, he called after her, "I'm here because I'm afraid something bad has happened to Mara."

55

DUBLIN - IRELAND

Finn and McCarthey drove to the hospital together. When they arrived at Siobhan's room, McCarthey waited outside and let Mr Drake see his wife first, a simple act of courtesy. Nonetheless, he made sure not to leave the couple alone long enough to discuss and domesticate the regained memory.

"Oh, honey I'm so happy your memory is back," Finn was to tell his wife the detective was there to see her too, but she interrupted him before he could finish his sentence.

"Oh, and now I might have lost it again as I can't remember the last time you called me honey," Siobhan smiled at her husband with a sweetness he had not seen on her face in a long time.

She was joking, but she was right. Finn instinctively turned his head to see if McCarthey was anywhere within earshot because, after the way he had interviewed him before, that could not have sounded good to him.

"Siobhan, do you remember what happened?" Finn impatiently asked.

"Pretty much and I can only tell you it's quite shocking!"

Finn took a step back, amused at how excited his wife was; like she was gossiping about someone else.

Finn's incredulity disappeared immediately, after all, it was Siobhan he was talking about, and she was like no other person. His wife could be annoying, but after everything that had happened, he now could see that it was the reason he loved her.

Finn bent over Siobhan and kissed her.

"You are unique; you know that? I can't believe I had forgotten that. I'm sorry I've been a lousy husband at times, but it won't happen again."

Siobhan was ready to reply with some jokes, but the expression on her husband's face and his deep green eyes shining like the day she had agreed to marry him, stopped her.

"I can be a pretty annoying wife myself. I love you too. I couldn't make it without you," she said instead, hugging and kissing him back,

A cough by the doorstep interrupted the little romantic moment husband and wife were having.

"Detective McCarthey," Siobhan exclaimed surprised.

"Oh, yes. When I went to call for Lola and Fergus, Detective McCarthey was there, and he has some questions for you. Well, we all have," Finn added as to justify the detective's presence to his wife, whose face suddenly darkened when she saw him.

Enda McCarthey didn't miss the change of expression on Siobhan Drake's face. There was no doubting she wasn't ready to talk to the detective, or she didn't want to.

"Mrs Drake, happy to see you are feeling better. The doctor said you had recovered your memory, and I need to ask you a few questions."

Finn made a move to leave his wife's bedside and let the detective get closer to her, but she grabbed his hand and stopped him, holding him there.

That was totally out of character for Siobhan. Finn stayed by her side.

She had gone through an awful lot, and maybe that bravery about what happened was more of a mask to hide how upset and shocked she still was by the experience.

"Well, there is not much to say, detective," Siobhan said, keeping her eyes away from her husband who was utterly puzzled. She had just told him she remembered everything and the details were shocking, but now, to the detective, his wife was saying she had nothing to add.

Finn threw his wife a questioning look in the hope of getting a sign of what was going on, but she ignored it and continued to talk to McCarthey.

"It all happened so quickly, and I only saw the aggressor for a few seconds. Not enough to be able to identify anyone."

The detective was dubious. From the reconstruction, Siobhan Drake must have found herself face to face with the assailant and at that close range, even a few seconds would be enough to imprint it in the memory. McCarthey decided not to say anything, but he asked her to go through the events for him.

"I had just returned home, and I was still in the hall when I heard a knock on the door. I opened it, and then everything happened. I felt a sudden pain, and after that, I don't remember anything else. I must have fainted nearly immediately. Only thing I can say is that the aggressor wore black clothes, maybe a hoody over a baseball cap."

Enda McCarthey kept writing on his notebook, and when he had finished, he confronted her, "But you were face to face with your attacker, at least for a few seconds. Enough to see his or her face, right, Mrs Drake?"

Siobhan was nervously shifting position in the bed.

"Yes," she started to reply like she was trying to gain time to think what to say next, "I guess, but I didn't. Maybe the fall has affected my memory, or it's the shock, besides I've never been much of a physiognomist..."

Now Finn knew for sure that something was wrong.

It only took a split second to his wife to fix someone's face in her head.

"So you are telling me that you can't remember the face of your attacker because of the shock, but you remember what he or she was wearing?"

Siobhan nodded to the detective, "You never know how your mind reacts to certain situations, right?"

Finn and Siobhan exchanged a panicky look. Only what they were fearing was different. While Finn couldn't understand why his wife was lying to the police and worried about the possible consequences; Siobhan was concerned her husband would blow her story.

Detective Enda McCarthey thanked them both for their collaboration and left.

He knew Siobhan Drake was hiding something, but he also knew he was not getting anything else out of the couple, at least for today.

"What the hell, Siobhan. What was that?" Finn nearly shouted.

Siobhan lowered her eyes and waited for Finn to calm down.

He sat on the bed beside her, ready to hear the truth, when a knock at the door interrupted them. Detective McCarthey was back. The blood drained out of the couple's faces.

Husband and wife looked at each other. They were both wondering how long the detective had been there and how much he had heard.

"Sorry to disturb you again, Mrs Drake, but I forgot to ask you about that run-in you had with your neighbour's friend. The Italian lady,"

Siobhan froze.

"It's probably nothing, and I think that lady had already

left when your attack took place, but it's just to verify the statements and keep my reports straight," the detective added waiting to hear Siobhan's side of the story.

Her version was pretty much the same as the one Lola and Fergus Owen had given him. He started to believe that the episode was insignificant and had no relevance for the investigation.

56

PONTE ALTO - ITALY

There was nothing that Giulia wanted to do less than to accompany the priest to her mother's house. Still, she did it to eliminate speculation and alleviate his concern about her mother's wellbeing.

Father Nello suggested Giulia follow him in her car, but she insisted they go together. The short drive together could give her the chance to learn more about what he knew and why he had to meet her mother that afternoon. It must have been something unmissable and so crucial that Nello refused even to consider Mara could have forgotten about it. If she was not answering the door and the phone it was because something had happened to her.

Giulia couldn't discover a thing. The priest was not easy to manipulate but, on the contrary, he was instead quite good at manipulating others, and Giulia believed that was what had happened with Mara.

Mara's car was still in the driveway. The front door was ajar. Something quite unusual because even if Mara never locked it during the day, she always kept it shut, particularly on days as warm as that one when most likely the air-conditioning was turned on inside. Nello and Giulia entered the house side by side, calling for Mara.

The house was silent. They passed the hall, walked the long corridor and stopped frozen. Mara's body was lying at the bottom of the stairs. Nello checked her pulse. She was dead.

He grabbed Giulia by the arms and moved her away from the scene. They waited in the sitting room for the ambulance.

Still not saying a word Giulia opened the gate and waited for the paramedics by the door.

"We arrived and found her like that. She must have tripped and fallen down the stairs," Giulia said, escorting them inside.

They inspected the body, but before they could take it away, they had to call the police. It was a routine procedure in cases of fatal domestic accidents. Once the police had assessed the casualty, they could move the corpse to the morgue in Belluno. Someone from the coroner's office or the station would have been in touch with the next of kin.

Giulia's expression betrayed her disappointment in hearing about police involvement. She didn't want them to snoop around her business.

"Do you want me to stay and wait for the police with you?" Nello's words and his concern were genuine. Giulia saw that, but she didn't want him there when the police arrived.

"No, thank you. You've done enough. I'll be OK."

* * *

Zamparelli was due to appear in court as a witness for the prosecutor in an old case. Piva was the only high-ranking officer available to go with one of the uniforms after the paramedics called. They could have been at the scene much earlier, but the only patrol car available at the time had a broken air conditioning. Piva refused to take it and sent to swap it with the one used to patrol the road into Ponte Alto, a notorious spot for drivers exceeding the speed limit.

When Deputy Inspector Luca Piva and officer Raniero Farinelli eventually arrived at the Kopfler residence, the two paramedics explained what had most likely happened.

Piva kindly introduced himself to the victim's daughter. After a brief assessment of the scene, he then released the body that was promptly lifted on the stretcher and loaded into the ambulance.

"If you don't need us anymore, we should go. In this heat, we better hurry bringing the corpse to the morgue," one of the paramedics said while the other had already positioned himself behind the wheel.

"Yes, yes, of course. Go," Piva waved the ambulance off and signalled Farinelli to follow him inside, where Giulia was waiting in the sitting room.

"I know it's not the best time, Miss Kopfler, but can you tell us what happened and what you saw when you arrived?" Piva asked.

Even if what happened was pretty clear, he still wanted to hear it from her.

Giulia just nodded with her head and took Piva through the events since she and father Nello arrived at the house.

"And where is this priest now?" Piva asked interrupting Giulia's account.

"He went home. He was pretty shaken, too."

"Is it normal for him to be around the house?"

Giulia could not decide if all those questions were simple routine, curiosity or if instead, the deputy inspector was implying something.

Giulia pondered every answer she gave. She didn't want to betray herself, giving away information that might bring the investigation in the opposite direction to what she wanted. It had been an accident: her mother lost her balance and fell down the stairs, as simple as that.

"Yes, they were friends for a long time. They had an appointment, but I don't know anything else," Giulia spoke nothing but the truth as she still didn't know the reason why her mother and Nello had to meet today.

Piva looked satisfied enough.

"Farinelli, did you get note of everything? And did you take some pictures of the scene?" Piva asked the officer turning away from Giulia whose body eventually relaxed.

"Yes, Sir. And the paramedics already sent the pics they took."

Deputy Inspector Luca Piva enjoyed being the one in charge, for once.

"I think that's all Miss Kopfler. I'm afraid your mother was the victim of an unfortunate accident. I'm sincerely sorry for your loss. Can we give you a lift home or is there someone you want us to call to stay with you? You should not be alone right now."

No foul play. Giulia was relieved and happily accepted a lift home. She would have called Carlo on her way there, except when she got her phone from her purse the battery was dead.

57

DUBLIN - IRELAND

Lola couldn't wait to see Siobhan and learn about what she remembered.

Fergus agreed to pick up the boys from school so she could have all the time she wanted to spend with her friend.

The impatience and excitement made her check her watch every minute, and the bus seemed to take forever to arrive.

When in proximity of St. Vincent's hospital, Lola rushed down the narrow stairs of the double-decker Dublin bus. She walked quickly through the large hall of the hospital and under the annoyed eyes of an older woman, who also was waiting for the lift, Lola kept pressing the button frantically.

"You need only to press it once, you know. It won't come any faster even if you keep pushing the button," the old lady remarked, making Lola blush and feel as embarrassed and ashamed as a teenager who's been caught stealing sweets in the local convenience store.

Lola lowered her gaze and gripped her hands on the handbag.

When the lift arrived, she politely stepped back and let the old lady go first. She hesitated a few seconds, not sure whether to go in and face her shame or wait for the next one.

"Now you are not coming in?" the woman called from inside, keeping the lift doors opened with her right foot.

"Oh, sure yes, sorry," Lola muttered getting in.

Lola hoped until the last minute that someone else would have taken the lift too. She didn't want to be alone in that confined space with that woman. She was too embarrassed. Thankfully the old lady got out on the first floor.

It wasn't visiting hours, but because Siobhan was in a single room, she was allowed visitors at any time of the day unless the doctors were in with her. Lola knocked at the door and went in, but the room was empty.

She went back to the corridor and looked for a nurse to ask about Siobhan. The nurse kindly explained to her that the patient was doing some tests, and she would not be back for a couple of hours.

Extremely disappointed Lola went back to the room, wrote a note and left it on the bedside table.

* * *

"Kevin," Enda McCarthey entered the station shouting the young officer's name on his way to his office.

"Kevin," he barked again from behind his desk.

"Kevin is not here, Sir. He's on night shift today," a shy voice said from the door. Garda Emma Connell had only recently graduated from Templemore College and lived in constant fear of Detective Enda McCarthey. A fear she couldn't overcome, despite Kevin's attempts to convince her that, once she had gotten used to his barbarous way of dealing with people, she would learn that the detective was a good guy.

McCarthey grunted a thank you and picked up the phone, "Kevin, I hope you were not sleeping."

"Well, Sir, I was napping as I'm on night shift."

"No, you are not anymore. You come to the station now as I need you." The detective hung up before Kevin could add anything.

When Officer Connell saw the detective approach her desk, her cheeks reddened, and when he stopped right in front of her, she froze.

McCarthey moved his reading glasses from his head to his nose and bent toward the young woman to read her name on the uniform. He should have known, but he couldn't remember.

"Officer Connell, take the next four hours off and, if you can, maybe use them to have a rest. You are going to be on night shift."

Emma's jaw dropped. She had never been on night shift on her own, without a supervisor and could not figure out if it was a punishment or a reward but, whatever it was, she didn't dare to object to the detective's order.

Half an hour later, Kevin arrived at the station, "Sir, here I am," he exclaimed, glad to have skipped a most likely boring night shift and even more pleased at the idea of the boss needing his help in the investigation.

"Sit, Kevin," McCarthey ordered, passing him some papers, "read the statements I took from the Owens this morning and then check the account I took from Siobhan Drake today in the hospital. Then tell me if you can find anything strange, anything that doesn't add up or any inconsistency."

Kevin carefully read the statements, and when he had finished, he lifted his head to meet McCarthey's questioning look.

"So?" the detective asked.

"That's very weird!"

"Right?" Detective McCarthey's tone was pleased with the

fact that his "chosen deputy" had come to the same conclusion as him.

Without saying anything further, the detective picked up the phone,

"Good Morning, I'm Detective Enda McCarthey from the Donnybrook Garda station. I need to talk to Mrs Siobhan Drake's neurologist. It's about her attack."

58

PONTE ALTO - ITALY

Deputy Inspector Piva and Officer Farinelli dropped Giulia Kopfler home. They waited for her to go inside the building and then drove off.

"So, that's how the other half lives eh?" the young officer couldn't resist saying, looking at the luxury tower and contorting his neck to get a view of the balcony of Giulia's penthouse.

"Yep." Piva answered, "I wouldn't trade that apartment with the shock of finding my mother with a broken neck, though."

"Nope!"

The two policemen entered the station, and since Zamparelli had come back, Piva went straight towards his office.

"Boss. How did it go in court?" he asked, popping his head inside the chief inspector's room.

"As expected, Piva. And you? They told me you responded to a domestic accident full inclusive of a corpse?" Zamparelli asked.

Piva took a seat opposite the inspector and gave him a detailed account of the events.

"So, you are positive there is nothing suspicious?"

"Yes, Sir. I honestly think it was just a regrettable accident."

Zamparelli nodded, and Piva stood up to go back to his desk, but before he could exit the office, Zamparelli called him back, "You haven't told me the name of the victim."

"I thought you knew already. The victim is a real VIP: Mrs Mara Kopfler. She owns the big hotel on the lake and half the town."

"Yes, I've heard of her businesses, and I met her in a couple of formal occasions. She wasn't old and looked in perfect health to me. I would never have thought she could die in such a stupid way."

"I know, sometimes you can have all the money and power in the world, and yet the destiny tricks you."

Carlo was at home waiting for Giulia, and as soon she slid the key in the lock, he went to the door.

Without saying g a word, she threw her arms around his neck.

He brutally pushed her away. He was angry. He had called her thousands of times, and she never called back.

It was only then she realised he could not know about Mara.

Giulia let herself sink on the couch, "My mother is dead."

Silence fell upon them. Carlo noisily swallowed his saliva.

"What you do mean she is dead?" he asked incredulously.

"Dead, gone, kaput! You got it?" Giulia said hysterically raising her voice. Feeling guilty for the way he attacked Giulia, Carlo sat beside her and in a calm and gentle tone asked her what had happened.

While Giulia abandoned herself to tears, many questions filled Carlo's head, and when she eventually calmed down and stopped sobbing, he had to ask:

"And you had nothing to do with this right? I mean it's not that you argued, and she fell..."

"No!" Giulia answered, "And I didn't come straight home after I left my mother's house only because I went to the bank and then back to the office. And then I wanted to relax, but the priest came and the rest you know."

Giulia sounded like she was justifying herself. In the beginning, Carlo thought that it was strange. He had expected her to be outraged by his question, but then he also thought she was probably still in shock and he had no reason to doubt her words but the police would, if they knew about the huge fight mother and daughter had, just a few hours before the accident. An accident that had no witnesses.

"Did you tell anybody about your fight with her?" Carlo suddenly asked.

"No. Nobody asked, it was an accident, that's it." Giulia replied, unburying her face from his chest.

"Good. Just don't mention it." Carlo added.

Giulia said nothing and watched him going into the kitchen and coming back with two glasses of chilled Pinot Grigio.

"Why did you go to the bank?" Carlo asked after he sat back down.

Giulia felt some panic rising inside her. She should tell him about the signatures but now was not the time. She didn't have the energy; also she wondered if, now that Mara was dead, Carlo needed to know.

"Everything is fine with the bank. Most importantly, we need to keep an eye on the priest. I still don't know how much he knows," Giulia had regained some rationality.

The tragedy of the moment had to leave space for practicality, "Also, I want to go back there and search the house. We need to be sure there is nothing that can be a link to my aunt and her murder."

"Right," Carlo agreed. He kissed Giulia on the forehead

and went to improvise some dinner while Giulia went to take a shower and change.

Neither Carlo nor Giulia was hungry. They both kept playing with the food pushing it in a circle around the plate until Carlo abruptly stood up, "Let's go."

Knowing he was over the alcohol limit, Carlo drove to Mara's house slowly and meticulously respecting the traffic laws.

* * *

Carlo and Giulia were searching Mara's office when they heard a noise that made them both jump.

"What the hell...." Carlo felt something against his leg.

"Leopold," Giulia exclaimed laughing.

"Jeez, I nearly died," Carlo said and immediately after apologised for the poor choice of words.

"It's OK," Giulia said, and then she bent to pick Leopold up.

"Poor Leopold, I forgot about you. But don't worry, you'll come home with us."

A dog was far too much work for Giulia, but she was sure she could happily meet a cat's needs, and in truth she always liked Leopold.

They were now in the house for over two hours. They had searched everywhere, and they had gone through most of Mara's papers, and they were both getting tired.

Carlo started to speak first, "Honey, we've looked everywhere and found nothing. I think there is no way she has left behind any connection to her past. I suppose it's safe to say that she's going to bring her secret with her to the grave. And as for that offshore account, it's a secret nobody can know about. We will figure out the codes to access it, or you will take a little vacation and go straight to the bank with the death certificate, then everything that is in there will be all yours too."

Carlo was right, and Giulia felt much better. She had to believe his words.

"I'm going to get Leopold's stuff, and then we can go."

When Giulia and Carlo were ready to leave the landline phone started to ring.

They both hesitated, and the phone stopped ringing, but before they made it out of the house, it was ringing again.

"Answer," Carlo suggested.

59

DUBLIN - IRELAND

When Lola walked into the house, it was extraordinarily silent. Extraordinarily and pleasantly calm. The boys' school bags were by the door, and Fergus's car was in the driveway, meaning they were home.

She stored her fit flops in the shoe cabinet by the hallway. Unless it was raining, Lola always wore them when visiting Siobhan at the hospital.

From the kitchen, where Lola went to make herself a coffee, she could hear the twins playing in the garden. They were nowhere to be seen, but the fact she could listen to them, it was enough to know they were OK.

Fergus was probably locked in his office. She poured a second mug of coffee and went up to him. He was wearing his Bose headphones blocking out any external noise, including his children but, from the window over his desk, he had a clear view of the treehouse where they were playing. He was on a call and thanked his wife with the movement of his head and a blown kiss.

Lola was exhausted. It had been another eventful day, starting with the unexpected morning chat with the detective. She went to the freezer to take four shepherd's pies out. She had no intention of cooking from scratch tonight or even cooking at all.

She left the containers in the kitchen sink to defrost; the microwave will finish the job if necessary and went upstairs to her bedroom.

She changed into a pair of wide-leg blue linen trousers, slightly outdated but incredibly comfortable to wear in the house, she threw on a long top and decided to lie down for a while.

She looked at the last Sam Black's book sitting on her bedside table undecided whether to read a few pages or not. She opted to close her eyes for a few minutes instead.

Nearly two hours later, Fergus stepped into the bedroom and found his wife fast asleep and noisily snoring. He tried to be as silent as he could, but a spontaneous giggle slipped out, and that was enough to wake her up.

"I was just resting my eyes for a minute," Lola said, rubbing her eyes unaware of the stripes of mascara that she was dragging around on her face.

"Sure!" Fergus said, laughing, "You were snoring, and I could see a bubble coming out your nostril like BooBoo Bear."

Lola removed the pillow from behind her head and threw it at her husband.

When she saw the time, she jumped to her feet, "I was only going to lie down for a few minutes. Gosh, I must have been exhausted."

"Yes, but now that you are as fresh as a rose, we'll make that phone call. Won't we?"

"Which call?" Lola asked, pretending not to understand.

One single look from her husband and the game was over. She had to call her aunt back, "OK. I need to pee, and I'll be down with you."

Lola got up and closed the bathroom door behind her.

When Fergus heard her steps on the stairs, he called from

the sitting room, "It's quiet here as the kids are having their dinner outside."

Lola put the phone on speaker, dialled the 171 to listen to the last voice mail Mara had left and then pressed the digit six to call back the number.

After a few rings and no answer, she hung up.

"I'll try later." It was hard to conceal the relief in Lola's tone, but all the same, she knew far too well that she was procrastinating and only postponing the inevitable. Fergus knew it as well, but he was determined to make her call.

"Come on, honey, give her time to get to the phone. Let's try another time and this time maybe let the phone ring a bit longer."

Lola looked at Fergus, defeated and nearly imploring.

"If she doesn't answer, then you'll try tomorrow," he said to make her feel better in some way.

Lola redialled the number and waited.

"Hello, who is it?" Someone had answered, but it wasn't Mara.

"Hello, is there anybody there?" this time, the voice was brusquer, and Lola recognised it.

"It's Giulia," Lola whispered to Fergus while covering the phone with her hand.

"Come on.... You can do it," he softly whispered back.

"Giulia? It's me, Lola," after a few seconds of silence, Lola continued, "I'm looking for your mother...."

"Well, well, well, have you sniffed some gain?"

Giulia's sharp tone and her reference to something Lola had no idea about, took her completely off guard.

"No, what .... What are you talking about?" Lola muttered before regaining control of her voice, "I'm calling because Mara left a couple of messages on my voice mail asking to ring her back."

Giulia stopped for a moment in silent pondering how to approach the matter.

"What did she want?" she asked, getting straight to the point.

-Had her mother been so stupid to mention something on the phone?-

"I don't know. Aunt Mara only said she needed to talk to me, urgently."

That was good. The old witch had not given anything away.

"Well, I'm afraid you will have to remain curious as my mother passed away today."

Both Fergus and Lola's jaws dropped, and they looked at each other astonished.

"Oh, I'm sorry, Giulia. I had no idea," Lola was genuinely speechless as the news had come out of the blue, but she couldn't say she felt sad. She felt nothing except annoyance because now she would never know why her aunt wanted to talk to her.

"You couldn't know," Giulia's tone was still sharp, but it had softened a little.

"Listen, Lola, I'm sorry, but I don't know what she wanted from you. I bet it was nothing significant. Maybe she had found something belonging to you in the attic and wanted to know if she could throw it away or not."

Carlo was desperately gesturing to his fiancé to cut the conversation short as she was now making flimsy excuses to justify her mother's calls. He didn't know Lola, but if it were him, Giulia's words would have made him suspicious.

"OK, I have to go now but if I find something I'll call you. You don't lose any sleep over this." Giulia abruptly hung up.

Fergus took the phone from his wife's shaking hands, "What was that?"

"I have no idea."

60

PONTE ALTO - ITALY

"What the fuck Giulia, do you want to give yourself away?" Carlo snapped as soon as Giulia hung up the phone.

She turned to him, half in shock by his reaction but too tired to snap back.

"What were those stupid excuses for Mara's calls. And the way you attacked her? Why not just tell your cousin that her mother was alive? I don't know Lola, but if she's not dumb, she must have guessed something is up by now."

Giulia listened to Carlo. His concerns were legitimate, and she agreed that she could have handled the conversation better, but she didn't think Lola had any suspicions.

"I know my cousin. She's a naive one. I'm sure she thinks nothing, and she'll forget about the entire thing soon. She's probably glad she doesn't have to talk to my mother and most likely she won't even come to the funeral."

"Well, I hope so because that will make things more complicated for us," Carlo replied, getting into the car.

"Don't worry, it won't happen, and if it does, I will take care of it."

The couple drove home without saying a word to each

other. The apartment was pleasantly fresh as they had left the air conditioning on before leaving. Carlo headed straight to the kitchen, "I'll get some ice cream, do you want some?" He offered a sign of truce.

Giulia appreciated the gesture, but she was too tired. The only thing she wanted was sleeping and emptying her mind of any thoughts.

"No, thank you. I'm going straight to bed. I'm exhausted, and tomorrow will be a busy day. I need to go to the hospital to see when the body will be released and then stop by at the funeral home to make arrangements. I also have to contact the solicitor for my.." she hesitated a second and then finished her sentence, "..her will." Giulia could not bring herself to say the word "mother". It was as if this way she could keep a certain distance from what had happened.

Carlo pulled her to him: "I love you. You know that, and I'll always be here for you." Giulia couldn't detach her body from his. She felt safe.

When in bed, despite her tiredness, Giulia struggled to fall asleep. So much was going on in her head. And the images of Mara's dead body kept flashing in front of her eyes. The feelings she was experiencing were so different: pain, sadness, guilt. Giulia had to confront her real self and learn to live with the consequences of her actions. But she also felt an extreme relief because from today she could stop being Mara Kopfler's daughter and be whoever she wanted to be.

61

DUBLIN - IRELAND

Lola and Fergus intentionally avoided going back over the phone call with Giulia while the kids were around. But, after they had settled them to bed, it was the only subject of conversation.

The evening was a warm and bright one. Lola went upstairs to get a shawl and then joined Fergus outside on the patio. He had prepared two glasses of whiskey and was waiting for his wife on one of the two deck chairs. They both took a sip of their drink, looking at the sky full of stars.

"Are you going to the funeral?" Fergus asked, stretching his free hand over the little table that divided them.

"Should I?" Lola asked in reply, genuinely expecting him to find a solution for her like he always did.

"I think it's not about what you should or shouldn't do, but more about what you feel or not feel to do."

"I didn't even go to my uncle's funeral, and he was the least evil of them all," Lola said unwrapping the Lindor dark chocolate that Fergus had left beside her glass.

"I think you've got your answer then. And I think you said good-bye to Mara many years ago already."

Fergus was right, but for some reason, Lola couldn't find

that sense of peace she hoped for. Before she knew it, the words came out of her mouth: "Am I a bad person?"

She knew she was not. Still, she couldn't help but feel a little sense of guilt for not doing what was socially acceptable and required of her, as her aunt had always taught her.

Even in death, that woman had the power to make her doubt herself, and that infuriated her.

"You don't want to go; you don't go! And don't even think about feeling the slightest bit of guilt about it. She made her bed," Fergus said like he had read his wife's mind.

"I know. It's just that, this whole thing is upsetting and confusing and I' d just like to forget about it...."

Fergus went to the kitchen to get the bottle of whiskey and another couple of chocolates. He refilled their glasses and toasted, "To relatives......only thing in life you can't choose."

"But you can stay away," Lola added, lifting her glass.

After a few minutes of silence, and with her mouth half full of the second chocolate, Lola suddenly muttered, "You know what's also bugging me?"

"No," Fergus answered, unwrapping his chocolate before his wife could lay her hands on that one too.

"That I will never be able to know what she wanted to tell me."

"Yes, well, that was weird. I mean someone doesn't call leaving urgent messages about some old shit found in the attic."

Fergus thought the whole thing was very awkward and suspicious, and even more so having heard Giulia's reaction.

"Exactly," Lola agreed, "my aunt would have just thrown them away and with immense pleasure. And then, there is Giulia. Maybe she was still in shock. Maybe I see things that aren't there but, wasn't she particularly adamant about discouraging me from any further enquiry and in a terrible hurry to dismiss me?"

"Yes, I had the same impression."

"Ah, I don't know. Maybe we read too many crime books," Lola laughed, trying to release her mind from thoughts and enigmas.

"Or maybe not," Fergus said with a pensive frown.

62

DUBLIN - IRELAND

Lola had tossed and turned for most of the night. The whiskey didn't help her sleep, but mostly it was the phone call with Giulia resonating in her head that kept her awake.

The alarm clock wouldn't go off for another hour, but she decided to get up anyway. There was no point lying in bed, staring at the ceiling. She went downstairs, switched on the percolator, and after grabbing a mug of coffee and a couple of digestive biscuits, she went to the sitting room.

She carefully closed the door to avoid the TV noise reaching upstairs and waking the rest of the house.

Lola kept zapping from one channel to another, eventually understanding why morning TV is often called trash TV. She stopped for a few minutes on a teleshopping channel where a young and overly muscular American couple advertised an abs machine with the power of transforming the floppy body of an overweight fifty-year-old into that of a fit forty-something. She gave one look at her forties belly and moved on to a replica of a Jerry Springer show where all the guests and the public were insulting a young mother accused of cheating about her baby's paternity.

Eventually, she heard the alarm from the bedroom and Fergus getting up. She waited for him in the kitchen with few pieces of toasts ready. If the drinks of the night before had the same effect on him that they had on her, he would appreciate the bread more than cereal.

"You look handsome," Lola said to Fergus when he entered the room fully dressed in a tailored Italian suit.

"Thank you," he kissed her on the neck.

"I have a meeting with a possible new client this morning. You remember I told you about that guy owning a chain of handmade shirts shops in London?"

Lola nodded with her head while pouring the coffee.

"Well, he's planning to expand to Ireland and Scotland and wants to restyle the look of the shops."

"That's great, and at the right time too, as you are nearly done up in the North, right?"

"Yep, and if everything goes well, maybe next winter we can drop the twins with my parents and go to NY for a few days. How does that sound?"

"Very, very good!" Lola smiled and imagined herself shopping in the Big Apple and browsing around its most famous art galleries.

"Don't take this the wrong way but you look tired, my love. And you were up early," Fergus said, looking his wife straight in her face.

"I couldn't sleep last night. My damned overthinking."

"Everything considered, it would be hard not to, darling. Have you changed your mind about the funeral?"

"No," Lola said glancing at Fergus like he was a Martian, "but I'm pondering to ring Giulia back and trying to find out what Mara wanted. The more I think about her words, the more I have a feeling she knows more than she is letting on."

"If you want my opinion, you either forget about it or find another way because from what I heard, even if your cousin knows what her mother wanted from you, she didn't sound keen to tell you."

"That's what is bothering me. Giulia's big effort to minimise."

Lola took the last sip of her coffee.

"Bah, maybe you are right, and I should forget about the whole thing. Try not to think about it and go on with my life as I did for the last twenty years," she said more to herself than Fergus.

"Let's start right now and change the subject, are you going to see Siobhan today?" Fergus asked cheerfully and desperately trying to distract his wife.

"Yes. I'm going with Finn this afternoon. Alahnna will mind the boys for a couple of hours. I'm dying to hear what she remembers, and she has asked to see me. Finn has been very secretive on the phone and told me nothing."

Finn Drake was feeling extremely uncomfortable with what his wife was doing, but he had no other choice but to pander to her. She was a very stubborn woman, and there was no way he could talk any sense into her. Hopefully, after she had spoken with Lola, everything would be over, and she could eventually come clean with the police.

He had told her that the detective was a smart guy and he had not believed for a second that she only partially regained her memory, but she insisted that she needed more time. She didn't want to reveal who her attacker was before she had spoken to Lola. They agreed that in the afternoon, he would drive Lola over to her so that they could talk and she could tell her everything that she had found out and everything that had happened. Finn understood his wife didn't want to betray her friend by talking to the police before her, but still, he thought she was playing a dangerous game. She could have been charged for obstruction of justice. Also, after all the effort McCarthey had put into the investigation, it honestly wasn't fair to him.

Finn even thought about going to the detective himself, but he knew that it was far safer to piss off Enda McCarthey than his wife.

The morning could not have passed slower in the surgery. The only thing Dr Finn Drake wanted was for three o'clock to come. He would collect Lola, bring her to the hospital, where Siobhan would explain how things were, and eventually, they would tell the guards. McCarthey would be happy, and hopefully, he would understand that Siobhan meant well.

"Thank you, Alahnna, and you two behave, OK?"

Lola kissed the boys goodbye and left. Finn was waiting for Lola outside, and as soon she was out of the house he rushed to open the car door for her.

She loved Finn's old fashioned way of approaching women always so mannerly. The man was a gentleman. Maybe not the most handsome and talkative but she could see what the bubbly Siobhan had seen in him.

"Thanks for the lift, Finn," Lola said, getting into the front passenger seat.

"Not a bother, Dear".

"Darling, there you are," Siobhan exclaimed widening her arms and inviting Lola for a big hug.

"I'm so happy to see you've recovered, Lola said sitting on the bed and gently squeezing her friend's hand.

"How is your memory? Do you remember everything? What happened? Finn didn't want to tell me anything. "

"Well, it's a bit complicated. I do remember everything, but before I say anything, there is something you must know."

Lola's look went from wife to husband.

"What's going on here? Should I be worried? Because I already had some fairly upsetting news yesterday and there is a limit to the amount of shit I can take in at once," Lola said half-joking and half-serious.

"Me too, but it seems of no importance to my wife here," Finn interrupted, not joking at all.

"Listen, it's not worrying at all, and it has nothing to do with you, but I needed you to know what happened before anybody else was informed."

Siobhan's introduction didn't relax Lola; on the contrary, it made her more anxious.

"Now ...." Siobhan was about to start her account of the attack when Finn, who had moved to the door to close it suddenly began convulsing and clearing his throat to attract the two women's attention.

"Honey do you want some water?" Siobhan asked. A couple of seconds later, it was evident that her husband didn't need water. He needed her to stop talking. Detective Enda McCarthey appeared at the door.

Finn had seen him in the corridor and tried to warn Siobhan. He had to know, but not like that.

"Detective!" the three of them exclaimed in unison like he was the last person they expected or wanted to see.

"Mrs Drake, Mr Drake, Mrs Owen," McCarthey greeted them with a nod of the head, "I hope I'm not interrupting anything!"

"No, just having a chat with Siobhan," Lola said genuinely enough to make McCarthey believe she was oblivious to whatever was happening with the Drakes.

An uncomfortable silence fell in the room, broken only by the noise of a chair's legs being dragged across the floor by the detective who, after positioning it right beside the bed, sat down. The message was clear: he was there to stay.

"Maybe I better leave now and let you talk with the detective," Lola felt she was now the third wheel.

"Thank you, Mrs Owen. Some developments in the case came up, and I need a word with Mr and Mrs Drake in private."

"Absolutely." And it was true, Lola was relieved to leave, even if she had not still learned what had happened to Siobhan.

"Will you be all right getting home? "Finn asked.

"Oh yeah, I'll call a taxi or fetch the bus. Don't worry. "

Siobhan smiled at her neighbour and friend and blew her a kiss, but her eyes showed no gleam.

63

DUBLIN - IRELAND

"How are you today, Mrs Drake?" Detective McCarthey asked with false courtesy.

Finn instinctively laid a hand on his wife's shoulder.

"How is your memory? Any improvement?" the detective asked again leaving no time to Siobhan to answer his previous question.

"No, unfortunately not yet, but the doctor said it might take another day or two."

"That's quite disappointing, but I need you to do something for me anyway," McCarthey continued.

"Sure, anything I can do to help," Siobhan said with staged confidence and hoping to see the back of the detective soon.

"Great, Mrs Drake, so I will tell you what I need you to do.... I need you to stop feeding me with bullshit." Enda McCarthey's voice was a tone higher than usual, and his gaze was fixed on Siobhan's.

Finn felt the urge to intervene and defend his wife in some way, but when he was about to say something, she squeezed his hand, which was still sitting protectively on her shoulder.

The detective had not finished, "See, Mrs Drake, this assault was strange from the beginning. I couldn't set my mind on a simple robbery gone wrong. I must admit that you are an excellent liar, and, in the end, you nearly convinced me that you were the victim of an unfortunate event and that, once your memory returned it would have been the end of it. Case solved. Except when the time came to tell me what had happened, you couldn't remember the details. Very peculiar, isn't it? So peculiar that I couldn't believe you."

"Detective this is far too much. My wife is the victim here," Finn had had enough. McCarthey promptly stopped his complaining and addressed him directly, "Oh, I know your wife is the victim Mr Drake, but she's also keeping the truth from me, and frankly, she should have consulted with you before staging her act. Maybe as a physician, you could have suggested not blaming it on the amnesia."

Finn and Siobhan looked at the detective dumbstruck.

"I did a little research too, " the detective's gaze was back on Siobhan, "and this kind of short-term memory loss you had experienced comes back in full and forever. There is no way you can only remember a fraction of what happened. I spoke to your neurologist, and he confirmed it."

McCarthey had laid all his cards on the table, now it was the Drakes' turn, and they knew it. Siobhan turned her face for a second to Finn, who smiled and nodded with the head. She took a deep breath and started talking, "OK, but please don't think I don't appreciate what you are doing, and I was going to tell you everything, I swear. I just needed to be sure first."

Siobhan then told the detective about the assault in every detail and also everything she knew about Laura. She also said to him that despite Lola's complaint about her paranoia, she knew it was her she had seen snooping through Lola's post. The woman had a strange way of looking at her friend. And then there were all those coincidental encounters between her and Lola. She decided to follow her and found out that nothing of what she had said to them was real. She was not a language student, and she didn't even live where she said. She had tailed her for an entire day and also took pictures. Siobhan didn't know who she was, but she believed she had an agenda involving Lola and when the woman showed up at her house wanting to talk, she panicked and sent her away threatening to call Lola and the police. From there, it escalated.

McCarthey stayed silent for a few minutes; he was processing all the information he had just received. The case was even more complicated than he thought. Mrs Drake knew who the assailant was, but not what she was up to. McCarthey also had severe doubt about her identity. For sure, this Laura woman didn't use her real name.

"OK, send me all the pictures you took, and I'll put a flag on this person, although I doubt she gave her real name. The good news is that we have her fingerprints, she had wiped the handle of the door on her way out but not the railing on the steps. I'll have them checked using the Interpol system, and with some luck, she might be in the records for some priors."

Siobhan kept holding her gaze low; she found it hard to meet the detective' s eyes. McCarthey stood up.

"Detective," Finn called after him when he had nearly reached the door, "what will happen now? Will we be charged with something?"

"I could charge you both with obstruction of justice. But that's not my priority at the moment. I need to find that woman and find out what her business here was and why she was so obsessed with your neighbour. Then I'll charge her for assault. After that, it will be up to the prosecutor."

"Thank you," Siobhan said, eventually looking at the detective.

"I'm only doing my job, Mrs Drake. Probably I would have done it even better and faster if you had not lied to me from the start. As for your possible charge, I only said it's not my priority at the moment, not that I won't proceed with it."

When he left the room, the Drakes eventually hugged each other and released some tension. They would face what they had to, but at least they got it all out, and it felt good.

"One more thing," Detective Enda McCarthey interrupted the couple's moment, "don't say anything to Mrs Owen for the moment."

"But... she must know. I mean, she has a right to know. She could be in danger," Siobhan protested.

"If that woman were going to hurt Mrs Owen, she would have done so already. Besides if you were so concerned with your friend's safety, maybe you should have told me the truth sooner as by now there would have been so much more I could have done."

McCarthey knew he had spoken harshly, but he had had enough of Siobhan Drake and her attitude.

"If Mrs Owen knows, she will only panic and worry for nothing, making things even more complicated. I want to avoid that, at least until we'll know more," the detective added and left.

64

PONTE ALTO - ITALY

"Steno Ferrari speaking," the coroner answered with cold professional tone but immediately softened when hearing Zamparelli on the other end of the line.

"Inspector, you certainly haven't been getting bored recently. I have on my table another body of yours."

"Yes, but that's a domestic accident, and I left it to Piva. I'm calling to see if you managed to reconstruct the face of the B&B victim. You said you would try."

At the beginning of his career, the coroner had lived in the States where he had worked as an assistant for a forensic anthropologist. He was not Temperance Brennan, but he knew his way around bones.

"I started, but then Mrs Kopfler arrived, and I had to give her my full attention as you know she was a close friend of the superintendent."

"That bloody woman! First, she complains because I'm not progressing fast enough with my investigation and then she holds up your office because of her friend lost her balance and fell down the stairs."

Zamparelli's annoyance was growing stronger until Ferrari said something that changed his mood.

"Well, my dear inspector, theoretically you might be right, and Di Fazio used her power to push her friend's case but, after I tell you my findings you might not be so annoyed that she did."

"What do you mean?" the coroner had now Zamparelli's full and undivided attention.

"Mara Kopfler was already dead when she fell down the stairs. The fractured neck was not the cause of death."

"Could she have had a heart attack and lost her balance? I mean at a certain age these things happen," Zamparelli asked still trying to make sense of the coroner's words.

"No. Mara's heart showed no sign of any damage or distress. She died by asphyxia, and to prevent your next question, no, she didn't have respiratory problems either."

Zamparelli said nothing; he knew there was more the coroner had to say and waited for him to continue.

"What alarmed me was the high level of triglycerides in her blood..."

"But that could be simply caused by age, right?" Zamparelli couldn't help but interrupt.

"Yes, indeed, and that's why I ordered some further tests. I am still waiting for the results."

"You are not implying she was murdered, are you?"

"No, inspector I'm only saying that it could be a suspicious accident and I'm looking into it."

The coroner's words were not of any consolation to the inspector. He knew that Steno Ferrari would have never wasted the tax payer's money on unnecessary tests if he believed it was nothing more than an accident.

* * *

"What do you mean they are performing an autopsy on my mother's body, and you don't know when I can have it back?" Giulia had been bounced from one department of the morgue to another all morning, and when she eventually found her answers, they were not in the least what she had wanted.

"You don't know who you are dealing with. We are family friends with the Superintendent!" She shouted at the phone before hanging up.

In reality, Giulia had no intention of calling Luisa Di Fazio to speed things up; it would only have shaken things further. The last thing Giulia needed was more police involvement and more interest in her mother's death. She was walking up and down her office trying to think about what to do next.

Going into the office that morning had been a mistake. Giulia couldn't focus enough to do any work. Wherever she went, someone was giving her their condolences and asking how she was or when the funeral would be. Giulia had no answer to either of those questions. She decided to keep the autopsy a secret. There was no need to feed gossip or speculation. So far, not a word about a suspicious death had been said, but then why request an autopsy?

Her thoughts were interrupted by Carlo calling.

"Please give me some good news," she said, answering the phone already smiling at the sight of his face on the phone display.

"Hello to you too," he greeted her before continuing, "As a matter of fact, I'm calling to give you good news. I just checked the bank account, and it's all there. I can pay the old contractors and sign the contracts with the new ones. We are right on track, and I know it's not the right time to celebrate, and it might sound insensitive, but we really should. We did it, honey!"

Carlo's excitement was contagious and just what Giulia needed at that moment. As for the inappropriateness of celebrating, with her mother's body still warm, she couldn't certainly say to be the most respectable grieving daughter either.

"Mother's last present," Giulia replied except her tone was

sadder than she intended. The line went silent for a few seconds.

"I'm sorry, honey. I can only imagine how it feels to lose the only parent you had left and in such an unexpected way. She was a witch, but she was your mother, and in the end, she proved her trust in you. Or else she would not have signed for the loan. She loved you, in her own way, and so did you." Carlo's words were genuine and sweet, Giulia only wished they were accurate as well.

Mara never trusted her daughter, and she never signed. She probably never really loved her either. In a way, Giulia was relieved that great Mara Kopfler was dead and out of her way. Except, the old witch made sure to fuck her daughter one last time because God knows what they will find with the autopsy.

Giulia so wished she could tell Carlo all this but how could she trust him to understand her feelings and worries? He was working class and the first of his family to go to university and do well for himself. His parents could not be any prouder of him. He fixed them up in a lovely flat in the nearest village where they had always lived and helped them here and there when their pension was not enough for unforeseen expenses or fancy holidays. Giulia had no idea if Carlo's parents were aware of his reputation when it came to business, but she had the feeling that it would not have diminished how proud they were of their son. He was lucky to have them. They loved him for who he was, unconditionally — something Giulia had never experienced.

"Yes, sorry, I have to go. I have another call. I'll see you at home in a while. Love you."

Giulia picked up the other incoming call. The number was unknown.

"Hi Giulia, it's me, Father Nello…"

"Father Nello, I'm sorry, but this is not a good time."

"Of course, I can imagine, and I won't keep you long," his

angelic, calm, wise and extremely superior manner of talking gave Giulia goosebumps. She waited in silence on the phone until he went back talking, "I was wondering when you are planning to celebrate the funeral. As a family friend, I would like to officiate, of course."

"You mean like my mother's friend! I'm sorry, but I don't think we can consider each other friends." Giulia had been purposely hostile, but she also wanted to provoke him to see if he would say a bit more about what he knew.

"No. I certainly don't want to impose my friendship on anyone."

"Good, you will oversee the funeral, but I'm still expecting news from the coroner."

"What? Has the body not been released yet? Are they performing an autopsy? Why? "Father Nello struggled to control his surprise. Giulia regretted her unforgivable slip before finishing the sentence.

"It's routine in a domestic accident, like calling the police. And now, please excuse me. As I said to you before, it's not a good time. I'm very busy," Giulia was desperate to put an end to the conversation.

How could she have been so stupid?

Father Nello had been a priest for a very long time and knew far too well that there was no autopsy performed unless there was something suspicious. Giulia had lied to him.

65

PONTE ALTO - ITALY

"Inspector, can you have a look at this? "

The mix of excitement and panic in Piva's voice immediately caught Zamparelli's attention.

The young deputy walked towards the inspector's desk and laid a sheet of paper in front of him.

"It's Mrs Kopfler's autopsy report."

"And you are not able to read it? Too graphic for you?" Zamparelli sarcastically responded without even looking at his deputy or the report but keeping his eyes on the computer screen. Having received no positive response from either the police HQ or the Interpol's database, Zamparelli's mood was beyond terrible. He could not find a proper lead for his investigation, and on top of it, he still didn't know who his victim was.

"I can indeed, but I think you'll want to see this for yourself, Sir," Piva answered dryly, and Zamparelli didn't miss the pride and outrage in his tone.

He had taken out his bad mood on the young officer again.

The inspector took the autopsy report in his hands and gestured to Piva to take a seat. It was his way of apologising.

After he had finished reading, without saying a word, he picked up the phone.

"What the hell, Ferrari? I just saw Mara Kopfler's autopsy report. You could have at least rung me!"

After their last conversation, the inspector had expected the coroner to call him if there'd been any relevant development, and he didn't hide his displeasure.

"You said Piva was dealing with it and I rang him," Dr Ferrari answered seeing no issue, after all, he had already given the inspector a heads up. It was up to the inspector and his deputy to share the info. As far as he was concerned, the body was officially Piva's.

"Yes, Piva was dealing with it, since you hadn't suggested it could be foul play," Zamparelli barked but immediately realised he was now upsetting both men listening to him.

The coroner didn't want to get involved in any of the officers' quarrel and was quick to point out he had followed the correct procedure. Piva, on his side, threw his boss a hurt look as if he had implied his deputy couldn't handle anything such as murder.

The inspector covered the phone receiver with his hand and whispered his apologies to his deputy, "Sorry Piva, I didn't mean to imply you are not skilled enough for the case. It's the political implications I'm thinking about."

Piva nodded, grateful for the apology, as he knew how hard the inspector was to admit his faults.

Zamparelli and Piva exchanged a look of mutual understanding before the inspector went back to the phone, "So someone wanted her dead?"

It was a rhetorical question, but Zamparelli still couldn't make full sense of what he had read in the report.

Who could hate Mara Kopfler that much?

"Pretty much as I say in the report. An overdose of barbiturates caused a high level of triglycerides. So, they drugged her, suffocated her with a pillow and then pushed her down the stairs to make it look like an accident."

"Great!" This was making things far more complicated, and the superintendent would be breathing down the inspector's neck even more.

"Poor woman, I met her a few times, and she seemed quite a nice lady," the coroner added to fill the silence between the two on the line.

Zamparelli had no time to praise the victim, "Steno, are you implying that we are looking for someone strong? I mean someone who could manage all that? Suffocate her, drag her to the top of the stairs and then push her down? "

"No. Anyone could have done it. With that amount of Phenobarbital in her body, Mrs Kopfler was half paralysed and couldn't put up a fight."

* * *

Zamparelli and Piva went through all the possible beneficiaries of Mara's death. At the top of their list, there was her daughter. Giulia had both the motive and the opportunity.

"So, how are we going to proceed, Sir?" Piva asked.

"How are you going to proceed Piva. The investigation is still yours," Piva's face lit up at the inspector's words, "you try to find out if Mara had enemies, she certainly didn't gain all that power and money without stepping on someone's feet. Check alibis, collect statements, etc. In one word, the usual. Only this time you'll have to do it alone. I need to focus on the B&B murder."

Piva could not believe his ears and felt slightly ashamed for the evil thoughts he had about the inspector.

"One last thing Piva. I want to be kept in the loop at all time. You will also inform me of even the most insignificant developments. Di Fazio will surely want to be informed. This thing is personal to her, and we must be sure that we feed her enough information to keep her quiet but not too much as to tempt her to interfere. Understood?"

Piva nodded from the door and left the inspector's office. Walking with his head in the papers, he bumped into someone, "Sorry, I didn't see you." Piva apologised as per an unconditional reflex but without even raising his head.

Only when he was back at his desk, he realised that it was Father Nello he had bumped into. The very same priest who had found Mara's body.

What was he doing at the station? It couldn't be a coincidence.

"Father Nello, right? "Piva got up from his desk and approached the priest who seemed lost.

"Can I help you with something?" Piva asked, curious to know why he was there. He had not called for him, not yet.

Father Nello seemed nervous, "Actually, I think I can help you with something. It's about my friend, Mara Kopfler."

"Follow me please," Piva said, leading the way to the inspector's room. He had seen Zamparelli leaving straight after they had finished talking.

"We can talk in peace here," he then added sitting down on the same side of the desk where Father Nello was seated.

Shorten the gap between you and the witnesses to make them feel at ease and more willing to talk. A technique Piva had learned in the academy, and that worked most of the time.

Piva was adamant about knowing what the priest had to say, but he knew he had to give the man time to gather his thoughts. He had to speak first and spontaneously. Pressuring him would not have helped; besides he was there by his own will. Father Nello wanted to talk.

"I heard there is an autopsy going on. Do you think someone murdered Mara?"

The first thing Piva wanted to ask was how the hell the priest knew about the autopsy, but then he realised that

Giulia had probably told him. After all, he was a family friend, even though he had the impression the young Kopfler was not particularly fond of him.

"I can confirm that there is an autopsy record, but I can't say anything more than that. Do you think someone killed your friend, father?"

"Well, I know that autopsies are performed when there is a suspicious death..." Father Nello cleverly avoided answering Piva's direct question.

"Indeed Father, but you used the word *murder*," Piva's tone was still calm and friendly, but he started to follow Nello closely.

The priest stayed silent for a few seconds and then eventually found the courage to say what was tormenting him, "Mara had planned to make some changes in her life. They were changes that would affect some other persons. Persons close to her. I can't say more. See, deputy inspector, what I know, I learnt it through the secrecy of the confessional. I would have never come here if it was sure that her death was accidental, but when I heard of the autopsy, I knew I had to come."

Father Nello stopped talking and dried his eyes that had begun to fill with tears.

Piva said nothing. It was not his time to speak. He gave the priest all the time he needed to regain his composure.

"I'm here to warn you not to leave any lead unexplored. Mara's past might give you some help, but you have to dig deep." Nello stood up and left.

He had said enough. Now it was up to the police to do their job, and he hoped they were good enough at it so that his friend would get the justice she deserved and the truth would come to light as she wished.

Piva watched the back of the priest without being able to say or ask anything else. He watched him leave the building from the window.

What was the priest referring to?

Piva was not yet sure about his next move, but he was sure of one thing: there was much more that had transpired throughout Mara Kopfler's life. Once he had his hands on what it was, then he would have his hands on who wanted her dead.

Only when he left the police station, did Nello have the feeling to breathe again. He got into his car and looked at the box on the passenger seat. Mara had given it to him to bring to the solicitor in case anything happened to her.

Nello felt a sudden sharp pain in his chest. The twinge of guilt. Mara knew she was in danger and went to him for help, but he had let her down. He had not been able to protect her, and now he had to live with the remorse. Unfortunately, the past couldn't be changed, but the present and the future could. The present and the future were still in his hands, and today he had made the first step in turning them in the right direction. Now it was time to take the second step.

66

DUBLIN- IRELAND

"You've got to be kidding me, Sir," Kevin said with an astonished expression after McCarthey had filled him in on the latest development from the Drake case.

"I knew they were hiding something. And what about Mrs Owen, what do you make of her? Do you think she is involved in any way?"

"No, I don't think so. Besides, she has no motive or interest." McCarthey genuinely believed Lola was oblivious to everything that was unravelling around her.

"Good, she looks like a nice lady to me." Kevin would have hated for Lola to be involved in something criminal. He liked her ever since the time he took her fingerprints. She was courteous and very polite, not snobby like most of the women on her road who randomly came into the station because someone had forced their brand new Mercedes SUV, or because they believed someone had kidnapped their miniature pinchers from the front garden.

"I think she was genuinely offering her friendship to that Laura woman. Assuming that is her real name, a thing I doubt,"

McCarthey continued, "I dug up a little bit on Mrs Owen's past. She lost her parents very young. An aunt raised her, but they were never close and so at the first chance she left Italy. The husband said they have no contact with the wife's family."

"So, you think she was just nice to an elderly woman out of Oedipus complex?" Kevin commented, trying to impress the chief with the reference. Unfortunately, his school psychology reminiscences were not accurate.

"Well, that applies more to men, Kevin; and it has to do with sex and jealousy," McCarthey corrected the young guard but stopped before digressing into a lecture about Freud's theories.

Kevin looked at his boss, disappointed there was no further explanation to come and put his notebook away.

"I think Lola Owen cannot help herself in front of elderly, motherly figures. She trusts them and projects the mother she never had in them. I mean she is one of the few women I know who loves her mother in law, from what I've heard." McCarthey added to make sure Kevin got the point.

"Yes, well, so basically Mrs Owen's only fault is being naive?"

"Basically yes, Kevin," McCarthey agreed.

"But, then, what's the connection? Could it have been just a random encounter between Lola Owen and our mystery woman?"

Something was missing.

"It could easily have been, but then something must have triggered the old lady. We need to find out who she is, and then we might be able to throw some light on the whole matter."

"Shall we start from the place where she was staying? She must have checked in," Kevin proactively suggested.

"Yes, you go there, I doubt she was so refined in her plan to use a fake ID. Let's hope so at least. Also, find out when she supposedly arrived and check the airlines. Getting past border control with a fake ID can be more complicated."

"I'm on it!"

Kevin got up, and at the threshold of the detective's office, he turned: "Oh Sir, I forgot to tell you. The system went back up working this morning."

McCarthey looked at him, moving his reading glasses back to his head like they were a hairband. The detective's ginger curls were well overdue a trim.

"What?" He distractedly asked, not understanding what the young guard was saying.

"You remember I told you the station router had gone, and we had to replace it?" McCarthey still looked at him like he was speaking a foreign language.

"Well, never mind," Kevin continued "now it's working, and I made sure everything is up to date. We lost the last two days of data, you know. But don't worry, I made sure those fingerprints reached the Interpol database as soon the system was back."

Now the detective understood what Kevin was on about, and went ballistic, "What the fuck, Kevin! So, you are saying that the prints from the Drakes' house have not been processed internationally yet?"

"They have now," Garda Kevin Farrell said taking a few steps backwards and leaving the office at high speed.

* * *

The day was lovely, sunny and warm. Lola's visit to the hospital had been cut short by the arrival of the detective, and so she decided not to go straight home. The boys were safe with Alahnna, and she could do with a walk.

She got off the bus in Ballsbridge, treated herself to an iced caramel mocha at the local Starbucks and used the Herbert Park Hotel's entrance to access Herbert Park.

While strolling around, Lola realised she hadn't thought about what Siobhan had to tell her, before the detective arrived. Typically, curiosity would have consumed her, but in fairness, it was Siobhan they were talking about. Siobhan always had something super important and exciting, that couldn't wait to be told. What annoyed her instead, was not knowing the details of the attack yet. But the fact that her friend was in good form was enough to put her mind at rest. She sat for a while by the pond and only when she heard the park warden starting to go around ringing his bell to advise that it was time to leave, she noticed how late it was. Lola stood up and began to walk towards the closest exit on the Donnybrook side.

She took her phone out of her bag to call Alahnna to say she was on her way home. The phone was still in silent mode from the hospital. There were two missed calls from an unknown number. Lola still had the phone in her hand when a text message came in. Again, anonymous.

She was now in front of the house, and the boys spotted her from the window. There was no time to read the text.

"Hi, is everything OK? Did they behave?" Lola asked Alahnna out of breath after she had literally jogged home.

"Of course, they were not a bother," the girl answered giving mother and sons a big smile.

"Your mum looked great," Lola said to the teenage girl that was now blossoming into a beautiful and smart young woman. The resemblance to her mother, more evident by the day.

"We were so worried. I never thought I would say so, but I missed mum terribly, and I'm looking forward to having her back home."

Lola motherly hugged Alahnna.

The girl already had her backpack on her shoulder, and one hand on the door handle when Lola handed her 30 euros.

"Oh no, Mrs Owen, that's far too much besides I minded the twins because you went to visit my mum."

Alahnna tried to give the money back to Lola, but she insisted for her to keep it.

"Your mum has nothing to do with this, and you've sacrificed some of your free time to mind my kids," Lola closed the girl's hand around the notes and waved her good-bye.

67

DUBLIN - IRELAND

"A toast to the new contract."

The meeting with the London client had gone well, and Fergus's company had won the contract. They would be starting after summer.

"I'm so happy for you," Lola said, sipping the pink Prosecco he brought home.

"And I'm so happy for us," Fergus said, raising his glass one more time, "with the money this job will bring, we can breathe a little."

Lola looked at her husband with that look she always gave him when he tended to worry too much about money. He had to learn to appreciate what they had more.

"I know, I know, we are doing well anyway, actually better than many others but still it will be good to have a bit more coming in."

"Indeed!" Lola agreed.

"What's going on with your phone? It's been beeping all evening with texts," Fergus asked when another text message beeped lighting up his wife mobile's screen.

"It's just old unread texts, and the phone reminds me to read them or erase them." Lola rolled her eyes annoyed.

"Maybe you should read them," Fergus suggested, "I'm sure there must be plenty of my texts too in that list," he then added laughing.

Lola showed the phone to her husband, "See, this has been driving me crazy all afternoon. But I didn't want to open it just in case it's a scam."

Fergus took the phone from his wife's hand, "Honey, did you look at that message properly?"

"No, why? Just erase it, would you?"

"I think you should read it before deciding what to do with it."

Lola took the phone back. She read it twice and then put the phone on the table face down.

"Fuck," she said.

"Yep," Fergus agreed.

"Now what? What's this? What am I supposed to do?" Lola was now standing, too nervous to sit still. She was on the verge of another hysterical cry.

Fergus went closer and handed her the phone, "Ring him back. I know it's late, but I don't think this can wait."

Lola sat back down at the table and put the phone on speaker.

It only took a couple of rings for the other person to answer.

"Lola? Is it you?"

Lola hesitated until Fergus squeezed her hand; she breathed in deeply and then she spoke. The conversation didn't last long.

Lola agreed to think about what Father Nello suggested and ring him back.

"Maybe you better get some whiskey," Lola said to Fergus, "...and chocolate."

"No, I don't think you need anything else to drink. You need your head clear. You have a decision to make, and it can't wait this time."

Husband and wife were still sceptical to the priest's words. Mara had confessed something which might have caused her death. Something about Lola. Something Father Nello could not say because of the secrecy of confession, but he begged Lola to come to Italy to learn more.

"More about what?" Lola was furious, how these people felt in the right to jump into her life and turn it upside down.

"Shit", she screamed. She had no intention of going to Italy to look for a truth she didn't want to know, nor did she care.

But then Father Nello mentioned Mara's phone calls. He knew her aunt had rung her, and he knew why, and at this stage, neither Fergus nor Lola could ignore those calls nor dismiss them as Giulia had tried to do.

"Can we just pretend nothing has happened?" Lola asked, mentally exhausted.

Fergus took his laptop and switched it on.

"What are you doing now? "

"I'm checking for flights."

68

PONTE ALTO - ITALY

Inspector Furio Zamparelli was driving home after spending most of the afternoon on the road, questioning possible witnesses who might identify the victim, but with no luck. She had been meticulously careful in not making herself stand out or been noticed, and this was still holding the investigation back because with no identity and no identikit to show around there was not much they could do. It was like the woman had not existed until someone had killed her.

"Piva," Zamparelli called out on the phone when his deputy answered, "how is it going on your side? I hope it's better than mine."

"Well, Sir, I had an interesting conversation with Father Nello,"

Zamparelli waited for his deputy to speak while rolling his eyes. He profoundly hated when Piva purposely paused to create an air of anticipation, "Piva, have you fallen asleep at your desk or do you want to tell me what the priest said?" Zamparelli had enough. He was not a man with a great patience, and even less so at the end of a long hot day.

"Yes, Sir, well he's the one who found the body along with

the victim's daughter, you remember. I told you..."

"Yes, Piva I do remember, I'm not an old sclerotic bastard yet. Can you please cut the bullshit and get to the point?"

Piva explained in detail his conversation with Father Nello. The young deputy's excitement was palpable. It was the first time he had to solve a murder on his own.

Zamparelli wondered if he was really up to the task and whether or not to leave him in charge but, there was not much else he could do as he couldn't manage two murders cases at once. The inspector asked how he intended to proceed. They agreed on a common strategy and, finally, the inspector was home.

He lived in a reasonably new apartment block. It was enclosed behind gates and had a modest amount of green all around. His flat was on the third floor and had one small balcony at the back and one, big enough to fit a table and some chairs, at the front. It was there he went after grabbing a chilled beer and a cigarillo from his secret stash. He always kept a packet for the odd smoke.

The front balcony overlooked the parking area. At that time of the evening, it was nice and quiet. Everybody had already gotten home, and they were probably having dinner. The majority of Zamparelli's neighbours were families; except for a couple of elderly ladies who were living on their own.

When he moved in, everybody welcomed him with great enthusiasm, like he could prevent any crime just by his presence. He learnt to smile back and gratefully accept Mrs Rui's pans of lasagne once a fortnight. He also learned to turn a blind eye to the young guy who used to smoke joints out of the bathroom window.

Lost in his thoughts, the inspector had not noticed a figure bending under the parking barrier and walking to stand directly beneath his balcony, "I need to talk to you. In private."

Zamparelli rose from the chair and went inside to buzz the door for superintendent Di Fazio.

69

PONTE ALTO - ITALY

Zamparelli woke up in the same lousy mood he went to bed with the previous night after talking with the superintendent.

As he had guessed, she was there about the Kopfler case. Superintendent Di Fazio wanted him to catch whoever had killed her friend, but considering the possible involvement of a family member, she also wanted him to be discreet. As far as the public opinion was concerned, media included, Mara Kopfler's death, had been an accident until otherwise irrefutably proven. Zamparelli was not surprised by those recommendations, but what he didn't expect was the order to remove Piva from the investigation and take it into his own hands. The inspector had agreed, there was no point to put up a fight, but he already decided not to follow the orders.

He knew the superintendent would keep a close eye on him and so he had to play it cool and in the smartest way possible.

That morning, as soon as he arrived at the station, Zamparelli called Piva into his office. After the inspector had finished updating his deputy about his previous evening meeting with the superintendent, Piva's facial expression was one of someone who had just lost their dream job.

"Come on, Piva, don't give me that look. I only told you what Di Fazio strongly suggested me to do. But I didn't say I'm going to do it, did I?"

The deputy's inspector's full-body immediately relaxed, but he still didn't say a word and allowed the inspector to continue talking.

"Listen, Piva. I can't afford to move again as a result of ignoring my boss's orders. The snow and the cold here over the winter and the humid and heat over the summer, I hate them, but I've gotten used to it. I've no intention to start all over again, maybe even somewhere further north. So, officially I can't leave you in charge of the investigation, but that is what I'm going to do in effect."

"Yes, Sir, I got it. Thank you, Sir." Piva stood up and was about to leave when Zamparelli stopped him: "Don't disappoint me Piva and don't get me in any trouble. You keep me up to speed on everything, and if you've any concern, you come straight to me."

"You can trust me on this, Sir." Piva stood straight in front of the inspector.

"I hope so," Zamparelli added, but his deputy knew he meant he could trust him, and this counted more than his name on the official papers of the case.

"Sir, before I go," Piva stopped by the door, "I asked around, and it looks like Mrs Kopfler had no enemies. She was well known and liked in the community. She was involved in many charities, and there were never any rumours about her private life, ever. Either she was a saint, or the lady knew how to protect her privacy. The only bizarre thing is about her sister."

Before Piva could continue, Zamparelli interrupted him with surprised curiosity, "Did she have a sister? Nobody ever mentioned it."

"That's the thing, Sir. Lorna Kopfler, the sister, was the family's black sheep. She had a troubled life and ended up drowning in the lake. She left a daughter behind that Mara raised along with her own. She lives abroad. Rumour has it that things were always tense between aunt and niece. She left as soon as she could."

A curious look appeared on Zamparelli's face, "And will this niece inherit anything now that both the Kopfler sisters are dead or will the entire estate go to Giulia?"

"I spoke with the family's solicitor, and from what he could tell me, without breaking client confidentiality, I understand that the whole estate will go to Giulia. Mr Kopfler, the father, left everything to Mara, not trusting the other daughter and the little she had to inherit by the law passed to her daughter, who renounced her share in exchange for severance pay to start her new life abroad."

"So, everything points to Giulia again."

"I'm afraid so, Sir."

The inspector and his deputy remained silent for a few seconds, each of them mentally pondering the implications of the case.

"Oh, and just out of curiosity, "Piva broke the silence, "you know that I told you that Lorna Kopfler had drowned, well the mother, drowned in the lake too."

"Dear Lord, what's wrong with that family? That's unreal! It's a soap opera script".

"Right," Piva agreed, before adding more details to the story, "and that's not all. The ones who remember those days silently suggest it was no accident. Even if there was never an official enquiry, they suggest that Ester Kopfler took her own life."

"I'm not surprised Piva; those were different times, and mental health was not valued as it is now. A suicide in the family could ruin their reputation forever. Considering the power the Kopflers already had, I don't think it took much effort for the old Mr Kopfler to cover everything up."

The inspector and his deputy had finished. Piva already had his hand on the door handle when someone opened it from outside and nearly smashed his nose.

"What the fuck, Farinelli, are you trying to kill me?" Piva screamed to the young uniform who had just barged into the office.

"I'm sorry, but I couldn't have known you were behind the door," the officer muttered apologetically.

"It's ok, Farinelli, he will survive. What is it?" Zamparelli asked with a particular urgency because it had to be something important for the officer to barge into his office without knocking.

"We have a match for the fingerprints in the B&B case," officer Farinelli eventually announced, "we got a match through the Interpol database. We don't have an identity yet, but apparently, the victim is wanted for a home assault in Dublin."

Still no name but at least it was a step forward, and they were not the only ones after her.

"Do we know who is working on her case in Ireland?" Zamparelli asked.

"Yes, Sir. Some Detective Enda McCarthey. He tried to ring last night as he got the dispatch too, but couldn't talk to anybody, so he left his name and number." Officer Farinelli handed Zamparelli a piece of paper with detective McCarthey's details.

"Brilliant, thank you, Farinelli."

* * *

There was only one thing Furio Zamparelli could thank his ex-wife for, and that was to have him enrolled in an English course.

In the beginning, he hated the idea of spending three evenings a week in a classroom with headphones over his ears, practising a language that had no appeal to him whatsoever. Still, when he started to speak fluently, all that effort proved its worth. Not to mention that after the divorce, it became an excellent way to impress the female tourists around Rome. But that was before his unwillingness to follow orders cost him his job in the capital.

The conversation between Zamparelli and McCarthey was brief but satisfactory, on both sides. The two detectives agreed to keep each other in the loop for possible developments

"Here," Zamparelli materialised at Piva's desk after printing the pictures McCarthey had sent.

Piva looked at the woman in the photo and back to the inspector.

"Yes, Piva. We managed to get a photo of our B&B victim."

"Where did it come from?" Piva asked

'Well, long story short, the woman she attacked in Dublin had taken a few pics of her. So, we still don't have an ID, but at least we know what she looked like before they smashed her face and made her unrecognisable."

"That's great, Sir. "

"I know Piva, something to work with, finally. I'm on my way to the Swhartzes' to see if they will confirm it's her. And then I'll start asking around if anyone had seen her."

" I wish I had a breakthrough in the Kopfler story as well," Piva said discouraged.

Zamparelli patted his young colleague on the shoulder and before he left, reminded him that the superintendent was waiting for a report by the end of the day.

70

DUBLIN - IRELAND

After speaking with the Italian inspector, Detective McCarthey decided it was time to inform Lola Owen of what was going on around her.

"Laura" had targeted her for some still unknown reason, and now she was dead. Someone had brutally murdered her. McCarthey didn't believe Lola was in danger, but he wanted to warn her. He threw the car keys to Kevin: he was driving. The young Garda had filled in papers all morning and couldn't be happier to get out of the station for a while.

"Should we not inform the Drakes that we are going to talk to Mrs Owen?" Kevin asked. McCarthey didn't bother to answer as if the young officer had uttered some nonsense.

"I mean, you told them to keep it quiet. But as we are going to speak to Mrs Owen now, there is no point for them to keep doing that anymore," Kevin felt to explain further, looking at the detective instead of the road and nearly going onto the path before swerving the car back onto the carriageway.

"OK, OK, I got it, Kevin," McCarthey said, compulsively pretending to brake with his foot on an invisible pedal, "Just keep looking at the road, will you?"

Kevin smiled and pulled up in front of the Owens' house.

"Let's talk to Mrs Owen, see how it goes, and then I'll talk to the Drakes. OK? I think they must be informed first of the fact that Mrs Drake's assailant is dead," the detective told Kevin unfastening his seatbelt as he made his point.

"Right Sir, I forgot about that!" Kevin said, slapping his forehead with his hat.

"You forgot about Mrs Drake's assault or about the fact that her assailant, who we were desperately trying to catch, is dead?"

That was the last blow to Kevin's pride. Next time he would think twice before suggesting to the detective how to do his job.

"No, but ...in a way maybe…I …" Kevin's embarrassment was heartbreaking.

"That's enough Kevin, just leave it, yeah?" McCarthey cut it short.

When the two officers rang the bell at the little pedestrian gate, they noticed that the Owens' car was not in the driveway. There was instead an old Volvo V70. When nobody answered, McCarthey lifted the rusty hook and led the way up to the front door.

"Can I help you?" a lady around her mid-sixties opened the door. Her face had sweet features framed by long grey hair impeccably blow-dried. McCarthey guessed she would be Lola's mother-in-law. She matched the idea he had made of her in his mind.

"Detective Enda McCarthey and this is Officer Farrell. We were hoping to have a word with Mrs Owen," McCarthey said, showing his badge.

"Oh," the lady standing before them was surprised, police don't show up at your doorstep every day, but then it was like she had suddenly remembered something. She patted the side of her head funnily and spoke again, "Sorry, of course, you must be here because of what happened to poor Siobhan.

How dreadful, but I'm sorry to tell you that my daughter-in-law is not at home."

"Do you know when she will be back? It's quite urgent; maybe your son is at home?" McCarthey asked, disappointed. Angela Owen was about to reply when a big shadow appeared behind her. Pat Owen, her husband.

"Who is it, darling? Please, whatever you are selling we don't need it unless it's a magic potion to cure my sciatica," he said rubbing his left hip and nearly closing the door in the two policemen's faces.

"Wait," Angela stopped her husband, "these gentlemen are policemen, they came to talk to Lola," she explained.

Pat Owen blushed and made his sincere apologies to the two guards. In a hurry to rescue his wife from possible salespeople of useless paraphernalia, he hadn't noticed Kevin's uniform.

"I was just about to tell them that the guys will be out of town for a few days," Angela said, shifting her gaze between her husband and McCarthey.

"OK then, here is my card, please tell Mrs Owen to call me as soon as she makes contact with you," McCarthey handed them his business card and left followed by Kevin, who signalled good-bye to the old couple by removing his hat.

* * *

"All this is crazy, and I can't believe we asked your parents to come over with no warning to mind the boys. God knows what they must have thought," Lola told Fergus struggling to keep her balance in the crowded aisle of the shuttle bus that was transporting them from the long-term carpark to the airport.

"Stop it. You heard mum and dad yourself. After we told them, they were the first to say you had to go."

"Exactly, I had to go. I could have gone on my own, and you know that. You didn't have to come."

Lola felt enormous gratitude to her husband for going with her, but she also felt guilty for all the trouble she had caused.

"I know. And you would have handled it perfectly well without me, but I wanted to come."

The bus stopped, and they got out.

The only tickets for a direct flight to the north of Italy at a reasonable price were to Bergamo.

Neither Ryanair and nor Aerlingus flew to Venice on the day, so they had no other options unless they wanted to change in Frankfurt, but that would take them twice the time and without saving any money. From Venice, there was a bus to Ponte Alto, but from Bergamo, there was no public transport going directly to the Dolomites. Their only alternative was to hire a car and drive nearly four hours. They had no time to book it online in advance, and so they would have to do it once they landed.

Lola had been unusually quiet for the entire flight. Her feelings were mixed: she was angry with a family that kept creating problems for her; she was terrified at what was awaiting her and felt guilty towards Fergus and his parents for having dragged them all into this big mess.

"Hey, you had no choice," Fergus suddenly said as he had read his wife's thoughts. She squeezed his hands and cocked her head on his shoulder, "I know, it's just that I hate all this. I really believed I left my past behind; you know?"

"Maybe after this, you will, once and for all."

"I hope so."

They both closed their eyes and fell asleep until the flight attendant woke them up, asking them to put their seat in the correct position for landing.

Bergamo's airport was one of the most trafficked in Europe, but also ridiculously small and unkempt. The air conditioning was not working, and they queued for over forty minutes to get through passport control.

The queue at the car rental kiosk was not any shorter. When their turn eventually came, Lola and Fergus weren't bothered about what car they got to rent, but it had to have air conditioning.

They split the drive: Fergus was going to drive for the first two hours on the motorway, and Lola would take over once they reached the primary roads. If nothing had changed since last time she was there, those mountain roads were steep and full of turns and undoubtedly more challenging to handle for Fergus who also had to get used to driving on the right-hand side of the way. They arrived in Ponte Alto at around ten in the evening. They hadn't eaten anything since they got off the plane, but the hot weather had made them lose their appetite.

It was late, and even if the last place Lola wanted to check in was her cousin's hotel, that seemed to be the best option. It was right in front of them as they entered the town and tired as they were, they hadn't the will to go around checking for other accommodation. Not for tonight at least.

The Kopfler Grand Hotel was still as Lola remembered it: lavish and intimidating.

The hotel was fully booked, except for a suite that was vacant until the end of the week.

"You can have it, but you will have to leave by Saturday," the receptionist told them politely.

"Perfect," Lola confirmed. She had no intention of staying long anyway.

"Massimo will bring your bags to the room, in the meantime can I get the kitchen to fix you something to eat? You must be exhausted and starving."

Fergus was particularly impressed by the amity of the personnel in the hotel, and at the same time terrified at how much it would cost when it came to settling the bill.

"Maybe your cousin should train herself in the same good

manners she trained her employees in," Fergus couldn't help but comment.

The couple took up the offer of something to eat, but instead of a meal, they asked for two big ice creams to enjoy on the terrace.

71

PONTE ALTO - ITALY

"Wow, this is a little bit like being on holiday, isn't it?" Fergus told Lola while drinking his orange juice and giving his custard cream-filled kraphen one last huge bite while enjoying the view of the lake from the balcony of their room.

"Yes, except it's not. And when Giulia knows we are here, she'll want to throw us out," Lola replied dryly.

"She can't. We are paying guests, even though I wouldn't mind a discount," Fergus laughed, patting his wife on the butt, who stood up to go back inside the room.

"Do you have Father Nello's address?" he called after her.

"Check on my phone. He sent it to me with a text," Lola said, disappearing into the bathroom to re-emerge fully dressed after a short while.

"Wow, you look lovely," Fergus spontaneously said to his wife, still with her phone in hand. Lola was quite pleased with the way the dress fitted her. She tied her sandals behind her ankles and jumped to her feet, ready to go.

"Google Maps says it's only a 15 minutes walk from here," Fergus said undecided whether as to take the car or not.

"Let's walk then."

Husband and wife left the hotel holding hands, but after a few minutes of walking, they had to let go as the heat had already made them both sweaty and sticky.

Father Nello's rectory was right beside the church. When they arrived, the cleaning lady was leaving. He offered them something to drink and told them as much as he could without betraying his vows. Unfortunately, there wasn't much to say but the fact that there was now an official murder investigation into Mara's death, and that reinforced Fergus's belief they had made the right decision to come.

Nello suggested Lola would go to the police, and despite her protests that she had nothing of any relevance to say to them, in the end, she agreed to go.

* * *

"Unbelievable, you should hear the tone of that inspector or deputy or whatever the hell he is," Giulia was still fuming after Piva had questioned her, "and that idiot of a superintendent cannot do anything about it, according to her."

Giulia was no fool and didn't believe for a second Piva's questions were intended only to exclude her as a suspect. He wanted to verify her alibi and how much she had to gain from her mother's death. Being Mara's sole heiress and having an alibi that was far from watertight, put her in a dangerous position and that was the reason, in the end, she rang the superintendent and appealed to her for some help.

Di Fazio knew she was moving on perilous ground. There was a potential conflict of interest because she and Mara had been friends. She had talked to Zamparelli already, asked for discretion, but this was all she could do. Giulia was on her own now. The superintendent had no desire to risk her career and pretty much told her so.

"Well, at least they have released the body so you can arrange the funeral," Carlo tried to calm his fiancé down.

"You are right, and thank God the loan has already been approved because until the murder investigation is over, I'm not even sure we can proceed with the reading of the will and the legal succession," Giulia said, standing up to go and get dressed.

Carlo understood what kind of pressure she was under, and he also knew she pretended to be stronger than she was. Still, her coldness towards her mother's death was something that made him uncomfortable. He had been no fan of Mara when she was alive, but again, it was her mother after all, and Giulia's apparent lack of compassion made him doubt her. Her alibi for the day of Mara's death puzzled him. She said she drove for a couple of hours, but he knew she was hiding something.

After she spent an hour learning about different types of coffins and their specifications, Giulia had enough. She picked the most expensive casket and let the funeral director decide on the flowers.

Her next stop was Father Nello to talk about a date for the funeral.

Giulia stopped at the pedestrian crossing in front of the church, and that was when she saw them: Nello, Lola and a man, who she took to be her cousin's husband. They were all getting into the priest's car.

She made a U-turn and followed them from a safe distance.

That was the road to the police station. Giulia kept hoping their destination was elsewhere until Father Nello's black Volkswagen Golf stopped in front of the big modern and architecturally ugly building. He conveniently parked in front of the entrance, and the trio went into the station. Giulia's fists clenched around the steering wheel until they were white and hurt, but she could not feel anything.

What was Lola doing there? And why was she going to the police with the priest? How much Father Nello knew? And what would he say to the police?

Surely it was not a coincidence that Lola came to Italy for the first time in over twenty years. The same way it couldn't be a coincidence that she was with that priest, the only one who knew the real story. Giulia had never really considered him a danger because what he knew he had learnt through the secrecy of the confessional, but what if he was ready to break his vows?

Giulia had lost any trace of clarity. Everything was blurry, and she was finding it hard to catch her breath. She waited in the car until she saw them coming out. She didn't know how long she'd been sitting there. She had thought of getting out of the vehicle to face them, but something stopped her. Fear! Was this the end of her?

72

PONTE ALTO- ITALY

"Father Nello," Piva exclaimed in surprise as he didn't expect to see the priest again after their last conversation.

"Good to see you, deputy inspector," Nello politely replied, shaking the officer's hand.

"I understand you are busy, Deputy Inspector Piva but I think you would appreciate a chat with this lady. Let me introduce you to Mara's niece, Lola."

Now things were getting interesting, Piva thought while greeting the woman in front of him and the man who introduced himself as the husband.

Piva invited them all to sit, as he sat back behind his desk too.

Father Nello was about to say something when a uniformed officer approached the deputy inspector's desk accompanied by Edda.

Father Nello was about to say hello to her, but she ignored him and went straight to face Lola, "Lola? Is it you?"

Lola took a few seconds to recognise the woman in front of her; Edda had aged so much.

"Edda..." Lola, said in the end, spontaneously hugging her. She had no resentment towards Edda. The woman never really fought to defend her or showed her any favouritism, but at least she had not contributed to making her life a misery.

Edda seemed reluctant and frostily freed herself from Lola's embrace.

Lola instinctively took a step back, slightly hurt by Edda's coldness. She blamed it on the shock of seeing her after all these years.

"Mrs Fano is here to give her statement," the uniformed officer said, speaking directly to Piva.

"Yes, of course," Piva said, pretending he had not forgotten and stood up to shake Edda's hand. Then he instructed officer Furlan to take the old housekeeper statement as he was unexpectedly otherwise engaged.

Following her husband and Nello's suggestions, Lola told the deputy inspector about the calls she had received from her aunt and also about the conversation she had with her cousin.

Piva listened to Lola in silence, but in his head, he was already trying to connect the dots.

The case grew more and more complicated by the hour.

"If you don't mind," Piva started to speak after he was sure Lola had finished with her account of the latest events, "I would like you to meet the chief inspector."

There was no way that Piva could keep this from Zamparelli.

Lola looked at Nello and Fergus, and they both nodded their heads.

Piva lifted the phone on the desk and dialled Zamparelli's direct line, "Inspector, there is someone I want you to meet. It's about the Kopfler case. Can we come to your office? A bit of privacy won't hurt." Piva tried not to say much on the phone but enough for Zamparelli to understand the urgency.

"Please, come with me," Piva stood up and carrying the case file led the way to the inspector's office.

After Piva made the introductions and summarised what Lola had told him, Zamparelli looked the woman straight in the eye, and she felt like she'd have to go through the whole thing all over again, just for the inspector's benefit.

What they had just learnt was not a real break in the case, but it was an essential piece of the puzzle.

Zamparelli thanked Lola, and while standing to shake everyone's hand, he clumsily hit the B&B murder file, which was on the edge of his desk, causing it to fall. Pictures of the crime scene and the victim were now scattered all over the floor. Piva knelt to pick them up as quickly as he could, and both he and the inspector apologised for the gruesomeness of the images.

Lola was staring at the pictures as if hypnotised. Fergus tried to make her look elsewhere, but when he looked down himself, he understood what had so obsessively grabbed his wife's attention.

When Lola eventually managed to take her eyes away from the pictures she exchanged a knowing look with her husband: Were they looking at what they thought they were?

Piva and Zamparelli were police officers long enough not to miss it.

"Mrs Owen, Mr Owen, is everything OK? Is there something you want to share?" Zamparelli made it quite clear that whatever it was that had upset them so much, he had also to know what it was.

"No... yes, I don't know...... sorry, I just thought I recognised something, but I'm sure I'm mistaken," Lola muttered.

"Maybe you are, Lola. Can I call you by your first name?" Lola nodded with her head, and the inspector continued, "But what if you aren't and what if what you saw, or what you know, could help the case? Sometimes we know far more than we realise."

Zamparelli sat back at his desk and gestured to everybody to do the same. Nobody was leaving until he was satisfied with what they told him.

"Now I'm going to show you some pictures, the same ones I dropped on the floor, and you will tell me if there is anything familiar," Zamparelli slowly went through all the B&B crime scene pics with Lola.

"This is all crazy. It can't be ..." Lola nervously started to speak.

Nobody interrupted her, and when she stopped for a few seconds, everybody stayed silent, leaving her all the time she needed to continue, but she didn't.

Fergus spoke instead, "I think my wife recognised a frame that looks exactly like one that we have." His poor Italian made what he said nearly incomprehensible to the inspector and his deputy. They both looked at Lola in the hope she would translate and explain further.

She took one of the pictures and pointed at the frame all covered in blood on the floor, "This picture frame. We have an identical one at home. Well, we had, because now it seems to have vanished."

"Are you sure Mrs Owen, I mean there might be a lot of the same frames sold worldwide," Piva commented back.

"Yeah, see I told you, it's a waste of time, and if you don't mind I'm tired now, and I'd like to go." Lola's annoyance at the way the deputy inspector had doubted her words was palpable.

The inspector threw a killing look at his deputy and then addressed Lola just when she was ready to leave, "Please, wait, tell me about your frame."

Zamparelli didn't know yet how Lola Owens could help the investigation, but he knew that he had to strike the iron while it was hot.

Lola Owen was a crucial part of the puzzle. He only had

to figure out how and she was about to throw some light on it.

"We used to have that same picture frame, by the front door and then all of a sudden one day I couldn't find it anymore. It's surely misplaced somewhere in the house, I mean who would steal only a picture frame, besides there were others on the same table even bigger, if they did it to sell the silver. But then someone must have got into my house without me realising it, and I doubt something like that could have happened." Lola genuinely believed in the irrelevance of her story, but the expression on the inspector's face said otherwise.

Zamparelli mentally went through the conversation he had with the detective from Dublin and felt an electric wave hitting his entire body.

With a frenzy of movements, the inspector took out another picture from the B&B case file, "Do you recognise this woman?"

Lola didn't have to answer; her reaction left no doubt.

Zamparelli explained that the woman she knew as Laura, had most likely introduced herself under a fake identity and that she was the murder victim. Inspector Zamparelli also revealed that he had been in contact with Detective McCarthey from Dublin, who confirmed it was the same woman who attacked Siobhan Drake.

"We still don't have an identity, but Detective McCarthey and I are making our best efforts to find out as soon as possible," Zamparelli concluded.

"So, are you saying she stalked my wife? And then attacked Siobhan? But why?" Fergus spoke slower and tried to be careful about his pronunciation this time.

"We don't know yet if the attack was planned or if it was merely the result of an argument, but most likely, your wife was the one she was after, Mr Owen. "

"That would explain why detective McCarthey called in yesterday looking for me, but we had already left. My in-laws told me about his visit, but I haven't had time to call him back yet," Lola said, still bewildered by the latest revelations.

"Yes, most likely," Zamparelli confirmed.

73

PONTE ALTO - ITALY

Giulia stormed into her office. She threw her bag on the velvet two-seater couch and let herself fall on it in despair. Things were getting out of control. Why was Lola in Italy, and why was she with Father Nello? And most of all, what did he know, and what had he said? Was he ready to spill the beans? Giulia had to know. Only then could she plan her next move, but before doing anything, Giulia had to let it all out.

She rang Carlo, the only person she could trust with this matter: " You won't believe who I just saw, my cousin Lola. She is here."

"What?" It took a few seconds for Carlo to register what his fiancé had just told him, "She might have come for the funeral," he said a bit too innocently and trying not to irritate Giulia any further.

"Are you stupid or what? After the conversation we had on the phone? And what fucking funeral? I don't even know myself when the funeral will be."

"I thought you went to the funeral home and also arranged things with Father Nello this morning," Carlo replied, swallowing his pride in front of Giulia's words. She was obviously in shock and furious. She had to take it out on someone, and he was there.

"Yes, and then I rang Lola, and she used teleportation to be here as soon as she could. What planet are you living on?" Giulia was now shouting. Talking to Carlo should have calmed her down, but it didn't. It looked like he was doing his best to upset her even more.

Carlo was starting to have enough. It took all his goodwill not to shout back while reminding Giulia that the only person who could have told the truth was dead and the other was bound to the secrecy of confession. There was nothing to worry about and as disturbing as the whole thing was, everything would be fine.

"Except the bloody priest was with her, and they went to the police station," Giulia barked.

Carlo eventually understood why she was so agitated. The situation was potentially explosive.

"And do you think the priest had betrayed his vows?" Carlo asked, trying to get a clearer picture of the gravity of the situation.

"That's what I'm planning to find out." Giulia now sounded like she was regaining control.

"But maybe he just said something, but not the full story. It will be hard for whoever to connect all the dots." Carlo could be right, but still, even a few words could lead the investigators to Giulia.

"Never mind whether he told the whole story or not, there will be questions and suspicions. And when they dig deeper into motives and who will benefit from my mother's death, I'll be the first suspect if I'm not already. And then what if they manage to connect Lorna's killing too?"

"OK, I got it. The police will look into you, but you have nothing to do with either murder, right?" Carlo immediately regretted his words.

"See, you suspect me too, so why wouldn't they?" Giulia's tone was defeatedly angry.

"Don't be ridiculous now. Of course, I don't think you had anything to do with your mother's or your aunt's deaths but..." Carlo tried to choose his words carefully. Unfortunately, there was no way to ease what he thought and what he had to say, "...You can't deny you've been acting very weird lately. As if you are hiding something and you are afraid. Afraid of something you can't even trust telling me."

Giulia didn't know how to reply. He was right. She was afraid, and she was hiding things from him, but the time was never right, and then lies started to build up. Now the time to be honest with each other had arrived, for the sake of their relationship.

Giulia took a deep breath and started to talk again, but this time slowly and calmly, "You are right. I'm keeping something from you, but I don't want to tell you over the phone. I'll be home in a couple of hours. First I want to pay a visit to Nello and try to find out where my cousin is staying and talk to her too."

* * *

Fergus and Lola turned down Nello's offer of a lift back to the hotel. They needed some time alone to process everything that was going on.

"Let me at least take you out for dinner tonight," Nello said in the full spirit of hospitality but also feeling responsible for having dragged the couple into this mess. They agreed to see each other at the hotel around eight and went separate ways.

The sky was foggy from the high humidity, and that made the heat feel even heavier. Lola sprayed more sun cream on her husband's arms and legs and started to walk back to the hotel. His fair Irish skin was already getting worryingly red.

They walked for a while without saying a word. When the couple stopped at a pedestrian traffic light, to wait for the green signal, Fergus broke the silence and asked his wife if and when she intended to see her cousin.

"I don't think I'll need to," Lola said, looking straight in front of her and making eye contact with the driver of the car that had just passed them. Fergus was about to ask his wife what she meant when the same vehicle which had captured Lola's attention made a sudden U-turn. A concert of angry horns followed and then the car pulled over. A tall, beautiful woman got out, but unfortunately, the expression on her face didn't promise anything good, and it didn't take a genius to guess who she was.

"Giulia," Lola exclaimed more as a warning to Fergus than a greeting to her cousin.

"What are you doing here?" Giulia went, completely ignoring Fergus who was standing there in the middle of what could quickly develop into a catfight.

"What has that priest told you? Did he call you because of my mother? Or did you talk to her but lied to me on the phone?" Giulia fired all her questions with ice-cold eyes fixed on her cousin's face.

Fergus was about to say something. Even if he had not entirely caught what Giulia had said and his Italian was not the best, he still felt he had to defend his wife. Lola touched his arm and stopped him, "It's OK. I can handle this."

"Listen to me. I flew over only to find myself involved in a big surreal mess that is not my fault and has nothing to do with me. I spent the morning at the police station. I don't even know why myself. So far, my day has been shitty enough without you attacking me and accusing me of things I can't even understand. Why I'm here is my business, and if I had the stupid idea to call you and maybe to see you as civil cousins might normally do, I now believe I should stay as far away as possible from you. This family is rotten to the core."

Lola made a promise to herself a long time ago: She would not allow any of the Kopflers to bully her ever again. They could still upset her and disrupt her life, as was the case now, but they could not victimise her. Not anymore.

"I couldn't agree more. You better stay away from me and this place. Get on the first plane and go back to where you have been hiding all these years." The fear of what Lola's presence could mean for her and the anger that things were not going as she planned, made Giulia overcome the surprise of seeing Lola so aggressive. She wanted to sound cruel, and she did. But Lola had no intention to step back, not this time.

"I didn't escape and neither did I hide. I simply cut the evil out of my existence. Where instead, I see you embraced it fully, as is the family tradition." Lola turned her back to her cousin and started walking away with Fergus by her side. She stopped after a few steps, Giulia was still standing there on the path when her cousin gave her the last blow, "And as for my staying here, I'll leave when it pleases me, not when an angry, bitter, miserable woman like you tells me to."

Lola could not believe she had just said that. Maybe those insults were excessive, but it felt so good. For once they were even.

Lola and Fergus kept walking, and a few seconds later, they heard a car skidding away. Giulia's.

Fergus gave a high five to his wife, "Honey, I missed most of it, but you sounded amazing."

"Was I too mean?" Lola asked a bit embarrassed.

"Not at all, you were great, and that bitch deserved it all. Whatever you said to her. Maybe next time talk slower so I can get more words," Fergus replied, throwing an arm around his wife's shoulders.

"Good, because it felt great to say all those things to her," Lola laughed as the adrenaline was still pumping in her veins.

"OK, enough of evil wife version for today. Let's grab an

ice cream," Fergus suggested smiling and pointing at the ice cream shop across the road.

The couple sat at one of the few tables the ice cream parlour had outside in the shade and started to lick their cones voraciously. Vanilla and mint for Fergus and banana and chocolate with whipped cream on the top for Lola.

"I think we should get the first flight back to Dublin. There is nothing else here for us to do. I said what I had to say. I heard what I had to hear, and as for Laura's story, Detective McCarthey will keep investigating anyway."

"Or we could stay and try to relax. Leave on Saturday with the direct flight from Venice. The boys are fine, and my parents are more than happy to mind them. We could use this time for a mini holiday. You know, to make this mess and all these troubles worthwhile," Fergus lowered his sunglasses and winked at his wife.

"You are incredible, relaxing like it's a little holiday in the middle of two murders and a family nightmare?"

"Yes, but we are done with that, aren't we? And after that evil performance of yours, I doubt your cousin will disturb us."

Fergus had a point, and Lola had to admit that it was tempting to spend a few days on their own in beautiful Italy, if only they were somewhere not connected to her past it would have been perfect but, as she always said to the boys, you get what you get and don't get upset.

"OK then, we'll stay until Saturday."

Lola smiled to a pleased Fergus and licked around her cone as the ice cream dripped on her hand.

74

PONTE ALTO - ITALY

"Edda, what are you doing here?" Giulia couldn't disguise her surprise seeing the woman leaving the rectory.

"Giulia darling, how are you doing?" Edda instinctively hugged her.

"I'm fine," Giulia said, not sounding persuading even to herself.

Edda caressed her face like she was still the little girl she used to spoil on the sly, "Everything will be fine."

Giulia stared at the old woman in front of her for a moment. Her words sounded so truthful, but Giulia didn't feel reassured and instead wondered if there was more behind them. Maybe Edda knew more than she showed.

Edda started to talk again, breaking the silence. Giulia wasn't listening, as her head filled with suspicions. When she managed to regain control of her paranoid thoughts, and started smiling at Edda pretending to have heard everything she had just said.

"Well, I better go now. I only came to ask Father Nello if I could sing in the choir for your mum's funeral, but he doesn't know when it will be yet." Edda concluded her monologue but didn't intend to leave until she had received an answer to the question hidden in her sentence.

"That's why I'm here. We don't have a date yet, but I need to talk to Father Nello about arrangements and something else," Giulia quickly replied.

"Good, take care of yourself Giulia. I might see you at the house maybe tomorrow or in the next few days?"

"Sure," Giulia replied, moving along in a hurry to end the conversation. The house was, in fact, another thing that Giulia had to sort out. She had no intention to keep that mausoleum. Everything spoke of Mara in there, and Giulia didn't need another reminder of how great and powerful her mother had been. She had already contacted an estate agent to list it but had not dared to tell Edda yet. Even after Mara died, Edda kept going to the house every day to clean. Giulia knew that to Edda it was more than a job. After she lost her family, it became her life, but she had no choice now but to let her go. Giulia pushed that thought away; it was a concern for another day. Now she had to focus on Father Nello. She approached the rectory's door and knocked.

"Giulia," Father Nello greeted her opening the door, "I guess you are here about the funeral. I know they finally released your poor mother's body."

"And that's not the only thing you know, right, Father?" Giulia pushed herself inside.

"I don't know what you are talking about," Nello replied, upset by her aggressiveness.

"Oh, I think you do, Father. So please don't play the part with me. I know my mother told you everything about Lorna and what she had done. But I also know she told it in confession, so I wonder what kind of twisted game you are playing."

"I'm not playing any game, and I'm a priest Giulia, I take my vows very seriously as much as my duty to comfort my parishioners and guide them to make the right decisions."

"Oh yes, and with Lola, what were you doing with her? Guiding her too? To the police?" Giulia got straight to the point, "Did my mother promise you money to help her fulfil her obnoxious plan? Is that what you are doing?"

"This is offensive!" The priest had no intention to let Giulia offend him and question his decency and integrity.

"No Father," Giulia continued pointing her index finger in front of the priest's face, "what is offensive is to see a man of the church betraying his cassock. If I can give you a piece of advice, stop before it's too late."

"I must ask you to leave now, Giulia. Maybe we can talk about Mara's funeral another day when you are calmer and less angry."

Father Nello opened the door and kept it open for Giulia to leave.

"You stay out of my business and my family's business, or else I'll destroy you."

Father Nello closed the door behind Giulia, her words and her gaze made him feel extremely uncomfortable, nearly afraid of what she could do or, of what she had done already. Maybe Mara's concerns were not unfounded. Calling Lola and going to the police had been the right thing to do, and now he was more certain than ever.

He checked his watch; there was still plenty of time before meeting the Owens for dinner. He could do with a short nap. It had been a long day, and he was not getting any younger. Father Nello was lying in bed, but for some reason, he couldn't get any rest. Giulia's words about her mother and her cousin kept resonating in his mind and flashes of the B&B victim kept coming up in his memory. There was something about that woman that disturbed him, and it was not the way she had died.

He had not said anything at the station because he didn't know what it was himself, but now, Father Nello suddenly realised what was so disturbing in that face: he knew it.

Everything made sense. Every piece of the puzzle was now in the correct place. He jumped out of bed, took Deputy Inspector Piva's business card and started to dial the number on it.

"Inspector Piva, it's me, Father Nello. I know who the B&B victim is! Please ring me as soon as you can."

Nello hoped Piva called him back as soon as he had listened at his voicemail and before he met Lola.

He wanted the police to know first, but surely he couldn't face an entire evening with Lola and Fergus without telling them what he had just found out. He sat back on the bed, looking at the peaceful nature scene outside, its apparent stillness, and he wished he could be part of it. Nello checked his watch and realised it was nearly time to go now.

He was tying his shoelaces when the doorbell rang. He rushed himself to the door full of expectations. He hoped that considering the urgency of his call, Piva had decided to see him in person.

"Oh, it's you. Have you forgotten to tell me something?" The priest's disappointment at not finding the deputy inspector at his doorstep, made him sound nearly rude.

"I'm sorry, but I'm in a hurry. I have an appointment," Father Nello added, not in an attempt to justify his tone but more to disengage himself. He was not in the mood, nor had he the time.

His visitor kept staring at him in silence.

Father Nello took a step back inside. Something was not right.

"What do you want?" He asked, but his words remained unanswered. The door closed, and he felt a sharp pain in his abdomen; he looked down and saw the blade of a kitchen knife penetrating his body and his blood dripping onto the floor.

75

PONTE ALTO - ITALY

It had been a very long day. Deputy Inspector Luca Piva couldn't wait to get home, throw himself under the shower and get ready for his date. Since the day he saw Zoe Falck at the Swhartze Guest House, he could not get her out of his head.

Unfortunately, the rule was a simple one: never date someone involved in a case. Luca Piva already broke it once, and it had been a disaster. He was not going to make the same mistake twice. The deputy inspector patiently waited until they cleared Zoe Falck from the investigation, and only then asked her out. Zoe had accepted his invitation in such a hurry that made Piva believe she was waiting for that call too. He shaved, sprinkled some cologne over his cheeks and jumped into a pair of jeans and a polo t-shirt.

While in the shower, Piva thought he had heard his phone, but ignored it. Tonight, he had promised himself not to let his job or anything else interfere with his plans. He was off duty, no exceptions.

The drive to Zoe's place took only 15 minutes. He knew she was still living with her parents and hoped she was waiting outside for him. Luca Piva tended to get uncomfortable around girls' parents. The greetings, the introductions, the pressure to make a good impression and, most of all, the feeling that once you had met the parents, things were inevitably getting serious. He stopped the car at the address she had given him, Zoe was waiting for him outside. She was stunning in that short black dress.

"Hi," Zoe opened the front door smiling and closed it nearly immediately behind her.

"Hi," Piva said back, relieved to be safe. There were no parents to meet.

The deputy inspector had booked a table in a restaurant further up the mountains overlooking the valley.

Luca and Zoe spent the evening chatting and didn't realise how late it was until one by one all the other guests had left, and the waiters started very discreetly to send signals that they had to close.

"I think we better go now before they throw us out," Zoe said, looking at the staff busily tidying up around them.

The deputy inspector asked for the bill and suggested going somewhere else. He was tired, but at the same time, he didn't want a pleasant evening to end.

"It's getting late, and we both have to work tomorrow. I say we better call it a night."

"Yes, maybe you're right," Piva replied. Disappointed, but knowing it was true as he hardly could hold back a big yawn.

When he stopped in front of Zoe's house, there was the usually uncomfortable silence and embarrassed uncertainty about what next, that comes with any first date.

"I truly enjoyed myself tonight," Zoe broke the silence. She smiled, kissed the deputy inspector on the lips and got out of the car.

When he arrived home, Luca Piva was in an ecstatic state, still feeling Zoe's velvety lips on his. He stripped himself naked and collapsed on the bed. He stared at the ceiling, smiling: The date has been a success. Not only had he managed to erase from his thoughts murders and murderers, but also Zoe Falck liked him. There was no doubt about it.

His eyelids were getting heavier, and when he was falling into Morpheo's arms, the sound of an incoming text message on his phone made his eyes open wide.

It was Zoe texting to know if Luca got home safe.

He did and replied so with the promise to call her the following day.

Piva was about to switch off the phone when he noticed he also had a missed call and a voice mail.

Father Nello's message sounded undoubtedly urgent. Piva checked the time, 1:30 am. Too late to ring him back. He would reach him first thing in the morning.

The following morning, on his way to the station, Piva tried to ring Father Nello repeatedly but never got an answer. His instinct told him there was something wrong. He made a u-turn and headed towards the rectory instead. Piva knocked on the door vigorously, and while waiting for someone to open, he tried to ring Nello one more time. The priest was not answering, but Piva could hear his phone ringing inside the house. The deputy inspector pushed down the door's handle. It wasn't locked, and he went in.

* * *

"Inspector, we have another one."

"Piva where are you. Why are you not here yet? And we have another one of what? I'm not in the mood for riddles this morning," Zamparelli replied cantankerously.

"We have another murder, Sir. "

"What? What is it now, an epidemic?"

"It's the priest, Sir. Someone stabbed him at his home."

"God Damn it. And we can't blame it on an unfortunate coincidence, can we?" A rhetorical question Piva knew he didn't have to answer.

"OK. I'm on my way." Zamparelli grabbed his linen suit jacket from the back of the chair and left.

"The guys in white are already processing the scene, and Ferrari is examining the body." Piva updated the chief inspector while handing him a pair of latex gloves and shoe covers.

"Good job Piva," Zamparelli patted his deputy on the shoulder and went to position himself behind the coroner.

"Before you ask, inspector, he presumably died between 7 and 9 last night, but it's hard to say precisely because of the heat. Stabbed twice in the abdomen, close range."

"So, he presumably knew his killer. What do you say, Doc?"

"Well, I would say so. As you can see, there are no signs of defence or struggle," Ferrari lifted father Nello's arms to show the total absence of wounds.

"Did he die instantly, or could he have been saved if someone would have found him earlier?" Piva asked, jumping in between the inspector and the coroner.

"Most likely no. I don't think so. The first stab was not lethal, but the second one perforated some of the vital organs and went so deep that the killer must have also made quite of an effort to remove the knife from the body." Ferrari closed his doctor's bag and stood up.

Piva nodded and walked off.

"And what about the weapon?" Zamparelli asked still following his deputy with his peripheral vision. He didn't miss that there was more behind Piva's question to the coroner.

"From the cut, I'd say a regular kitchen knife."

"A weapon of chance. Maybe the killer didn't come intending to kill. They argued, and things got out of hand,

and he or she grabbed a knife from the kitchen," Zamparelli suggested.

"No, I think the killer brought the knife along. From the blood on the floor, Father Nello was killed here. If he had an argument with the killer and the killer went to the other room to get a knife, why didn't the priest run?" Ferrari stated authoritatively.

"Yes, it doesn't make sense. I'm sure the guys in white will confirm there isn't any knife missing from the knife block or the drawers in the kitchen," Zamparelli agreed.

The inspector and his deputy went back to the station in separate cars as they came. As soon as they arrived, the inspector ordered his deputy to follow him into his office.

"OK, now can you tell me what's wrong with you? What was that question to Ferrari? And your face, like you had seen a ghost? Well, I suppose you had, but it's not the first time."

Piva took a seat in front of his boss, took out his mobile and played the message Father Nello had left on his voice mail.

"I didn't hear it until it was too late to call him back. I called him this morning first thing, but he never answered. My instinct told me something was wrong, and that's why I went to the rectory before coming to the station."

The inspector said nothing.

"I could have saved him. If I had picked up my phone if I had checked my missed calls. His death is on me." Piva struggled to keep his emotions at bay.

Zamparelli was not good at consoling people, but he felt sorry for the guy.

"Listen to me, Piva. Recompose yourself please. You know I'm not good with emotional situations, but I can tell you one thing: the priest's murder had nothing to do with you. You would have been too late anyway. You heard Ferrari; the second stab was lethal. There was no way you could have saved him, no matter how early you had arrived at the scene. His death is on whoever stabbed him."

Piva lifted his face. Rationally the inspector was right, but he still felt an atrocious sense of guilt.

"Now, Piva, doing this to yourself won't do any good either to you or the investigations, which are now three. Do you want me to blame you because you should have answered your phone? Well, yes, I could, and you could have been more alert considering the mess we have on our hands, but you didn't have to. Once you are off duty, you are off duty. You can't work 24/7, and you can't let the job take over your private life. Trust me on this. I made that mistake, and I paid a hefty price for it."

Piva was grateful for Zamparelli's understanding.

He had expected the chief to lose it and blame him, instead, he didn't, and he also shared something about his private life, which was still a mystery to everybody at the station. Piva recomposed himself and sat up as straight as he could. It was time to set his feelings and remorse aside and get back to work.

"Do you think the three murders are all connected?" the deputy inspector asked even if he already knew the answer.

"I'd like to say no. But I know they are. The question is, how?" Inspector Furio Zamparelli started to feel defeated.

"If we only knew what Mara Kopfler told Father Nello," Piva said investigating possible scenarios in his head.

"Whatever it was, it is harmful enough for someone to kill to keep it quiet!"

76

PONTE ALTO - ITALY

"Are you sitting inspector? Because if you aren't, you'd better do so," Dr Steno Ferrari sounded overexcited.

"Now you are scaring me, Steno," the inspector blurted out.

"You must be, to call me by my first name," Ferrari couldn't help the joke.

"Doc, I guarantee you you'll be scared too, but of my reaction, if you don't tell me what you are ringing me for," Furio Zamparelli was in no mood for jokes.

"I know who the B&B victim is!" The coroner said loosely concealing the pleasure in his voice.

Zamparelli shifted uncomfortably in his chair, feeling a sense of Déjà vu: the same words Father Nello had spoken.

"I have to warn you Doc, the last person who said that ended up on your table."

The coroner didn't know what Zamparelli was talking about, but it only took a look at the body in front of him to connect the dots: "The priest?" he asked.

"Yes, but I will fill you in later, go on now. Who is she and how the hell did you find out her identity?" Now the inspector's tone had that hint of excitement and urgency that Steno

Ferrari had expected to hear since the beginning of their conversation.

"OK, inspector. Sit tight. I'm pretty sure your victim is Lorna Kopfler."

"That's impossible. She died nearly forty years ago."

"I know, it sounds crazy, but DNA doesn't lie. "

"Are you sure, I mean, it could have been contaminated in the lab or something?" Zamparelli tried not to sound doubtful towards Ferrari's professionalism, but it was hard not to be incredulous.

"No. I'm positive. Mara's and Lorna's bodies never came in contact, and neither did the samples of fluids. They share 50% of segments, and you see, that only exists in the case of siblings. And because there wasn't a third sister, it has to be her."

"But how did it come up only now? Those results should have shown up from the autopsies as soon they were performed?" Zamparelli still could not believe what he was hearing but, he knew that without being one hundred per cent sure, Ferrari would have never said anything.

"I didn't do the autopsy on Mara Kopfler myself. My assistant did. I ran the toxicology tests and focused mainly on her bloodstreams because of the drugs she ingested before she was suffocated. I never looked at her DNA. Well, there was no reason for me to do so. But today, I was filing the reports away, when something caught my eye: the victim from the B&B and Mrs Kopfler shared the same DNA," the coroner explained.

"This is beyond imagination. You are telling me that Mara Kopfler staged her sister's death or Lorna herself did it with the cooperation of her sister and nobody ever questioned the events?" Zamparelli was now massaging his temples as he felt like his head was exploding.

"I suppose even if they never recovered the body, nobody had any reason to question Mara and Renzo's account of the events. They gave a meticulous and plausible version of what had happened. Lorna was depressed; she tried to kill herself and her baby. Renzo managed to save the baby, Lola, but he had no time to go back for the mother who drowned. Nobody had seen anything, the only two witnesses were Mara and Renzo, as Lola was only an infant. The police just took their story for granted. Everybody knew how troubled Lorna was. And that was it. Like mother like daughter if you want! Sad but true!"

"I don't understand. Why in all these years had Lorna never contacted her daughter? And how is it possible that nobody recognised her once she came back?"

"Well, Zamparelli, that is your job to find out. What I can tell you is that the two women were sisters. I can also tell you that Lorna's brain was damaged. She had dementia. Maybe she came back to amend her past before it was too late." The coroner suggested proudly of his investigative instinct.

"Yes, but someone stopped her before she could."

Zamparelli finally knew who his victim was, but this seemed to generate more questions than answers.

"Oh, Zamparelli, before you go. I've not said anything to the superintendent yet. I thought you might want to deal with that yourself. I mean when and how to inform Di Fazio."

"Thank you, I appreciate that, and the work you have done, Steno."

* * *

Piva had just arrived at the Kopfler Grand Hotel to find out that the Owens were out. He left a message for them at the reception to call him back as soon as possible. He didn't want to break the news about Father Nello over the phone, that they were not answering anyway.

"Piva, did you reach the Owens yet?" The deputy inspector had just got into his car when the inspector called.

"No, they were out. I'm coming back to the station."

"Do you know where they are? "

"They just went for a drive. That's what they told me at the hotel. They are not answering their phones, so I left a message asking to contact me as soon as possible."

"OK, you get your ass back here as soon as you can. Something came up that can eventually bring our investigations forward. All three of them. In the meantime, I'll send someone to find them and bring them to the station."

Piva pushed his right foot on the accelerator and drove careless of the speed limit towards the station.

"Can I come in?" Piva popped his head halfway into Zamparelli's office.

"Come in and close the door, Piva. Have you heard back from the Owens?"

"No, Sir. Nothing yet. Poor guys, what a fucked-up mess," the deputy said, taking a seat at the inspector's desk.

"Well, Piva, I'm afraid that what they have been through so far, is nothing compared to what is now coming their way."

"What do you mean, Sir? Do you think they are in danger too?" Piva asked alarmed.

"I can't be sure, but they could be," Zamparelli's facial expression and tone were undeniably serious while he updated his deputy on everything Ferrari had found out.

"Jesus Christ," Deputy Inspector Luca Piva exclaimed rubbing his face with both his hands.

"Listen to me, Piva. If you think about it, it all makes sense. Even the picture frame Lola thought she recognised. It has to be hers. Lorna stole it from her house to have a picture of her daughter and her family. She was not stalking Lola. Lorna's interest in her was not malicious. The woman was only trying to approach her daughter. Reconnect with her."

"Of course, and she did it only now because she could not wait. She had no time left before her dementia would degenerate," Piva added, and continued, "but Lola Owens thinks her mother is dead,"

"Yes, Piva. Because Mara had told Lola the same story she had told everybody else. "

"But what did she say to Lorna to keep her away for so long?" Piva still could not make sense of this.

"This is what I think happened," the inspector continued to talk, "Mara and Renzo didn't just save the baby from drowning but also Lorna. Keep in mind their mother took her own life too. Depression runs in the family, or at least a certain fragility for sure. When they realised she was totally out of control, they made her disappear, probably to some psychiatric clinic abroad. I suppose in Mara and Renzo's mind it was for the best. Lorna could get the care she needed, and Mara could take control of everything: family, business, assets. "

"But what about Lola?" Piva interrupted. The cruelty of depriving a child of her mother was something beyond comprehension for him.

"Lola was a problem with an easy solution. Mara told her that Lorna took her own life and avoided further enquiries from the child." Zamparelli theory was legit, but to Piva, there were still too many holes in it, "And Lorna? I mean she knew her daughter was alive, even admitting she was mentally unstable, she must have tried to contact her daughter over the years."

"Yes, and she most likely did. But as resourceful as Mara was, she must have dismissed her sister's requests saying Lola didn't want to have anything to do with her. Or something like that. After all, who would want to keep in touch with a mother who first tries to kill you and then abandons you for years? And so, Mara went along with her lies as long as she could."

"Until Lorna discovered she had dementia," Piva eventually made sense of things," and that is when things got complicated. Mara always had significant power over her sister, but Lorna's desire to see her daughter and talk to her, probably even to ask for forgiveness, before her illness destroyed her, was stronger."

"Precisely. And that must have triggered Lorna's return to Ponte Alto. What Mara had confessed to Father Nello was certainly the truth about what she had done. I think that was also what she wanted to tell Lola. Maybe she felt the call of her conscience or, more probably, Lorna gave her an ultimatum. Either Mara came clean herself, or she would have exposed her."

"That's a motive, Inspector."

"Yes, Piva. And guess whose interest it is not to have the truth to come out?" Zamparelli grinned.

"Giulia Kopfler!" the two officers said in unison.

"I don't see anybody else who could have a stronger motive or opportunity, and she has a very weak alibi for all three murders. That should be enough to search Giulia's office, her house and Mara's."

Zamparelli victoriously picked up the phone to call the judge.

77

PONTE ALTO - ITALY

The patrol car with Lola and Fergus Owen had just arrived at the station.

"You start talking to them. I want to call Detective McCarthey. He needs to know sooner rather than later," Zamparelli told Piva, who was leaving the chief's office to join the Owens in one of the interrogation room. Not a cosy place but at least nobody would disturb them in there.

When the deputy inspector entered the room, Fergus could not disguise his anger. In the best Italian he could muster, he harshly complained about the way the uniformed officers forced them into their car and brought them to the station with no explanation, and then dumped them in that hole of a room like criminals.

Piva had no words to express his sorrow for the couple and everything they had gone through, and even less so, to tell them the latest developments. He presented the facts in the most straightforward way possible. Neither Lola nor Fergus said a single word nor interrupted him once.

They held hands and listened to the deputy inspector with wide, shock-filled eyes. Eyes that Piva would hardly ever forget. It was not the first time the deputy inspector delivered bad news to the victim's family, but this was not going to fade in his memory.

When Zamparelli made his appearance, his deputy had just finished talking. The atmosphere in the room was surreal. Lola stood up and headed for the door. She didn't ask for permission to leave, but nobody objected.

Fergus followed his wife, and before stepping out, he turned toward the two officers whose mortification was genuine, "Sorry."

Lola felt empty and exhausted as she had never felt before. She hugged her husband burying her face in his chest, grateful he was there with her. On the drive back to the hotel, neither of them said a word. Only when they were back to their room did Lola start to cry. Fergus held her tight and let her weep until she had no more tears to cry.

"Am I supposed to feel something? And if so, what am I supposed to feel?" Lola asked her husband, raising her face to him. Her red and swollen eyes showed suffering he had never seen before.

"You are not supposed to feel anything else but what you feel, honey. Feeling one thing rather than something else doesn't make us a good or a bad person. It only makes us who we are." Fergus was heartbroken to see his wife in such agony.

"I'm not sad because Lorna is dead. I'm not sad because Mara is dead. And I'm not sad for the priest either. He dragged me into all this. I'm angry, and I feel betrayed. Am I a monster?"

"You are not!" Fergus answered with the sweetest of tones.

"But I come from that family; there must be something evil in me too," more tears filled Lola's eyes.

Fergus lifted her face gently and delicately wiped her tears away.

"Now listen to me. You are one of the kindest people I know. You have nothing to do with that family. You left before they could poison you with their venom. Your aunt did nothing but make your life miserable. You owe her nothing and for sure, not grief. As for your mother, I can't tell you what to feel, and honestly, I can't even start to imagine what you are going through right now. But when I met you, you had no mother. She was dead long before now. It's sad. You are entitled to feel sad and angry against those who had taken her away from you for all these years. But honestly, I don't think you can miss what you've never had."

Fergus had to summon all his will to sound calm because right now, he felt the most intense rage he had ever experienced in his entire life. He was furious with every single member of the Kopfler family and everyone else involved in this nightmare that was causing so much sorrow to his wife.

Lola felt reassured. Her husband was undoubtedly right, and he was rational about it all.

Out of exhaustion she eventually fell asleep, but nightmares and worries tormented her rest. Lola had so many questions, and some of them would probably never find an answer.

Lola wouldn't miss the mother she never had, but she would forever wonder how different her life could have been knowing that Lorna was alive.

The following morning when she got up, Fergus was already dressed and on the balcony, speaking on the phone. The balcony door was open, and she could hear him talking, presumably to Angela or Pat.

Lola felt relieved it had been Fergus who told his parents. They had the right to know, and she wanted them to know. They were the only family she had ever had, but still, she could not help but feel embarrassed. It was not her fault, they would never judge, but once again, it was her messy family that spoiled everybody else's existence.

How nice it would have been to have a typical ordinary decent family and two parents like Pat and Angela.

The only thing that made Lola feel better was the fact that everything she never had herself; she was making sure her kids would have. The thought of the twins made her smile, and suddenly she missed them so much. She went to the balcony and whispered to Fergus to ask his parents to put them on the phone.

Ireland was an hour behind, and they most certainly had not left for school yet.

"Mum, are you crying? Why?"

Lola wiped her eyes, "No silly, why would I cry? I'm afraid I caught a bit of cold here. Now you better go to school, you don't want to be late on the last day of school, right? I'll talk to you tonight."

Angela took the phone, "Lola darling, I don't know what to say except that I love you. You are like a daughter, and like you were my own daughter, I'm telling you that everything is going to be OK. Time is a healer."

"I love you too, Angela."

The only words Lola managed to speak before she started weeping again.

78

DUBLIN - IRELAND

McCarthey strived to understand what Zamparelli had just told him. This was far beyond imagination unless you were a screenwriter of some South-American telenovelas. He called Kevin into the office and repeated the whole story to him.

"Wow this is crazy, but at least we can close the case."

"Well, yes, I suppose so, Kevin. I only have to inform the Drakes, and then we can forget about this damn case," McCarthey said, stretching his long bulky arms behind his head.

"And what about Mrs Drake? Are you going to do anything about the fact that she lied about her memory?" Kevin asked, already at the door.

"No. I convinced myself she did it for all the right reasons and, frankly, everybody has already suffered enough in this story. There will be no mention of this in the records."

Kevin looked dubious; he was not comfortable on omitting pieces of information from the official papers.

"Believe me, Kevin. It's the most considerate and gracious thing to do, plus it will spare us all a lot of hassle. Unless of course, you want to stay on the case filling in paperwork for another good while," McCarthey said, reading Kevin's face.

"You are probably right, Sir." The thought of himself sitting at the desk submerged by more paperwork, made Kevin keen to agree with his boss.

With that, McCarthey switched off his computer and left. He didn't take Kevin with him to speak to the Drakes as he had planned to go straight home afterwards. It was Friday, and he had promised his daughters to take them out for ice cream.

When Siobhan opened the door, the detective nearly didn't recognise her.

Her impeccable makeup was applied with undeniable expertise. Her hair perfectly tied in a bun on the back of her head with only a few locks coming wildly down on the side. She was not dressed to impress but to be comfortable and yet chic. White full leg linen trousers and a matching tunic on top embellished with a long coral necklace.

"Detective!" Siobhan said surprised to see the officer at her doorstep and not sure if it was a good or a bad sign.

"Mrs Drake, I'm glad to see you are well enough to be home."

"Thank you. You have no idea how good it feels to be home and in my own clothes, rather than in the hospital nightgown," Siobhan replied, laughing. McCarthey's chirpy tone had relaxed her.

"I can imagine," Enda McCarthey laughed back. The woman was incredible and so not an obvious match for her husband or at least not from the exterior but as they say, opposites attract each other. And just when the detective was trying not to laugh at the mental image of Finn Drake boringly watching the evening news sitting in his favourite armchair while his petulant wife talked to him from all over the house, he, in person, appeared behind Siobhan.

"Honey, who is it?" and immediately after, "Detective," he exclaimed in surprise too.

"Mr Drake," the detective extended his hand to shake Finn's.

"Has anything happened?" Finn asked quite directly.

"Well, there is something I think you should know. About the case."

Siobhan and Finn invited McCarthey in and had him take a seat in the sitting room.

It was a pontifical room, full of antique furniture, two big three-seater couches facing each other, and in between them a coffee table made of glass and marble.

Enda McCarthey lost his balance when taking his seat as the sofa completely swallowed him in.

"Sorry, it's an old couch, but we love it, and it's excellent for napping in," Finn Drake giggled aloud.

"I see," the detective agreed, bringing himself into the straightest position possible and having to rethink some of his opinions about Dr Drake.

"Oh my gosh. I still can't believe it," Siobhan commented after the detective had told them the entire story about Lorna/Laura and about how her sister faked her death.

"And how is Lola? She must feel tremendously confused. Oh my gosh, I can't even imagine how the poor thing must feel. This is the most atrocious family story I've ever heard."

Everything in Siobhan's body language was exaggerated, but it was not fake: she was genuinely a walking drama.

"Yes, well I suppose finding out something like that would shock anybody. I haven't spoken to Mrs Owen yet. My colleague from the Italian police did."

"And do Fergus's parents know yet? As you probably know, they mind the twins at the moment. Should we go talk to them?" Siobhan asked.

McCarthey suggested keeping the whole matter to themselves for now. Most likely, Lola and Fergus had informed them by now, but just in case they hadn't yet, it would be sensitive not to mention anything.

The detective's visit was over. He stood up, and the Drakes walked him to the door. Finn and Siobhan Drake waited for him to get into the car and waved goodbye. The detective had to admit that he was starting to like the couple, despite their oddities.

He turned on the engine and the speaker phone.

"Start getting ready and thinking about which ice-cream flavour you want, I'm on my way."

79

PONTE ALTO - ITALY

"Damn priest, I've been trying to call him since yesterday about this bloody funeral," Giulia threw her mobile on the couch and went outside to the balcony with her cup of coffee.

Carlo was in the kitchen, still making his coffee and deciding whether to join his fiancée or stay away from her. He felt she needed a bit of space.

The stress of recent events had inevitably affected their relationship as Giulia's nerves were beyond tense but, what put the icing on the cake, was the previous night's confession about the forged signatures. Carlo had done things he had not been proud of throughout his career, and some of them were at the limit of legality. But what Giulia did was far too much, even for him. She indeed secured them the loan they needed but at what price? If someone found out, they could charge her with fraud, with him as an accessory. He could say goodbye to his business. And if this were not enough, the discovery of these actions would have given her one more motive to want her mother dead. Carlo was still furious with Giulia.

Their previous night's conversation and the fight that followed kept coming back into his mind. In the end, she had found a way to blame him. She said he had cornered her, and he put her under pressure. She had no choice but to do it, for him and to avoid him being eaten alive by the loan shark and lose his business.

Carlo thought it was all bullshit, and if she expected gratitude from him, she was wrong.

He went to the sitting room and switched on the TV. He was still too upset to face Giulia. She, on the other hand, was still consumed by her pride and had no intention to make the first step towards reconciliation.

"Giulia, Giulia…Come over here. Now!" Carlo screamed after the news started.

"Hey, is it too much to ask for you not to scream at me like that?" Giulia came in prepared for another fight.

Carlo was staring at the screen. Giulia was about to lash out as he first rushed her in, and then continued to watch TV ignoring her. Only when she looked at the screen too, she understood.

They were showing images of Ponte Alto's church, and rectory and a body in a white bag brought away. Someone had stabbed Father Nello Santini to death.

Giulia's jaw dropped. Carlo turned to her: his face had an expression that she had never seen before.

"No, no, no, wait a minute," she said, "you don't think I've something to do with this? Carlo, you can't seriously think I did something to the priest." Giulia took a step back. As bad as they had fought the previous night, and even considering her recent behaviour, she could not believe Carlo could ever suspect her. He was the man who was supposed to love and support her.

Carlo had repressed all his doubts until now, but the killing of the priest could not be a coincidence. In one way or another, anyone who had been in Giulia's way to control the family business had somehow ended up dead. He felt disgusted at even the idea of such a suspicion, but he couldn't ignore the facts any longer. Giulia had lied to him and the bank, and she did it magisterially. What else could she be lying about? To protect her interests, she went as far as to commit fraud. Could she have pushed herself as far as murder too?

Giulia kept looking at him with a wounded look, that failed to call for any mercy from Carlo, he didn't trust her anymore.

"What Giulia? What should I think? Do you want to tell me?" Carlo was shouting, his face red.

"What do you want me to say? I don't have to defend myself, or at least I thought so. Not with you. You know who I am and what I'm capable of or not," Giulia screamed back with a violence that left Carlo astonished.

"No Giulia, I don't know who you are or what you are capable of. Not anymore."

Giulia was losing the only man she had ever loved, and she knew it.

"Listen to me, I know I should not have forged those signatures, and I shouldn't have kept it from you, but Mara would never have signed. I know you don't want to hear it, but I did it for you and us."

Giulia broke into tears, her cry was desperate, but Carlo couldn't tell anymore whether she was acting. Part of him wanted to hug her and tell her that everything was going to be alright, but another part of him could not trust the woman in front of him, not anymore. He left and went to the bedroom to get dressed.

He sat on the bed and tried to collect his thoughts. In fairness over the last few months, he had pressed Giulia to get that money. What if she genuinely felt desperate to help him? And in exchange, he questioned her integrity and morality and even accused her of murder.

When Carlo reappeared in the sitting room, Giulia was sitting on the floor, still sobbing. Her back leaned to the couch; her legs bent to her chest wrapped by her arms to hold them.

She was shaking like a bird who had fallen from the nest.

Carlo sat beside her, "I'm sorry. I'm so sorry. I don't know what came over me. I should never have said those things, and I should never have doubted you". Carlo could not hold back the tears himself.

Giulia looked at him. In her eyes, there was no rage, nor disappointment, no pain, just a gleam of hope. The hope that things could go back to where they had left them.

"I was wrong. Will you ever be able to forgive me?" Carlo implored taking Giulia's face in his hands.

"And you? Would you ever be able to forgive me and trust me again?" she asked in response.

"I already did!"

That was it. Was it for real, or was it an illusion? Whether out of trust or convenience, Carlo and Giulia found their way to a new start. They were both survivors in their unique way, and they always managed to fall on their feet.

No more talking was necessary. They made love right there, on the floor, wildly and tenderly at the same time. Whatever broke between them, had left its place to a new even stronger bond.

While Giulia was getting dressed, Carlo started to prepare something to eat, but disappointedly Giulia had no time to stay.

"Sorry. I have an appointment with the estate agent at my mother's house."

"Is it not a bit too early?" Carlo asked.

"Probably yes. But a property like that is not easy to sell. My mother had received a few offers over the years that she always turned down. One in particular, very recently, and they are still interested." Giulia answered, picking at the pineapple Carlo was chopping.

"Then, you better go."

"If they give me what I want, we can close the bank with that money and not have to worry about anything anymore," Giulia kissed Carlo on the lips and left.

80

PONTE ALTO - ITALY

Even if the flight home was not until the following morning, Lola was packing. She could not wait to leave Ponte Alto. Fergus had arranged to book a room in one of the hotels close to the airport, where they could spend the night after dropping off the rental car.

Lola's head was still a mess, but the worst thing was not feeling any closure after this entirely sloppy affair.

"I was thinking," Fergus addressed his wife while still looking out the window as if in this way, his words would upset her less, "that maybe you should talk to Giulia. And by talk, I mean confront her. You need to know, you need explanations, or else you will never be able to leave all this behind. And as far as we know, she is the only one still alive that can give you those answers that you deserve. Or at least throw a bit of clarity on the whole matter."

Fergus turned to get a glimpse of Lola to see her reaction.

She had stopped packing. Her fist tight, and her gaze lost in the void.

-Was she angry at him? - Fergus had no idea how to interpret his wife's body language.

"You know what honey? You are right. Let's finish packing, and then I will ask the receptionist for her number. We'll get her on our way out of this bloody town." Lola's reaction pleasantly surprised Fergus, "That's my girl," he kissed her while helping to finish packing.

When Lola and Fergus went down to settle the bill and check out, Lola asked for her cousin's number with the excuse of saying goodbye to her and hoping the girl at the reception didn't know the two of them were not on speaking terms.

"Of course," Nicoletta, the receptionist, replied and scribbled Giulia's number on a sticky note," it's a pity Miss Kopfler is not in the office this morning, she had an appointment at poor old Mrs Kopfler house, to sell it." Nicoletta had offered more pieces of information than Lola had hoped.

"Well, it looks like we'll have to pay a visit to my aunt's house then. Another pleasant ride down memory lane for me," Lola said sarcastically climbing into the car.

* * *

"I know this is not what you were expecting from the investigation, but at the moment, this is where it's going. Everything unequivocally points to Giulia Kopfler. I'm not sure if she killed them all or if Mara killed her sister and then Giulia killed her and the priest. But this is what we have at the moment."

For Zamparelli the velvet gloves were off in how he would be dealing with superintendent Di Fazio. He had no intention of letting her influence his investigation or manipulate the evidence they had.

"I understand. And as much as it hurts, I have to agree with you."

"You do?" The inspector could not disguise his surprise as he was sure the superintendent would have hindered his line of investigation.

"Yes, Zamparelli. What did you think? That because there

was a friendship over the years, I would have played around with the investigation and the evidence? I'm a woman of the law. I certainly asked for your discretion, and you have been discreet. I can't deny I'm shocked and sad for where the investigation is leading, but I also want the truth to come out and the culprit behind bars." The superintendent's tone betrayed some outrage.

"Thank you, superintendent, and just to clear the air, I didn't mean to question your integrity." Zamparelli felt he owed her that.

"No hurt feelings inspector. Did you get your warrants?"

"Yes. The judge didn't feel we had the grounds to justify an arrest warrant but certainly one for a search. We will be turning Giulia's house and office and Mara's house upside down until we will find something. As I believe Mara was paying for her sister's silence, we should find bank statements, and I'm pretty confident that something will also emerge from Giulia's properties to connect her to the murders too."

"Good. I want the searches conducted simultaneously and discreetly, particularly the one at the hotel." The superintendent ordered.

"I don't have enough men. I can organise two teams and start with Giulia's apartment and office, but if you want us to search the Kopfler residence at the same time, you must send backup from Belluno."

Superintendent Di Fazio thought for a second how to tackle the situation and then confidently answered, "OK, you start with Giulia's home and office as planned, and meanwhile, I'll organise and send a team to help with Mara's residence."

"Thank you." Zamparelli hung up the phone.

He took his gun from the first drawer of his desk, where he always kept it when he was in the station, and loaded it before going to organise the search teams.

"Listen up people. We have warrants to search Miss Kopfler's apartment, her office and even her mother's house. The superintendent wants discretion, so no sirens. I need you to split up in two teams. I'll go with one to the apartment in Via Galbusera and the other will be coordinated by Deputy Inspector Piva and will search the office at the hotel. A third team is coming from Belluno to help to search the Kopfler's residence. The superintendent will let me know when they are ready, and I'll meet them there. Now, remember, Giulia Kopfler is our top suspect, but she has not been charged with anything yet. Go easy, don't screw up. Don't give her ground for complaint, but turn those places upside down until you find something. Look for possible evidence that links her to any of the three murders and anything related to her finances; her strongest motive is money."

Chief Inspector Furio Zamparelli and Deputy Inspector Luca Piva left the station in two separate cars followed by a patrol unit each.

81

PONTE ALTO - ITALY

Giulia had arrived at the Kopfler residence purposely in advance to be sure that everything was in order.

She opened the gate so that Mr Gava, the estate agent, could drive straight in.

When Giulia slid the key in the padlock and realised the front door was already unlocked, she knew Edda was there. Giulia didn't want her around, at least not until she had the chance to speak to her.

"Edda?" Giulia called from the hallway. She received no answer but spotted her mother's study's door ajar.

She pushed the door wide open and caught Edda behind Mara's desk.

"What are you doing here?" Giulia asked more unfriendly than intended. Edda justified herself, saying she was tidying up.

"Inside my mother's desk's drawers?" Giulia was sure she had seen Edda hurrying to push the top drawer back in.

"One of the drawers was jammed, so I only pushed it close."

It was a plausible explanation, but still, Giulia had a funny feeling that Edda was not telling the truth, and she could swear she had seen her hide something in the front pocket of her apron.

"Whatever. Now, why don't you go home? Take the Friday off, besides there is nothing really to do for you here." Edda left the room and went to hang her apron in the kitchen and take her purse.

"Leave the gate open as it is when you go, please Edda. I'm expecting someone," Giulia shouted after the old woman as she watched her leave from the front sitting room window.

Edda was getting too old to work. She would have been happy to retire, in the end. Giulia had also already agreed with her accountant on a considerable sum to give her. Edda would live the rest of her days with no financial worries.

There was also another reason Giulia was happy to see Edda go: she could not handle her much recently. Edda had acted strange, like today in her mother's office, and her attachment to Giulia had gradually grown to be a sort of obsession. Giulia wasn't a little girl anymore, and she wasn't even a substitute for her late daughter. Maybe in the past, she used to appreciate Edda's favouritism and attention, but now she was a grown woman, and it was weird.

The noise of tyres on the gravel brought Giulia back from her thoughts. A few minutes later, Mr Gava's voice was calling for her: "Miss Kopfler? Are you here?"

"Mr Gava," Giulia cheerfully greeted him, shaking his hand.

"Shall I give you a full tour?"

"Wow, I've been here before, but because your mother never wanted to sell, I never had a chance to go any further than the hallway. This house is impressive!" The estate agent exclaimed once they were back downstairs. Without wasting words, Giulia asked him if he still had those interested buyers that he had mentioned on the phone.

"Yes, I do. They are still keen on the house, indeed. They just had to wait so long, while they could have bought any other property, that they feel to renegotiate their offer," the estate agent, in contrast to Giulia, was playing out a strategy.

"Mr Gava," she interrupted him, "we are both business persons, and we are both here for a reason today. I want to sell, and your clients want to buy. It's just a matter of price at this stage. I suggest we talk straight. It would save us both some time."

Gava blushed and agreeably took out a purchase proposition from his briefcase. Giulia was more than satisfied. The numbers met her expectations, "I'll have my lawyers check the contract, but I'm more than positive that there will be no obstacles to seal the deal. I'll be in touch with you early next week."

Giulia and Gava shook hands, and she walked him to the door.

She waited for him to drive out of the property and went back inside to grab her purse and car keys from the sitting room.

"What the hell.." Giulia exclaimed when back to the hallway. She was sure she had closed the front door behind her, and now it was wide open.

* * *

"Here we are," Fergus said when they arrived in front of Mara's house.

"Look, she might be waiting for me already," Lola said in an unsuccessful attempt of humour staring at the open gate. They drove through and parked right beside the front door.

"I'm going alone. I think I have to do this on my own," Lola said, trying to sound calm.

"Ok, but I'll be out here if you need me."

Lola stopped at the threshold, turned to look at her husband and smiled. Fergus kept his eyes on his wife until she disappeared inside the house.

Lola's legs were shaking, and the strength she had felt before her entrance was about to abandon her. Being in that place after so many years brought back too many memories. Memories she had fought so hard to forget. She sauntered along the corridors. The house had not changed much, and the oppressive atmosphere was still alive, even after Mara had died. She passed the kitchen and Mara' s studio.

The sitting room door was closed, but through the glass door, she could see someone sitting on the couch. It could only be Giulia. Lola twisted the handle and started to call her cousin's name while entering the room. Giulia couldn't answer. She had some brown parcel tape covering her mouth, and her hands were tied behind her back. There was an open cut on her right temple, and the blood that dripped mixed with the smudged mascara on her face made her look like a Halloween mask.

Giulia's eyes were wide in terror but also trying to say something. It was too late for Lola to understand the warning. The sharp tip of a knife was already at her throat.

"We were hoping to have a private conversation, but as you are here, you can join us." The voice was familiar.

Edda pushed Lola on the couch beside Giulia.

"How can you do this to me? After everything I've done for you?"

Edda asked Giulia, removing the tape from her mouth.

"Is this all because I'm selling the house?" Giulia's words came out as a whisper.

"Of course, it's not, you stupid cow. It's about loyalty! You are no better than your mother. You use people, and when you don't need them anymore, you get rid of them."

Giulia tried to calm Edda down. She mentioned the more than generous sum she was planning to give her, but the fire in Edda's eyes was not fading. She had lost control.

"I don't care about money. My life is here, taking care of this house, this family, you."

"But Edda, you couldn't possibly have thought you could stay here forever?" The absurdity of the situation made Giulia speak without thinking whether her words were upsetting the old woman even further.

"I've been like a second mother to you. You were like a daughter to me. And you knew it and used it to your advantage." Edda's eyes were filling with tears, but it was hard to understand if it was because of the extreme state of rage she was in or because she felt hurt.

"Edda, you are wrong," Giulia tried to justify herself.

"Shut up!" Edda shouted, brandishing the knife in the hair right in front of Giulia's face.

"I comforted you when your mother mistreated you and then when she had that crazy idea to tell all about Lorna; I took care of everything. To protect you."

Giulia and Lola looked at each other.

"You knew?" Lola asked

"You don't talk now. I will deal with you later. You are like your mother. Looking for trouble your entire existence. Greedy useless parasites. Could you not stay away? No, you had to come back and now look at the consequences."

"Edda, did you kill Lorna and my mother?" Giulia asked, terrified of the answer far more than the knife that flitted in front of her eyes.

"I had to, but I did it for you, darling," Edda's voice softened but in a crazy twisted way that could only add fear to the situation.

"Come on, Giulia; you can't deny you were happy when Lorna was not a problem anymore. And forever this time. But then your mother wanted to tell anyway. I heard her calling Lola on the phone and then talking with Father Nello. I had to stop her before she ruined your life any further." Edda sighed and sat on one of the armchairs opposite the two cousins.

Giulia started to cry.

"It's a bit late now to cry, isn't it, Giulia?" Edda's tone was again sharp and cruel.

"All I wanted was for you to be safe and happy and I nearly did it until you decided to turn your back on me." Edda walked closer to Giulia and slapped her in the face as hard as her old body allowed her.

"You hypocritical, selfish brat."

Lola jumped in her seat, causing Edda to turn towards her.

"And you. Poor little Lola. In fairness, you haven't many faults. But you should have stayed in Ireland with that lovely husband of yours."

Lola was afraid for herself but was also worried for Fergus. A long time must have passed, and he should have come looking for her unless something had happened to him. Tears were uncontrollably running down her face.

Edda took a step closer to her too and aimed the knife at her abdomen.

"I'm sorry honey; I've nothing really against you, but like Father Nello, you know too much now. You really shouldn't have come here."

The glimpse of craziness in Edda's eyes was terrifying.

Lola instinctively brought her hands to her stomach.

Philip and Alex were smiling at her, maybe for the last time.

82

PONTE ALTO - ITALY

After his wife disappeared inside the house, Fergus took out his mobile and browsed around emails for ten/fifteen minutes, but then he started to get hot in the car. He got out and strolled around the garden.

Fergus was still pondering whether to go in and check on Lola or not when he heard voices coming from one of the rooms on the ground floor. It could only be Lola and Giulia.

Fergus walked toward the window the voices were coming from. He crouched down a little so as not be seen from inside. The scene that presented itself to him made him wonder if he was hallucinating because of the heat. His wife and her cousin were held hostage by the crazy old housekeeper.

He dropped to his knees with his back against the wall.

He was not a man of action, and the woman had a knife that, despite her elderly age, still gave her a massive advantage over him. He started to panic. He had to do something. If something ever happened to Lola, he would never be able to forgive himself.

As silently as possible, he went back to the car where he

had left his phone. He went through the last few calls and found Piva's number.

The deputy inspector answered immediately. Still, Fergus was so frantic in explaining what was going on that the officer could barely understand a single word the Irish man was saying.

Fergus gave up on his attempt to ask for help and decided to go in. He slammed the car door shut, and just when he had done so, he heard the noise of engines approaching. Fergus instinctively turned. Behind the dust lifted by the gravel, he saw an unmarked car followed by a police patrol car.

Fergus ran towards Zamparelli who was climbing out of the lead car, "Inspector, did Piva call you? Did he tell you what is going on in there? We need to save my wife."

Zamparelli looked at Fergus, barely understanding what he was saying in his delirium, "Now, calm down, Mr Owen. We are here to search the house, what are you doing here?"

Fergus felt they were losing precious time, but he had to tell Zamparelli, or else nothing could progress. Zamparelli, who was starting to believe they were never going to see the end of this mayhem, turned toward the search team ready to go in.

"Listen up people. Never mind the search. We have a possible hostage situation."

The entire squad went back to the cars and donned their bulletproof vests before getting in line in front of the chief inspector for orders.

"No noise, you and you, come with me through the front door. You, you and you go through the back."

"You, Mr Owen, stay here. You do not come inside for any reason. Everything will be fine." Zamparelli turned his back to Fergus and went in.

At the back of the house, the two officers found the door locked and delayed their entrance because they had to break a glass to reach the inside handle.

Zamparelli and the others entered the house and followed the shouting. The three of them were now outside the sitting room.

Zamparelli signalled the two uniformed officers to cover him and barged in.

"Drop the knife and turn around with your hands above your head. We have surrounded the house," the inspector shouted.

An awkward silence fell in the room. Like in a slow-motion movie, Edda brandished the knife and lowered it, aiming at Lola's stomach. Zamparelli fired a shot and along with the other officers ran towards the two cousins.

Giulia's head wound was only superficial. One of the officers untied her hands and escorted her outside.

Zamparelli looked at Lola's hands, still pressed on her stomach. The blood was everywhere, but it was not hers. It was Edda's, who fell over her after being shot.

Lola looked up and saw Fergus by the door.

After he heard shooting nothing could keep him from going in.

His eyes terrified and fixed on the blood on his wife.

Zamparelli, who had kneeled to move Edda's body away from Lola, turned towards Fergus and reassured him, "It's not your wife's blood. She is unharmed."

The inspector walked husband and wife outside without making any remark about the fact that Fergus was not supposed to come in.

Two ambulances entered the property followed by Piva's car.

"Well, you missed the action, Piva. But you are on time to call forensics and lend me a pair of handcuffs," Zamparelli said to his deputy.

"Giulia Kopfler you are under arrest for fraud and obstruction of justice." Zamparelli closed the handcuffs around the young woman's wrists.

The search of her office more than the house had revealed evidence extremely profitable to the case.

"Wait," Lola's voice had eventually come back.

"Can I talk to her a moment please?"

The officer who was escorting Giulia to one of the patrol cars looked at the inspector who nodded in agreement.

"Why did your mother do that? And who knew? And why did my mother never look for me?" Lola could not possibly leave without trying to have some answers.

Giulia had nothing left to lose and started to talk:

"I only found out recently. I swear I always thought Lorna had drowned. Why my mother did it? Avidity, or maybe because she was ashamed of her sister. As for why your mother never looked for you, simply because she thought you didn't want to see her. That's what my mother told her. And as naive as Lorna was, she believed her; or maybe she felt she was better without you. After all, she tried to kill you once, didn't she?"

The smirk on Giulia's face was something Lola would never forget. Like she was pleased to give her a final blow. The ultimate humiliation. Lola was sure it was Giulia's way to make her pay for her downfall as in her twisted mind, all of this was because of her.

* * *

Lola and Fergus were escorted to the station where they had to give their statements. Lola also had to hand her clothes in as evidence, not that she was keen to keep them anyway. All she wanted was to wash the blood off and change into a clean outfit.

They let her use the station changing room where she could shower and change but not before the forensic team had collected a swab of her DNA, and of the blood she had on her. They also checked for residues under her fingernails. It was hard not to feel victimised.

Eventually, Fergus and Lola were free to go.

A uniformed officer drove their rental, while Zamparelli insisted on driving them himself to their hotel near Venice airport. There was no way he could have allowed either of them to drive after everything they had been through earlier.

The drive was less than two hours. The conversation was sparse and basic, mainly between Fergus and the inspector. Lola was in the back seat still feeling in a state of shock; she didn't know why anymore.

Every once in a while, Fergus threw a look at his wife through the rear mirror. She was quiet, looking absently out the window.

He would have paid a million euros to know what was going on in her head, and if she would ever be the same woman she was before all this. He would have paid any amount of money in the world to be able to go back in time and rewrite history.

83

DUBLIN - IRELAND

Doctor Auberdeen was one of Siobhan's oldest friends, and this helped Lola to trust her from the beginning, despite her reluctance to see a therapist.

After they returned from Italy, Fergus had firmly insisted that his wife would talk to someone, and in the end, she gave in.

That morning Lola had to be with Doctor Auberdeen by ten.

She walked the twins to school and came back home to give the house a quick tidy up before leaving. Fergus was in London for the day. He had gone to the airport in a taxi so Lola could have the car. Doctor Auberdeen had her study in Monkstown, where she lived. It was not far from Donnybrook but very poorly served by public transports, and as a consequence, Lola preferred to drive there.

She gave herself one last look in the mirror and grabbed the car keys from the bowl on the console table by the front door. She had removed the picture frames, too hard to look at them. She had replaced them with a silver bowl for the keys and a big vase always filled with fresh scented cut flowers.

When she was about to leave, the doorbell rang. It was the postman carrying a parcel.

Lola was not expecting anything, but the name and the address left no doubt; the parcel was for her. Her curiosity was stronger than her concern for being late to therapy. She went back into the house, down to the kitchen and grabbed the pair of scissors from the knife block.

Only while cutting the seal, did she notice the parcel came from Italy. She hesitated a second and then finished unwrapping it.

There was a letter attached:

-Lola, if you are reading these words of mine, it means something has happened to me before I could talk to you face to face. I never expected to harm anybody; I only made the decisions that I thought were best for my family and me.

Would I make the same decisions again? I can't answer that, and I can't change the past.

Would I be saying all this to you if your mother had not shown up at my door threatening to expose me? I can't answer that, either. But she did, and here I am not able to withhold this secret any longer.

Your mother was weak and could not look after you. At the time, you were both better off without one another. Then when she recovered from her darkness, it was too late. The web of lies had extended too widely. Lorna was dead for everybody, and so she had to stay dead.

In the box, you will find all the letters she has sent you over the years. I never gave them to you. Why would I have? As far as you were concerned, she was dead.

I don't know how she found you, but she did. Maybe in the end, after all, you were meant to meet. I won't ask for your forgiveness, just for your understanding. Mara-

Lola kneeled on the floor. Her tears were wetting the paper in her hand. She opened the box and took out the bulky pack of letters tied together with a ribbon.

* * *

The drive to Doctor Auberdeen never felt so long, and neither did the wait to be called in.

Eventually, Lola was sitting inside the therapist's office.

"I just received these," she said, handing the letters to her therapist.

Doctor Auberdeen read Mara's letter first, and slightly tilting her head looked Lola straight in the eye, "This gives you answers," she said, and passing her mother's letters back to Lola continued, "but these will give you the closure you are looking for."

Doctor and patient went through the letters together. They had all been sent every year on Lola's birthday, and they stopped when Lola turned eighteen. In the letters, Lorna kept apologising to her daughter for her weakness. She regretted not being able to be a better mother, but she never suggested they meet. Never did she say she had tried to find her.

Doctor Auberdeen felt Lola's pain. The answers she had found were not the ones she wanted. Her mother had never really looked for her until it was too late.

"How can someone say that they love their children but do nothing to find them? She rejected me over and over again," Lola cried out in a mix of anger, resentment and sadness.

"She didn't reject you; she rejected herself as a mother. But I suppose to you it makes no difference. Your pain is still the same."

"Oh come on, even if someone tells you that your daughter doesn't want to see you, would that stop you from trying?"

Lola could not believe the therapist was, if not defending Lorna, finding rational justification for her behaviour.

"I can only answer for myself, Lola. Not for your mother. You need to accept what she did and what she was. Only by acknowledging the reality of things, whether you like it or not, you will find closure and with it some peace."

Maybe Doctor Auberdeen had a point there. And also Angela always said that you couldn't control the way others behave, but you can control the way you react to it.

"You have been unlucky Lola, neither Lorna nor Mara served you as a mother, but you must not victimise yourself because of those two women. You must see yourself for the gentle and yet strong woman and brilliant mother that you have become, despite those two women. Now you know the whole truth. Good or bad, never mind. The truth always has thousands of angles. The important thing is that you have no more excuses to stay anchored to the past. You have to let it go and fully embrace your present and future."

Dr Aberdeen was right.

Lola stood still for a few minutes and then she gathered the letters together, including Mara's, she tied them back up with the purple ribbon and walked to the big fireplace on the other side of the room letting the flames devour her past.

EPILOGUE

Dear Lorna,

I'm a wife and a mother.

I've never been your daughter, and I'm not ready to become it now. Maybe one day I will, but I can't say.

I know it's not entirely your fault, I know you paid a high price but I did too and for sins that weren't even mine.

The line of the family's black souls ends here, with me.

Lola Owen

AKNOWLEDGEMENT

First of all I want to thank my readers as it is only because of them I can call myself a writer.

Thank you to my technical support team, Sara Jane and Hugh Doolan and Petra Fransas. They are the testimony that sometimes mixing business and friendship works.

Thank you to the talented Debbie Boettcher for creating Black Souls' amazing cover, but also for supporting me along this writing journey. Distance can't stop friendship.

Thank you to my editor John Laiche who had taught me so much.

Last but not least, thank you to my husband and daughters who patiently shared me with my Mac.

Edited by TSSI Editorial Services jlaiche@earthlink.net

Cover by Debbie Boettcher www.indiebookcovers.weebly.com

ABOUT THE AUTHOR

After a degree in history and philosophy in Italy and some experience in human resources, the author moved to Ireland in 2003 with her husband. She worked a few years in the financial services before she decided to go back to her old passion: writing.

She is currently living in the little village of Balrothery with her husband, two daughters, two dogs, and a foster who comes and goes.

Her next murder mystery book will be out summer 2020.

ALSO BY SABINA GABRIELLI CARRARA

Fields Of Lies, Book 0 of The Seacross Mysteries

Printed in Poland
by Amazon Fulfillment
Poland Sp. z o.o., Wrocław

52934184R00192